A PREDATOR AND A
PSYCHOPATH

JAY KERK

A PREDATOR
AND A
PSYCHOPATH

A Dark and Twisted
Psychological Thriller

Jay Kerk

Jay Kerk

CONTENTS

CONTENTS

CONTENTS

4

JERRY

CONTENTS

Special thanks to M. for her support going through my manuscript.

Thank you, the reader, for purchasing this book and for investing your time into reading it.

If you like this book, please take the time to rate it and write a short review. Having reviews and ratings for such books are key to their success.

Follow me on social media if you want to know about my upcoming work.

Thanks again and happy reading!

PART

1

JASON

CHAPTER

1

PAGE DR. THOMPSON

The screams resonated through the front door of the psychiatric hospital, building four. In the hall, three nurses in scrubs tried their best to keep the man pinned to the floor. Next to them, a leather armchair lay on its side. The receptionist waited on the phone, eager to hear a reply.

"Morning, Dr. Thompson. Mr. Stankovic is having another fit. We gave him a shot." she blurted.

"When he's out of it, transfer him to my clinic."

"Your clinic? Not the ward?"

"No, not the ward." He hesitated for a second. "Let's try something different."

She hung up, and Dr. Thompson thought about how cruel life could be to some people. How many fits could Jason Stankovic take? They have been happening closer together compared to when they occurred initially.

I woke up, and I'd had a deep and uninterrupted sleep, but my back ached. I was lying on a leather sofa, and I could smell stale cigar smoke.

I turned and saw Dr. Thompson behind his desk, and my anger built up inside me. In a split second, I sat up straight and put one leg over the other, folding my arms to show composure and pride. The office was filled with wooden furniture and countless books, and I always wondered if people actually read them or used them solely for decoration.

I grew fond of the man and his skill, but I didn't trust him, trust was my scarcest commodity.

"Hello, Jason. How are you doing?" He hadn't looked at me yet, still tidying his desk by rearranging documents.

Like shit. "Fresh as an early morning bagel. How about yourself?"

"I'm doing well." I recognized his tricks by then, how he let the silence expand until I did most of the speaking. Well, not this time.

Two minutes passed. "Would you like something to drink?"

"Whiskey. On the rocks. Please." *Would be phenomenal.*

He chuckled. "Not possible."

"Gary, I would like to go home. Whatever you think I am suffering from, I'm fine now, and I would like to leave this place, this instant. I miss my family." Filled with anxiety as

I waited for his reply, I knew anything I did could give him information. My legs started shaking.

I tried to distract myself as he sipped his drink. Gary Thompson was a psychiatrist, my psychiatrist, but not sure how long I'd known him. Maybe about a month since this nightmare started. He was in his late fifties, and he wore a ridiculous, out-of-fashion goatee.

"I don't think you are ready."

The words fell heavy on me, but I expected them.

"Tell me how you're feeling and what you're thinking. Why did you snap at work? What happened to you?"

I needed to put on a performance, perhaps threaten him. "Listen Gary. I won't succumb to this bullshit. I want to leave, so draft the papers. I'll sign anything."

I waited. He didn't reply or react.

"You can't keep me here against my will. I'll call my lawyer, and a big lawsuit will come your way, buddy. I'll make sure you bear the consequences. Unless—" I put my finger up. "Unless I'm satisfied by my immediate release. Then I won't press any charges."

A desperate attempt, but still worth trying.

The silence expanded. The motherfucker smiled, enjoying the control.

"Jason. How *are* you? What's going on inside?" He said in his usual calm voice.

"I'm frustrated. I'm furious. I'm being held against my will." We smiled at each other. "And I resent you." In previous sessions, we agreed I would voice my emotions, whatever they were. I took advantage of that every now and then.

"The thing is that you're in a tricky situation, and we're here to help you," he said. "Do you know where you are?"

"I'm in a psychiatric ward. A prison."

"You're in Jackson's Psychiatric Functional Rehabilitation Center," he said.

"Let's call Lisa, please. I can give you her number,"

"I don't think that will be possible," he said impatiently.

"552 223 1414. Luke Anderson, my lawyer. No further discussion at this point."

I stood and moved toward the window. We were on the third floor.

"Please don't think about escaping." He sighed. "You'd need to break the reinforced glass, and there wouldn't be enough time to get out. Guards can arrive here within a minute."

I slowly walked away.

"Jason, you've hit a rough patch, and the situation you are in is *complicated*. I'll need you to work with me so I can help you heal. Let's start with small steps. It's half-past six now, and you slept for ten hours. Do you feel well rested?"

Mental Note 1: Complicated situation.

"I'm still tired as if I need more sleep. What is this complicated situation?"

I tried to set up a *quid pro quo* situation and hoped he would play along.

"Too soon to tell you everything. The mind works in a way difficult for us to understand, compartmentalizing what we experience. The incident is buried inside you, and every time you face the facts, you regress to the initial stages of basic functioning." He moved to the armed chair, and I instinctively took the chaise longue. *I sat and babbled in the same chaise long before.*

Mental Note 2: The truth is buried inside me.

"You sound as if I'm broken, but I'm not. You paint me as ill, deranged, paranoid. I'M NOT!" I wondered how many crazy people screamed they weren't crazy. I imagined myself running down a street in a robe, shouting, *"I'M NOT CRAZY! I'M NOT CRAZY!"*

"I didn't say so. I said you're in a complicated situation, and you're here to heal. We are here to help you."

"My memories of my life are intact. I know who I am and what I do. I remember everything," I grew angrier, and I could throw a few punches at this guy.

"Not everything. You clearly don't remember what happened," he said.

"382, give me a 3-digit number, Gary. Please."

"693."

"382 times 693 is 264,726," I said proudly.

Don't speak shit about my mind.

He looked uneasy, irritated.

"Enough diversion, Jason."

"My total assets are worth $22,782,000. Do you want money?" I pushed more.

"STOP!" he said. "Our time is limited!"

Mental Note 3: We do not have time. Why the fuck don't we?

"I appreciate your grip on numbers." He softened his voice as if he pleaded with me. He leaned forward. "The processor is a part of your mind. The psyche is another part. Your processor is intact, but your psyche is not."

He smiled and extended his arm to place his hand on my leg; I jerked backward.

"Let's try something else. Tell me about any new dreams you've had."

"Mmm. None. None that I can remember." I will not give you a thing to hold against me.

"What is your occupation?" The neutral tone, the *quid pro quo* was back.

"I work in finance at CyberCrews. I'm the CFO," I said. "Can we call Will or Amanda? Or Lea?"

"Who are they?" Zero sincerity in his voice.

His question infuriated me, but I held my nerves. I answered, "Will, my brother, Amanda, my sister, and Lea, my daughter. Can we call them now?"

"No, also not possible. We will see when you improve." He said.

"What the fuck do you mean *we'll see*?"

So much for holding my nerves.

"Calm down, Jason. When you're better, we'll call. What year is it, and how old are you?"

The truce was back on. "2016. I can't tell you the exact date, I would say October. Did something bad happen to my family or to me?"

"Yes."

The word took some time to sink in, hearing the confirmation depressed me.

"Are you exercising regularly? Tell me about your exercise routine and your current weight."

"I do a few weights training per week, a couple cardio sessions, and one muscle and joint stretching session. I keep my weight around 195 pounds. That's been constant for the past four years or so." I felt some pride, but considering the big picture, I thought he tricked me into a comfort zone. "What do I need to do to get out?"

He jotted down a few notes, then stared me in the eyes and said, "Now we are talking. We'll build a schedule and a rhythm to follow, and we'll make zero contact with the outside world until you're better. I'm certain things will come back to you in no time. Just be patient." He stood. "Come, I want to make you some chamomile tea to help you relax." He was enthusiastic and sincere, but overselling it.

Mental Note 4: Zero contact with the outside world.

As soon as he stood up, I jumped to my feet.

"Yes, come watch me make the drink." He shook his head.

I followed him a few steps to the corner. He opened a sealed water bottle. They could inject those, or even reseal them after tampering with the contents.

"Don't be paranoid. I'll refresh mine, and we'll drink together." He heated the water and served us.

I eyed his desk as we moved toward the seats. I saw a handset phone and a mobile. This could be my break. If I can knock him out and make my calls, I might be out of here in thirty minutes.

"Please don't think of the phones. I switched one off and disconnected the other," he told me without turning, continuing his steady steps. "And don't attack me. Again." He took a seat and smiled at me.

We sat in silence, and the hot vapor from the cup made me nostalgic for winter, snow, and family gatherings.

His remark about the phones shocked me. How did he know my thoughts, and when did I become so predictable?

Mental Note 5: Is this a cognitive experiment? A telepathic kind?

He grabbed an electronic tablet from a drawer in the coffee table, and said, "The WiFi is turned off for the sake of our meeting. But I can teach you a little about the facility and myself."

He wanted me to trust him.

A half hour passed as he told me about his years in education, his first clinic, his relationship with his patients, his colleagues, and lastly, the purpose of this unit in Jackson's Functional Rehabilitation Center. He only took the most severe cases and got involved in new research in psychiatry and modern cognitive enhancement. He saw me getting restless when he talked about the research.

"See, Jason, I'm your doctor, and everything I do is for your benefit. Give me your time and faith. You're not a research subject, I assure you that enrolling you as a subject in any study is neither legal nor ethical without your consent or the consent of a legal representative." He walked over to the desk and grabbed a folder.

He came back, and I still didn't say a thing. I watched and recorded mental notes.

He took a paper out of the folder. "This is a letter from your lawyer, Luke, about your condition and the legality of your stay here. Read it. Surely, you'll recognize his signature and some intimate details."

The letter from Luke said I wasn't well and everybody missed me, and he wished me well and hoped I recover soon. He also told me he gave the facility his consent to treat me. The signature was his, and he included our safe phrase, "Springfield times."

I trusted Luke with my life; we grew up together and always stayed close. Did I trust him with my money?

Mental Note 6: Consider the likelihood of Luke being compromised. Motive: money?

Unwell. Crazy. Insane.

How the hell did that happen!!!

Mental Note 7: If someone wanted to access my fortune, they could frame me for a crime. Or fabricate my insanity.

"I know what you're thinking, Jason. Just relax now, and later you can go over the facts. Now let's play chess, and afterward we go over your treatment plan." He was eager to continue the play he orchestrated.

You know nothing, my friend.

Can he access my thoughts? Can he predict what I am thinking?

Mental Note 8: Remember if you signed for any experiment for mental predictability.

He set the table. "Before we begin, tell me how much you trust me if ten is the maximum and one is as much as you would trust a hungry lion."

My processor went into action mode, and the calculations started.

"Remember my merits, and this law-abiding facility, and Luke's note, and apply the number of circumstances causing a person to develop a mental illness or suffer from a nervous breakdown." He paused, and I knew the rest: death, drugs, accident. A Cheating partner. Cancer. Bankruptcy.

I grew fond of this guy. Apparently, he knew his customer well... He spoke my language.

"I would say for merits and law and circumstances, seven out of ten. I'll leave the rest until later," I said, "define mental illness."

"Many forms of mental illness can cause a break from reality. The disease doesn't matter, what *matters* is the result of a disruption in a person's perception of reality. However, if this disruption continues, we then search for the root cause."

What happened? What is the plan?

I used to think chess is prestigious, designed exclusively for computational minds, but skill got reduced to a set of algorithms so simple that the most primitive computer can beat the most intelligent human.

I beat him with some effort. He set the board aside, and we resumed our conversation.

"Can you please tell me what happened? And I miss Lea a lot, can we call her?"

"Every time we tell you, you end up having a major setback. This time we want you to try to discover what happened, and I will personally help you. I brought you this device for taking notes. No connectivity, only an electronic notepad you can lock. Before your last setback, you were taking notes, memorizing them and then destroying them. And the next day you would write them down again and destroy them before bedtime."

The notepad might come in handy.

He continued. "Here is the plan for the next four or five weeks. Just imagine the world has come to an end. There is nothing outside of your room or your mind. You owe yourself this time to heal. I want you to take your medication, on time. I want you to exercise as often and extensively as you used to, and we'll add some variety like swimming and yoga. And there are a few books for you to read."

He started well, but I became anxious towards the end. I wondered whether I didn't believe him or didn't believe myself.

I didn't reply.

"Come with me." We moved to the corner near the door. "Please stand on the scale."

161 pounds???? Really??? I've lost thirty-five pounds!

"Something's wrong. I haven't weighed less than one-ninety in a decade." *Shit, shit, shit.* "I need a mirror, please."

I remembered the movie about a crazy man who didn't recognize himself in the mirror; the main actor had significantly changed his body weight to fit the role.

I was a broken man. My tears poured down my cheeks, and I realized I must surrender to whatever happened. Dr. Thompson put his arm around me as I sobbed, but I jerked out of his embrace, driven by pride.

"Jason, it is okay. I want you to put your confidence in me, and then maybe we can get you back on your feet. What's the last thing you remember before being here?"

He paused. I cursed him silently for putting me in such a weak position. "Come lie down and relax your body."

I answered truthfully. "I remember working on something in my office." I closed my eyes. "The forecast for 2017. I'm thinking about getting out of this suit once I get home. This tie annoys me on sunny days."

"Okay, good. What else? Take your time, please." He said.

"My deadline is close, and I need some input from the managers in the Western area. I said I would give them 'til Monday. The day is... Thursday."

I didn't want to share the truth yet, not before I tested him.

"I grab my bowling shoes. I want to relax for an hour before coming back to the office."

"Oh, please don't lie. I honestly don't know what I have to do to gain your trust." Dr. Thompson sucked on one cheek and shook his head. "Enough with the lies."

Sweat formed on my back. All my instincts told me I shouldn't share the rest, but regardless, I did.

"I leave work early. I want to go home and spend time with my family. I miss them. I'm hungry and want a fresh meal. The last thing I remember is driving into the driveway and parking. I don't recall getting out of the car."

"Great. What happened afterward?"

"Nothing. I don't remember."

Something happened. Otherwise, what the fuck are we doing here?

"Do you recall the time of the day?"

"I left work at 2 p.m., the drive to get home is around thirty minutes."

He drew a deep breath in, "How would you describe your relationship with your daughter, Lea? How do you feel toward her? Are you two close?"

"We are close. Close friends. I'm proud of her. She's everything I dreamed she would be. I know parents shouldn't push their children toward something, but with her it's different. We have this special connection, I take her advice and she takes mine. We are lucky to be like this."

"Are you in love with her?" He leaned forward like investigators do.

Fuck you. "No. I love her a lot. I'm so attached to her—she's always on my mind. But I'm not in love with her, and I won't go into how insulting your question is."

Mental Note 9: Lea...

The silence expanded, and I broke it. "She puts me in a trance state, and I want to give her everything in my life. I want to be near her as much as she allows me to be. She has an attractive aura, with a mix of intense beauty and calming presence. I love her, but I'm not in love with her."

"Did you ever engage in any physical relationship with her?" he said.

I sat on the edge of the chair. He leaned back defensively, out of my reach. I imagined myself slapping him and pulling him by the hair to the floor. "No fucking way. No. Fucking. Way. You're one crazy asshole. Where is this coming from?"

"They're standard questions," he said. "I'm exploring all angles."

"This session is over," I said and stood up.

PLAY ALONG

The trip to my room was a walk of shame; I imagined myself as a defeated beast, a gorilla being dragged back to his cage in the zoo, overpowered and helpless.

The room was sickeningly white, with a TV mounted to the wall, under which there was a shelf with a DVD player, discs, a bed and a small desk. A camera hung in the corner above the door, and below the camera stood a sink, a toilet seat and a small cabinet.

The nurse gave me pills, and they knocked me out within ten minutes, while I recited my mental notes for the morning session.

I woke up early. The sun hadn't risen yet. I did my morning stretches for fifteen minutes, powered on the notepad, and set up a complex password for the device. Dr. Thompson had said four weeks.

I went over my mental notes and took my time putting things together, controlling my breath. Inhale one, two, three, four. Exhale slowly.

The sun rose above the horizon as I wrote down my initial thoughts and plans.

Findings:

Unlikely to be a government operation or mind study.

My case concerned altered perception, undoubtedly severe. What caused the weight loss? How long had I been here?

I buried the truth inside me, so I must have seen something happen, or I took part in what happened.

Explanations: Did someone hit me on the head? Or had an accident led to my amnesia? I could have fallen on a hiking trip or been in a car accident. Was I drugged? Or did I try a new drug?

Motive: Money? Hate?

Luke couldn't be compromised, and he wouldn't betray me. I knew him well, and he wasn't the type unless he'd been putting on a fake face for over three decades.

Plan:

· Ask the staff and other patients what happened.
· Be healthy and regain my muscle mass.
· Meditation and breathing: try to induce a hypnotic state in which I can recover memories.

- Call Luke: Check the phones. Use the least secured one.
- Escape plan: Study exits and entries, check cameras and access cards.

I waited in silence and timed my breathing. I focused on making the most of the day. I heard footsteps — time to go.

Her name tag said Norma, and a man accompanied her. He didn't wear a name tag. She wore scrubs, and he wore gray overalls.

We walked through the hall, eight doors down, up two flights of stairs and into the breakfast hall. I counted over forty patients having breakfast, and no children. Behind the counter stood three kitchen staff, and four security personnel each positioned on every exit of the hall. Eight nurses floated around the room and cared for patients. On the walls, two television sets were mounted, each displaying something different, and both speakers blasting sound.

While filling my tray with food, I spotted a staff phone on the wall behind the counter.

The noisy hall annoyed me and reminded me of school playgrounds. I selected an empty table, and I took my time eating. I needed to gain weight.

An old guy sat next to me; he dressed funny.

"Heya, bright sport. How you doin? All well?" He said. I didn't intend to alienate him-he might be the craziest person on earth. Here, people behaved as weird as they wanted.

"Good. How about you? Do you want my chocolate pudding?" I would waste no time in building allies and identifying weak points. Simple transactions forged the best relationships.

"I'm doing *okaaay*. It's non-pancake Tuesday, and I told Gary I want pancakes every day." He reached for the pudding and removed the seal. "What brings you here, sport?"

"I don't know," I said. He held the spoon in midair and glanced at me. "No, really, I don't seem to remember. I swear. Do you know?"

"Are you the guy who killed his squad?"

What a waste of time, the guy is bananas.

"Not me," Wait, be patient.

"I don't know. But you're most welcome here. You can get married here, start a family. I can look after your children." He stood up to leave.

"Wait. What's your name? Why are you in a hurry?" I waved for him to sit.

"They call me Sandals," he pointed down at his sandals.

"So, what is this place? Who is in here and why?" I asked — *worth a try.*

"When your wires burn, they bring you in here." He pointed his finger to his head, opened his eyes, and rotated his arm. "Cuckoo," he whispered.

"So nobody here is in for addiction problems? Cocaine? Heroin?" I asked. None looked the type, but it was still better to ask.

"Nope." He licked the spoon thoroughly. "Well, sometimes they bring in a rich young fuckup. Most of them look like you."

"Ok. Anyone here got cancer?"

"Nope. Huh, uh." He shook his head.

I placed my hand over his. "Thanks. I will always give you my pudding."

Afterward, we headed for a restroom break, to be followed by a gym session.

"Norma. Yeah, hi. Can you please tell me what happened to me?"

"Mm, I can't Jason." Her high-pitched voice unsettled me. "Only Dr. Thompson knows the details, and we have strict orders not to discuss anyone's past. Our role in the treatment is solely to create daily stability."

"Not even headlines?" I asked and smiled. She didn't answer. "Is my family okay?"

"I truly don't know. We know nothing about our patients. The place is a rehabilitation facility, so you make healthy habits, do enjoyable work, take control of your everyday life, and bounce back," she said.

Yeah, right. Tra la la la and ta-da!

"Okay, I hope the routine helps. Oh, before leaving, please tell Dr. Thompson I want to see him soon, preferably today."

"You're scheduled to see him on Thursday afternoon, which would be in two days. Do you want to speak to him over the phone in the afternoon or early evening?"

"Okay."

She handed me over like a criminal to another nurse with no name tag and zero interest in my affairs, but he got the job done and delivered me to the gym.

I would spend two hours cycling and weight lifting, then move to the sauna and steam rooms and finish in the jacuzzi or with a swim. The staff monitored our movement from the surveillance room, and I'd bet they had a phone inside.

Most people here were in their twenties, or over fifty years old.

During lunch, I concluded that the cafeteria staff phone was too exposed to be used, and all the windows fenced with iron bars. They operated the exits by access cards, in and out, and none operated by buttons. A distance of about two hundred yards separated the building from the guarded front gates.

Escaping was impossible.

The best chance to call Luke was from the surveillance room, but I would need a diversion to force the personnel out of the room. And only one person must be inside. Otherwise, one could respond to the distraction and the others could still prevent me from making the call.

If I jammed the outer door to lock Sandals in the steam room, he would press the emergency button. But I would risk his death, and I didn't want to injure him.

What if the nut-bag slipped and broke his neck?

I hated being handled by the nurses. They moved us like cattle, and they monitored us while we swallowed our pills, forcing us to spread our mouths open with our fingers afterward.

"Hey, Jason. Ready for the call?" Norma was always excited.

"Sure."

"Hello, this is Dr. Thompson."

"Hello, Gary. Fancy a chess game? A Jameson on the rocks?"

"Hi, Jason." He chuckled. "And please call me Gary."

Oh my, he had a sense of humor. The robot can take a joke.

"Seriously now, I want to speed up the process. I think I'll be fine." He didn't reply, but he sighed. "I'm meditating and…"

He cut in. "I will adjust our schedule to speed matters up; we'll meet every other day instead of weekly."

"Okay. Sounds fine."

I went with Norma to the common area, but I didn't want to mingle.

"Some people like to eat their dinner here while watching TV and there are many games, board and electronic," she said.

"Yeah, we can catch the 7 p.m. news on Channel 2."

"Actually, we don't have network cable, but there are many DVDs. You also can borrow one to watch in your room." Her enthusiasm resembled the Caesar's palace reception.

Live games and VIP tables on the 1st floor and over six thousand slot machines on the ground floor.

"Okay."

I put food on my tray, taking four puddings.

"Hi, Sandals. How are you doing old pal?" I took a seat next to him.

"Heya, sport, how are you?" He seemed tired.

"I'm good. Missed you in the gym but hoped to catch you here."

"Oh, I got no juice left to exercise." In the evening he looked even older. I'd put him down to be around 60.

"Who said exercise? Come relax in the steam room or the jacuzzi." *Please take the bait.*

"Yeah, I need to relax. Let's go now." He stood up.

"No, not now! Tomorrow at 11 a.m. You meet me there. Here, take these two puddings." He took the puddings without hesitation. "Why can't you get your own pudding?"

"I'm on insulin. I keep telling the doctors I don't care; I should choose what I eat, but they won't listen. How long do they think I can live?" He turned the spoon around inside his mouth and licked forcefully.

"You don't need to worry. I can constantly supply your pudding if you can do me a favor. A small, simple favor."

He eyed me suspiciously, stopping the spoon midair for effect, trying to be funny. "I'm listening."

"When you're in the steam room, I'll go into the sauna, and you count to a hundred and press the red button. I want to see what happens and how quickly they respond."

"Sport." He gave me the side eye. "*Are you trying to escape?*" he whispered. I stayed silent.

"Can't do it," he added.

"Can't press the button or can't escape?"

"Both. Others tried to escape during my time; I stopped counting. And escape where? The police will bring you back in less than a day." He puffed some air.

"The police are colluding with them?" I said jokingly.

"Yup, the pigs are their best mates."

"Ok, how can I make a call?"

"Duh, the visitors' area. Haven't you been? We all go at 4 p.m.." How stupid of me, surely the facility included a visiting area. But likely they wouldn't let me in without supervision.

"Mm."

Well, well, new horizons.

"We can agree about the button situation," Sandals said.

"What do you want in return? I'm open to anything, but tomorrow at 11 a.m. is not negotiable."

"One month of pudding," he held his finger up.

"Deal." We shook hands, but I had my doubts. He wasn't reliable.

Day 2

No major updates. I tried to obtain news from another nurse, but she gave the exact same response as Norma.

In the morning, I bargained with Sandals for three months' worth of pudding if he faked chest pains to stall the responding staff. He agreed, and I promised him another three months if he could alert me in time.

"Alert you? How can I do that?" he protested. I told him to say something funny or even to shout my name.

A few minutes to eleven. I waited in the pool area, and right outside the door was the entrance to the surveillance room. When Sandals presses the button, I will walk casually in the hallway. When the surveillance guys responded, I must be quick enough to enter the room before the access-controlled door closed. The timing was crucial. I could miss the entrance.

I wore one of the white robes places nearby, and I splashed some water on myself until I looked as though I had just come out of the steam room. Sandals passed by me and entered the room, and a minute later I heard Sandals screams: "Help me! My heart! For the love of God, help me!"

His screams sounded ridiculously fake.

The alarm went off.

I counted to three and moved through the pool door into the hallway, walking purposely. The surveillance room door opened from the inside, and a guy ran toward the pool area. The door almost closed, but I grasped the handle.

I entered, and thankfully; the room was empty.

I found the phone on the desk. I dialed the number and waited.

"Hello, this is Helene. How may I help you?"

I hung up.

All these phones were part of the internal network, I should have thought of that.

Think fast.

I tried 9, and 0, and 1 to access an external line, but none worked.

I tried 111, got the same voice, "Hello, this is Helene, how may I help you?" Same response.

"Hi." I deepened my voice. "This is Richard from surveillance. I'm new here; could you please remind me how to dial externally."

"Oh sure. 1318, wait for a few seconds, and you will receive a line."

"Thanks."

Superb. Now we're talking.

I dialed Luke's number; three rings and went to voice mail, so I left a message. "Hey, asshole, this is Jason. Come pick me up; I'm in Jackson's rehab facility, something occupational. The treating physician is Gary Thompson. Prepare a lawsuit, Luke."

The sooner he heard the voice message, the sooner I would be out. Maybe this afternoon, tomorrow at the latest. Luke moved mountains with his legal work.

Sandals screamed erratically, but they stopped the alarms, so I had little time.

I tried Lisa's number twice. Disconnected! So was Lea's!

I tried Luke again, and he answered, "Hi, Luke Anderson."

"Luke, this is Jason. What the fuck is happening, man? Please come get me. Who put me in here?" My heart pounded through my chest.

"Heeeeey, buddy." He sounded surprised by my call. "I can't, bro. It's court-ordered. How are you? We miss you a lot. Are you feeling better?" He was sympathetic.

"Yeah, much better. How is my family? Are Lisa and Lea ok? I called them, but their lines are disconnected."

"Yeah, they're great. They miss you. I guess they got new lines; I'll inform Lisa about the lines. Are you getting better, sticking to your meds?" His worry was genuine.

"Please, if you can't get me out then come see me. I've got to go, but I'm waiting for you," I hung up.

Things didn't add up. Why would they buy new phone lines?

I swiftly got out of the room and headed to the pool area.

Sandals' bad acting caused quite the laugh, the staff gathered around him grinning as he tried his best to prolong the fit on the floor while naked. The scene cracked me up.

He spotted me and said, "Sport, nobody believes me. Chest pains almost got me, but they disappeared just this minute. This second." He opened his eyes wide to fake a massive surprise. "Poof." He gestured with his hand.

FACING THE DEMONS

The time to meet Gary finally came. Scrubs led me to Dr. Thompson's clinic. I wondered why he didn't come to where I stayed. I still didn't figure out how often we met before. As I waited impatiently for him, I scanned the office, looking at his stupid statues and collectibles.

The footsteps preceded him, and he entered.

Wow, what happened to him?

"Hello. How are you, Jason?"

He walked over to his desk with heavy steps, almost shuffling. The right words evaded me, his appearance shocked me.

"I see you *like* my ensemble today." He settled in his seat and sighed.

He lost his hair, goatee, and thick eyebrows. All gone! He was yellowish.

Oh my god, he has cancer.

"No, nothing. Hello. I'm doing well, how are you?" I sounded like a robot. The sentences came in fractions.

"Chemo." He exhaled. "We recently discovered cancer in my pancreas, at an advanced stage. I have little time left. Estimated to be a couple of months, up to a year, or a couple of years at best." He pursed his lips.

Despite being a physician, he was still human, and death scared the shit out of him. If what comes after death didn't frighten you, the cessation of your life and your existence distressed you.

"I'm so sorry, Gary." I walked toward his desk and offered my hand. Reading the expressions on his face difficult without his eyebrows, but the tears forming in his eyes gave away his emotions.

Fuck. Never easy.

I leaned forward and whispered to him in a breathy voice, "I see dead people." I hoped he saw the movie.

He broke into laughter, and I smiled.

"Seriously, doc, I wish you a painless recovery. Stay hopeful, you never know, maybe you can beat this." He nodded.

"The reason I wanted to speed up our process is obvious. I want you to be strong and ready before I'm gone."

Okay, I can trust this guy, or I should. He was dying, so I doubted he had any malicious motives.

"Okay. So, what's wrong with me?"

"Let's start stepwise, how about an exchange of questions? We have a couple of hours. I combined my lunch break with our session, so let's place our orders."

He treated me with respect, as an equal, no longer as a challenged and struggling patient. I appreciated that.

"Do you have a family? Did you tell them about your condition?" I asked as we sat on the couch, half turned to face each other.

"No, life passed me by, and I lost interest in having a family." He looked down. "I lived with a long-term partner, but we couldn't conceive, or rather *I* couldn't, so after years of happiness, she eventually left. I respect her decision. Or at least, I do now."

The silence grew, and I gave him his space. I wondered if he wanted his ex-lover to spend the remaining time he had with him, or to be next to him on his deathbed.

"So. Based on the current turn of events, I'll take a different approach, an unorthodox one. You think you spent one month here, right? And you work at CyberCrews, hmm?"

"Yeah."

Where is he going with this?

"Keep an open mind with me here. I'm going off the books, so whatever you think you can't handle, inform me. Share the early signs of discomfort, don't hesitate."

Whatever you say, man. Just shoot.

"Did you love your wife? And how long did you suspect she had been cheating on you?"

"I love her. I *love* her a lot. I really love her."

A defensive answer.

I fixed my eyes on the floor; how could you love some-one who cheated on you? "Three months of suspecting, and one month certain," I said. "I still love her a lot."

"Do you think you're capable of committing a crime?"

"I'm capable, in terms of ability. Did I ever commit a crime? I guess most of us did! Mostly traffic related, some tax-related, such kind of stuff."

"Did you ever follow her? Are you able of committing a violent act? Are you good with your fists?" I didn't like his changed tone.

"Listen to me, tell me what *I* did or what *you* think I did, and I can answer these questions. I don't like your tone." I got mad, but I didn't want to lose my grip on my nerves.

He is testing how I handle provocation!

"Do you remember the trust fall?" I shook my head. "You close your eyes while your friend stands behind you. You fall back and entrust your friend will catch you. I want to do a similar thing today. Save me the energy, Jason. Pretend I'm putting on an act." He leaned forward, smiling.

"Okay, let's do this," I responded.

"Answer, please."

"I never followed her, although I dreamed a lot about following her." Flashbacks involving cars ran through my mind. "I'm not capable of committing any violent act. I never hit anyone, and I despise guns of all sorts."

"You're able, in terms of ability,"

Well played, sneaky.

"Yes, able physically. But I never engaged in any fight, and I never owned guns."

"Tell me your most vivid dream about following Lisa. Please."

"It's daytime, and I borrowed one of Luke's firm's cars, a regular sedan. I'm angry, and I approach a gas station, but I can't make through the details and dates. The images are blurred." I wanted to stop, so I lied. The vividness of the images made me doubt whether they might be real.

Dr. Thompson didn't reply. He floated to his desk and brought out a small folder, locking the drawer behind him. His movement was labored, every action requiring a lot of energy.

"Have a look at these photos. Highway and gas station cameras confirm you stalked her."

I examined the photos, I became lightheaded and nauseated, and I felt difficulty swallowing. My fingers got cold, my heart raced, and cold sweat formed on my forehead.

"I'm having a panic attack," I said anxiously.

"Ask your monkey mind to stop. Don't start the analysis. You are measuring the possible harm done by talking and therefore the liability falling on you. Take a few deep breaths, and order your mind to stop. Trust me. No consequences and no calculations of any kind. Consider this an *off*-the-record session."

A few minutes of breathing helped.

"Close your eyes and breathe. In cases of compartmentalization, we want one reality to meet the other without conflicting and causing another crack in the psyche." He waited for a minute. "If one of the possibilities is true, the possibility becomes a fact belonging to the past. Let's get familiar with *this* fact and try to accept it."

A few more minutes passed before he continued.

"You said you never followed her, but apparently you did. And you said you never committed a violent act. See where I'm going? Perhaps you did, but you don't remember."

What is this, delivering a knockout?

Our food arrived. We sat in silence, neither of us eating, for different reasons.

I summoned whatever energy left in me. "Let's start again, please. Did I hurt my wife?"

"Okay. So, here's the thing. We've tried introducing the facts for a long time now, and each time you shut down again. We tried quite a few times. You've been here for a long time, in case you're wondering."

"I don't recall," I tightened my lips, and barely swallowed because of my mouth dryness. He observed my reactions, looking for clues whether I lied when I had no clue about what went on.

"Whatever I tell you, try to focus on some present consciousness, like our newly formed friendship," he said. "What will you say if I told you, you've been here for ten years?"

"I wouldn't like that fact, and I'd demand an explanation for why I am kept here against my will," I replied.

"No, forget the laws and rights and whatnot. Would you commit suicide if someone imprisoned you for life?" he asked.

"No. Life doesn't stop, you can do a lot, discover and change in oneself. When your power fails you, then maybe..."

He interrupted. "So, the physical presence or the period is not the driving factor, correct?"

"I guess not." I shrugged my shoulders.

"If I told you ten years passed while you are here, how would you feel?"

"I'd be miserable because my mind would definitely be broken." I considered the possibility before but admitting to Gary was tough. "I'd worry about my cure, and... and I would be grieving over the lost precious time I could have spent with my family."

"You are expressing well. We don't need delays going around the subject. We are not yet sure of the diagnosis, but your psychosis is transient so far. Before you arrived here, the physicians narrowed your diagnosis down to two possibilities. Luke transferred you here because our center is specialized in treating conditions like yours."

I stared at the ceiling. My mind raced: Luke got me here. Who is the man at the gas station? What is "a long time" in here?

"Don't let your mind drift, come back. Focus on the present."

"How long have I been here?"

"You should tell how long. You're a very resourceful man, Jason. You pulled a smart stunt in the pool area." He laughed.

"What stunt?" How the hell does he know?

"Luke called. Watching the clip of Sandals faking the heart attack was hilarious, but I am impressed by your planning and execution." He made a ring with his index and thumb, gesturing perfection.

"Thank Luke for me," *Traitorous Luke.*

"Trust Luke and me. This is for your benefit. And the moment you allow me in is when I can start helping you heal," Dr. Thompson said.

The panic attack persisted. My heart didn't slow yet, and I held my palms under my thighs to hide the shaking. I became cold.

"I think you're innocent. I want to set the record straight." He said graciously.

"What? Am I accused of something?"

Innocent of what, you slick shit?

"No, you are not accused. Now let me ask you this." He moved on so quickly. I doubted if any kind of therapy worked at such a fast pace. "CyberCrews fired you. Do you remember?"

"No, they never fired me. No way I'm being fired. I work hard, and I always go above and beyond."

"Not *being* fired. The company has already fired you. The situation wasn't normal. They wanted you to stay, but you stopped showing up, and they sent you many letters and contacted your lawyer. They appointed an interim person to replace you for some time, but you never showed up again, so you were eventually let go."

I tried my best to digest what he said, but the whole story seemed unreal or fabricated.

"And your *disappearance* from work happened three months before the termination. They must like you to have waited for such a lengthy period." Dr. Thompson stopped for a minute. I was speechless. "We must establish a time-line. In June, you stopped going to your office, but you still put on your suit and disappeared daily. In early September, you trailed your wife around. They admitted you to a hospital on September 14 and transferred here on December 22."

He went to his desk again, and I jumped to my feet and chased him. We both froze and locked eyes, like deer before they lock horns. A surge or a current of energy built up inside me.

Fired? Daily disappearances? Followed Lisa?

"I will take something from my drawer. Calm down." Dr. Thompson drew a deep breath and then removed a small key chain with an electronic lock similar to a garage door remote. "And if you assault me or try anything stupid, I'll press the alarm button, and all of this work will go down the drain. Now, you don't want such a setback, do you?" He spoke calmly.

I slowly took three steps toward the door, relaxed my shoulders, and placed my hands behind my back and locked my fingers.

"Here, read the letter."

This is HELL.

How can the letters start in June until termination in August? And why don't I remember? Why?

I only remembered the day I left work early and drove home.

"I remember none of these. I remember driving home from work."

"Yes. Work. A new job, a different one, but not Cyber-Crews," Dr. Thompson exclaimed. "Luke confirmed you didn't need your job anymore, he said you worked on a special project. Do you remember anything related to your work?"

I shook my head.

"Do you remember renting a new office?"

I didn't answer this time. Honestly, I couldn't be sure, I sat at many desks in my life.

"What the hell did you do during this time?" he said abruptly. "You can't lose three months of your memory like this. Simply not possible. And now, so much is at stake.... So you remember what you want to remember, what suits you, what protects you."

"I don't remember." I raised my voice. "You either believe me or not. I can't force you."

"Try, at least. Where were you on the 4th of July? Anything? Try, close your eyes and try."

I closed my eyes; the darkness unsettled me.

An idea crossed my mind: insects can't imagine the consciousness of an animal, and the most intelligent animal can't imagine the consciousness of a human. I could not understand what people around me understood. Something had died or burned inside of me, and I couldn't think like my old self. I remembered Sandals expression, "burned wires."

I heard Dr. Thompson moving to his desk, the lock clicking, and papers rattling.

"Open your eyes." He gave me a newspaper. "It's 2017, Jason. You have been here for five months, add the three months before coming here, of which you remember nothing. Eight months are absent from your mind, my friend. You must understand why."

Fuck you. I'm not your friend.

I read the newspaper, and the tears rolled down my cheek. The year *was* 2017, and Trump won the presidential race. Doctoring such a paper could be done easily, you could get excellent quality for a hundred dollars.

He held out a tablet. "You might not believe the paper, so instead give me a couple websites you trust."

"Harvard," Damn. A headline read *Top Takeaways From 2016.* "Try Roscosmos please."

"It isn't loading," he sighed.

"Try Roscosmos.ru, not .com," The Russian version of NASA. The date checked out too, news banners from 2017 moved across the screen. In English, the header read *IN SPACE WE TRUST.* Yes, like the dollar.

Without asking me, he played videos of him and me on the tablet, and my stomach turned upside down at the sight.

I stood up and moved away, I swerved to the right, and then to the left. I became nauseous and cold, my hands shaking, but I found the trash bin and vomited.

IMPURE TRUTH

I woke up in the white room. I couldn't remember how I got here, but I remembered the discussion from the day before, and it left me in an unshakable foul mood.

A nurse visited me holding a handy phone. "Hi, Jason. Dr. Thompson for you." He signaled with his eyes: *Come on.*

"Hi, Jason," Dr. Thompson said. "I'm looking forward to our meeting tonight. One question, please. Remind me—how old are you?"

He intended to check whether the news destabilized me, pulling me back to the repression zones and to amnesia.

"Don't worry. I remember everything. The year is 2017, for confirmation."

"Great. Let's continue over dinner and a chess game." He chirped.

"Okay."

I thanked the nurse smiling courteously.

Around 7 p.m., they escorted me to the clinic. Dr. Thompson wore a V-neck white cotton shirt. On his forearm, a faint small tattoo said I.B.G.F. I never saw him in casual clothes. Someone added a small bed in a corner of his office.

After the greetings, I asked him about the ink. "What does your tattoo mean?" I thought it related to a gang or a sort of mantra reminder.

"Nowadays, it's a reminder of buoyant youth, but at the time, the letters meant Intelligent. Brave. Greedy. Foolish," he numbered the words on his fingers.

"Did you come up with the wording or get it from a famous person?"

"I did," He smiled.

We ordered dinner, but eating turned into a task; a nourishment need and not an indulgence for the taste buds.

"Tell me about the dream."

"We agreed it is not a dream." I gave a smirk. Afterward, I gave in totally. *Be my guest; let's dive to the unknown.*

"Any other dreams? Weird or recurrent?"

"Yes. I had this one few times. I enter a funeral home, and as I'm walking down an aisle, I see many friends. I reach the first row where my family sat. I see Lisa and Lea, and Lisa signals me with her head to check the casket. I move toward the casket; the view is zooming in a surreal sense, like in a movie. I open the casket, and I see myself inside. I turn back, and there is no one there, and the room is pitch black."

"Okay. Any other dreams?" he asked while jotting down a few notes. I responded with "none".

"Did you ever use drugs? Specifically, in the last year leading to the event?"

"I wish to say no, but unfortunately, I did. In high school and college, I smoked marijuana, nothing too dangerous, but I enjoyed the experience. And then for a decade, I used nothing. I read a book a while ago about acid being used in very low doses. I'd been taking small doses for a year before I lost my memory. Acid supposedly makes you more creative in your work, promote lateral and creative thinking." I felt ashamed of sharing this reckless behavior with a doctor.

"Acid. Hmm. Lysergic acid can cause psychotic episodes at recreational doses, but it isn't well-studied in smaller doses."

"So, could the drugs be the reason for all this? Are the effects reversible?" I asked eagerly.

We may have found the reason for this nightmare.

"Did you take a high dose?"

"No, I never did high doses."

"It could still be the cause. Maybe you took a high dose during the period you can't remember." He took a deep breath in. "What defines a human being? How do you rate modern people, a man or a woman?"

"The questions deserve deep thinking, but off the top of my head, I would say their footprint in life, work achievements, family, faith, values, and standards. How they take care of their body and what they give back to the community. The definition varies from one person to another, and one place to another. Whether they recycled." I chuckled.

"So, a mistake does not define a person?" he asked.

"No," I said.

"Even if the mistake of taking a drug led to an unwanted side effect?"

"Well, most mistakes don't define the person. You can't make a judgment based on such a small act. You would be overlooking years of effort, thought, memories, and emotions."

"What if taking the drug also leads to a lapse in judgment or some injury to oneself and others?" he asked.

"Tough one. Like driving under the influence of alcohol? In my opinion, the act defines you because the act endangers others."

"DUI is a well-known crime, but I can't say the same about acid. Let's say you're here because of a medication side effect. This is easier to accept than being here because you killed someone while driving drunk."

"Yes. Obviously." I shrugged my shoulders.

"The side effects of alcohol are well-known, but people don't foresee the consequences. Let's say you took a bad batch of acid and you attacked someone without awareness, I wouldn't be too hard on you, and you shouldn't be either. Mistakes happen, and they're part of who we are. We can learn to accept our mistakes."

We fell silent for a minute; my mind raced through possibilities. Then he said, "You must accept your mistakes, whatever they are. You must accept that sometimes we do things based on the situations we're in, and we aren't fully aware of the consequences at the time."

The food interrupted us. Neither of us had the energy to discuss the matter further, intention and culpability, we needed rest.

"So, let's continue. Take a few deep breaths and relax your body." After two minutes, he added, "So, to repeat the facts, you were taking lysergic acid, and you discovered your wife's cheating, and you don't recall the last few months. Right?" I nodded. "Did you hurt your wife?"

I didn't answer. I mean for fuck's sake; it *was* possible. I wondered what hurt meant.

"Did you *HARM* your wife?"

"No. I don't remember I did. I wish I could remember."

"I'll tell you what happened. You cracked. You suspected she started an affair, and you stopped going to work as a reaction to the betrayal. And you followed her to be sure, and once confirmed, you acted." He sighed. "You killed her."

"Nope. No. That didn't happen. I would never harm Lisa, even if she cheated on me. Is she okay? Did I hurt her?" I stood up and paced the room. "I would never do anything bad to her. *Kill my wife*? Never. Never. I'm a pacifist, and I love her more than anything."

"You can't be certain, though."

"No," I said. "We have an open dialogue about everything, including sex and urges and needs. Sure, we get jealous and possessive, but rarely compared to other people. What holds us together is not whether she or I engage in a five-minute sexual *act* ending in a twenty-second orgasm."

"An open dialogue doesn't mean you accept cheating though, right?"

"We put in the effort, and the open dialogue protects us from diving into fights over a biological need. So, when our sex life slowed down, we came up with new ideas and acted on them. I pitched a threesome, but she wasn't interested. She said she wouldn't mind if I did something on the side without her knowledge."

"This is one-sided. The deal takes care of your urges and desires, but not Lisa's. Did she ever discuss her needs?"

I thought about whether she was okay. Did I kill her? I genuinely hoped I hadn't hurt her.

"No, we didn't discuss her need. Still, I can't imagine myself hurting her. I don't believe you, whatever it is I've supposedly done. I do not believe your stories. I love her so much. When I followed her, I wanted to make sure she was cheating, not to hurt her, but to open a discussion." After a minute of silence, I said, "I wanted to focus on winning her back. I thought she wanted my attention through her actions. She is not a lavish woman who went on wild trips, she just needed me to be myself again. Like a wake-up call."

"Okay," Dr. Thompson said. "Let's change courses. Tell me about the moment when you felt most proud and the most peaceful moment you recall—either, or both, whatever you prefer."

"A proud moment? When I ran after a dog off its leash in our community. I ran for three miles after her. I searched in the bushes, behind ramps, and then I spotted her. The run exhausted her, so I approached slowly and hugged her. I waited until her owners came. They were looking for her around the block. Some people wouldn't regard the chase as something big, but I do. I used to own a dog, and this made me happy."

"When did you own a dog?"

"I got him from middle school until the first years of my marriage. Let's go back. What happened? What did I do?"

"I'll tell you later," he said. "Lea, Lea, Lea. A beautiful girl. How old is she now?"

"Fifteen. No, sixteen." I remembered. *2017*.

"Has anyone told you anything about your relationship with your daughter?"

"What do you mean told me anything?"

"Did anyone talk to you about your relationship with her? Or perhaps advise you about how close you were?" He took his time choosing his words carefully.

"Like an intervention? Are you serious?"

"No, nothing like that. Just drawing your attention to certain parts of your relationship with her."

"Lisa told me our close relationship is weird. Nothing else. Luke told me a couple of times we are too close, and I should give her some space."

"Did they specify what close meant?"

"Lisa said we tell each other everything. I guess she felt excluded. Luke said we text a lot, and we stay connected all the time. I guess he hated the interruptions when we met. Nothing notable."

"Why do you call her 'babe' and 'love'?"

"Who told you? How do you know about that? And what the fuck does it matter?"

"After the *accident*, the police took your phone and checked your messages with her. Who takes his daughter on a date? Tells her to dress up? Do you think such behavior is normal?" He mocked me, intentionally provoking me.

"Many mothers call their sons babe, and whether I say babe and love to my daughter is no different. I regularly take her on dates because I love her a lot. But I'm not in love with her," I said, and my chest got tight. I wanted to cry. I was vulnerable and exposed. In my mind, my relationship with Lea was a healthy one. I would not accept the insinuation from Gary.

I said, "Whatever you're hinting at, just don't. It isn't true. I would never lay a hand on my wife, and I would never abuse my daughter. I'm careful not to say anything hurtful to her, let alone hurt her in such a way."

I was frightened. The truth of my intimate relationship with Lea was out in the open. What right did Dr. Thompson have to expose me?

"In your texts, a peculiar one drew my attention, you told her to wear the tight red dress." He stopped for a few seconds. I controlled my reactions. "Did you enjoy looking at her body? Did you feel an urge to do something sexual with her?"

I laughed sarcastically. "No. An absolute no. Fuck you, this is over. I'm leaving." I walked to the door that was locked. I turned back to face him. "If you say anything else about her, I will punch you."

"Jason. You just said you aren't a violent person." He flipped a page in his notepad. "A pacifist."

I took a deep breath. "You wouldn't judge our proximity and intimacy if Lea was a person with a disability. Or a recovering addict. Isn't that right? You would even say such parenting is an example to be followed by other parents."

"Did you enjoy when she told you about her sex life? Whom she sleeps with—and how?" He questioned with disgust.

"If she told Lisa, you wouldn't judge. You would admire how close they are, how they share everything. I'm protective of Lea, and I respect her privacy. I never obliged her to tell me, never pressured her. She shares when she wants, and I listen, I advise... Fuck you, Gary." I tried my best to focus on breathing. "I never enjoyed her telling me."

"Why didn't you enjoy?"

When I didn't answer, he raised his voice. "I asked why didn't you enjoy? Why were you annoyed when she told you about other men kissing her, groping her, lying with her?"

I wanted to hit him with something, ideally an ashtray. Instead, I froze. I held my breath.

"Because it made me jealous. There. Satisfied?"

I'm sorry you're sick, but fuck you.

My throat tightened. I could have cried.

"Jealous!" he said. "Why? Because you're in love with her?"

"No. What father would feel okay about his daughter sleeping with men? I'm jealously possessive, protective, but not jealous to be her lover."

"I don't believe you," he blurted out.

"Fuck you, asshole. This subject is off the table. You aren't allowed to utter Lea's name anymore."

He stood and went to make another cup of tea. He didn't use a tea-bag this time. Instead, he used something he'd brought with him.

"What happened to me?"

"You killed your wife," he said dispassionately.

"No way. No. Don't say that." I didn't know how to react or what to do.

"I'm not kidding. Here, read this newspaper."

It was true. I didn't know what to think. Must. Breathe. The room grew darker, and I passed out.

CHAPTER

5

BROKEN

CHAPTER 5:

BROKEN

I woke up in my room drained of energy, and anxiety took over me. "My mind is a tool, my mind is a monkey, and I control it," I repeated to myself as I paced the room.

The calmest among us transforms into a savage under the right circumstances, but I couldn't believe I killed Lisa without remembering. I wished someone would intervene and confess this was all a bad joke, the worst one.

My thoughts spiraled until we reached Dr. Thompson's office. On the way, I kept my head down, embarrassed to look people in the eye. Although I knew no one in the place, I cared for their opinion of me.

The room stank of old people smell. *The cancer is spreading,* I told myself. Dr. Thompson sat on the couch looking yellower than last time, skinny and frail.

I lied down and closed my eyes wishing this nightmare would stop. Lisa's voice echoed in my mind, "Ask for help, never shy away. We all need help at some point." She used to tell me whenever I hit a rough patch or passed through one of my low periods.

"People fear losing control over their minds because others take advantage of them, steal from them, abuse them. But the *true* risk to the individual comes from the one losing control." Dr. Thompson said.

"True."

"Did you fight with Lisa?"

"Yes. All married couples fight. Our fights were normal, in frequency and intensity. I thought we could separate for some time, not because of cheating. We wanted different things at different stages of our lives. Lisa always asked me if she should go away for a month or two. But once the separation happened, she wanted to punish me, she asked me to move out and stay away from the family."

"So, you're remembering now," he said.

"Ask, don't imply. Please." I grinned. "I remember emotions and thoughts, not incidents and dates."

"Okay. Continue please," he said.

"I wanted to try new things, to travel for a month to a foreign country, write a play, or be part of an experiment."

Paranoid ideas tried to sneak in: *What if this is an experiment?*

"When did this talk take place?"

"I don't know, but during the period in which I stopped going to CyberCrews." I looked at the floor.

"Do you remember where you went instead or with whom you met?"

"Nothing. Just that I stopped going to work. I also remember the letters the company sent," I said

"What happened afterward?"

"I packed a suitcase and left, but I slept at home once or twice per week, in the basement on a foldout bed. And I always returned home for dinner. Lisa refused to talk claiming I abandoned my family." I paused. "I remembered something, I became fond of the basement because of the autonomy while staying close to the family."

"Continue."

"A few times I sneaked into our room to watch Lisa during her sleep. How could I kill her? I would never harm her. No way."

I imagined what Lisa's family had said about me to the press, on TV shows, in court. Lisa's brother, Brent, would have been the meanest. Her family tried to build a relationship, but I neglected their attempts. I kept wondering whether they would have forgiven me if I'd done anything to Lisa. *I* didn't hurt her, but some sick part of my mind, my other personality. Not me.

Lea's forgiveness was the most important thing. Could she look past this? My eyes filled up. "So, Lea isn't speaking with me. Is this why we can't call her?"

He didn't answer.

"Where did they bury Lisa?" I didn't recall whether she preferred cremation.

"She's in a cemetery near your home," he said. "Would you like to visit?"

I wanted to so badly. To apologize, to cry, to hug the gravestone.

"Yes. Can we go today?"

"Not today, but soon. I sense you're drifting, many thoughts are coming to your mind, and that's normal." He changed his tone. "Let's talk about Lea."

"No. Let's talk *to* her. Call her. I want to hear her voice."

Full panic mode kicked in. Did I meet Lea in court? I imagined her causing a scene, calling me names. I became dizzy and close to losing consciousness again. I extended my arms on the sofa for support.

"Speak up, don't hold your emotions in," he said.

How can I tell him what went on inside me?

Fear paralyzed me. Did somebody hurt my baby? Or worse, did I hurt her?

He put his hand over mine. "Jason. Speak up. We must work together, or you'll suffer. Don't be afraid."

"Is my baby okay? Is she injured?" Tears rolled down my cheek.

"She is not okay," he said.

I succumbed to the floor breathing shallowly. I crawled on my knees to Dr. Thompson, and I studied his face, trembling with fear. "Is she dead? Tell me she's okay. Tell me she's alive. I beg you! Tell me she is okay!" I whimpered.

He didn't answer, and I understood. After a while he said, "she is dead, Jason. I'm very sorry. I wish the truth were different. I wish I could tell you she is okay, but she's gone."

I became numb. I lied on the floor and the tears poured down my face. My chest ached. I remembered the broken heart syndrome, when people died from a terrible breakup or heartache.

Please stop and let me die.

I wished I had never wasted a minute away from Lisa and Lea.

Once on my feet, I became nauseous. Dr. Thompson spoke about grief, acceptance, and finding a reason to live.

Revenge will be a good reason to live, afterward, I'll die in peace.

"How did she die?" I asked.

"Someone shot her."

Did Lisa kill her? If she did, therefore killing Lisa made sense. Actually, the only reason I would ever hurt Lisa was if she harmed Lea. But why would she? The whole story made a little more sense.

"Who shot her?"

Dr. Thompson didn't reply.

Is it possible? No way.

"WHO SHOT HER?" I cried.

He pursed his lips "Lisa did."

"No way. NO WAY. They love each other. Lisa devoted her entire life for Lea. No. This isn't real, this is not real." I slapped myself and screamed, "WAKE UP! JUST WAKE UP!"

"Jason. Calm down. Calm down." I was about to faint.

He grabbed my hands. "Jason, you must stop, this is exactly what you do whenever we reach this stage."

"This isn't real." I sobbed until I coughed hard. The room grew darker.

"Jason, don't sleep."

Dr. Thompson moved my legs to rest slightly above the level of my head.

"Jason, open your eyes."

I lied on the couch, conscious.

"Relax. Breathe."

"What happened? Why would Lisa shoot her?"

Dr. Thompson showed me a few photos of the crime scene at our home, I saw the blood spattered on the walls of the doorway, but no bodies.

"This is not real." I wanted to wake up, I slapped myself harder. Enough pain. "Wake up. Wake up!"

I had never prayed much before, but at that moment, I pleaded to any higher non-human existence. Give me my family back and take everything else. Let them live. Let me see their eyes one more time. I want nothing else anymore.

Everything faded away. How stupid of me to leave their side every day for work.

"Are any memories coming back?" he asked. "Are you remembering what happened?"

"No," I said.

"Search deeper. Breathe, I don't want you to faint."

I closed my eyes and imagined winter time, when Lisa and Lea used to squeeze next to me on the couch until they pushed me off.

Why would Lisa kill Lea? Lea did nothing to harm Lisa or our family. They never fought and hardly argued.

"What do you think happened?" Dr. Thompson asked after a while.

"I can't think of anything. Lisa adored Lea. Lisa told her she was better than both of us. And parents want to see their children become better than them, right? And then to fucking bury them. Unbelievable." I wept. "Unbearable. Oh, god." I puffed air through my mouth.

"What might have happened?" he asked.

"I don't know. I have no clue why. Did Lea do something? Did she kill someone, run over someone? Drugs?"

I got dizzy again. "What if the shooting was an accident? No other valid explanation, must be an accident. Lisa shot her by accident."

Dr. Thompson walked to his desk and took out something from his drawer. He came back with a newspaper and a tablet.

He took a seat next to me on the couch. "Jason. I'm so sorry for what happened. You had a beautiful family. Moving forward seems unreasonable today, or tomorrow. But with time, you can move forward." He sighed. "I'll tell you what happened."

I held my breath. I didn't know what to hope for; I knew what I didn't hope for and the list was long.

"Check this." He handed me the paper and my hands trembled. A short article written in the local journal, and the title read:

HAPPY FAMILY. THINK TWICE.

ESTABLISHED COMMUNITY WOMAN KILLS DAUGHTER OVER AFFAIR WITH FATHER! FATHER KILLS THE MOTHER!

"What? Is this real? Are you serious? This is disgusting. Unacceptable. Why are they allowed to spread such spiteful news? INCEST? How is this possible? This isn't real! This isn't real!"

"CALM down!" Dr. Thompson yelled, and I froze, surprised by his shriek. "Stop. Just stop saying this isn't real. The universe is not conspiring to doom you. *This* is what history put down, the records, the court documents. This happened." He pointed at the newspaper.

"I choose not to believe because I remember none of this. No way," I said.

Dr. Thompson was already typing on the tablet. "Look." He pulled up the same story from different resources. "Remind yourself you were under the influence of a substance. Maybe with a different personality. You started an affair with your daughter, and your wife learned about the relationship, she fought with your daughter and killed her. You came in and saw Lea's body, and couldn't accept what your wife had done, so your rage took over, and you killed her."

"But I can't believe I would do anything to Lea," I said. "Probably Lisa acted on jealousy. I don't know. I would never harm them."

"The police found your DNA."

"What do you mean, my DNA?" Again, my heart pumped aggressively. I felt each beat in my neck, gut and arms.

"The police retrieved DNA from Lea's body. Your DNA." He waited for a second.

"No. Nooooo. This isn't real. THIS ISN'T REEEAAALLL." I pounded on my head and screamed more. "What DNA?"

"Sperm. She wasn't pregnant."

I curled up on the floor in the fetal position, humming and grunting in pain. I heard chatter and screams. I vomited next to my head and rested in my place, and then I perceived people were moving me.

MATHEW

Denial? They're gone, and I don't deny this.

I assumed everyone imagines losing a family member, accidents happen, my heart skipped a beat when an unfamiliar number showed up on my phone's screen. The anxiety peaked whenever I came too close to crashing into another car, or when Lisa said an idiot nearly pushed her off the road.

I woke up in Dr. Thompson's office drenched in sweat from a nightmare, and he slept in his bed. Vandals had spray painted our house: they wrote CRIMINAL in red paint. FUCKER and RAPIST with black spray. ROT IN HELL, PEDO in yellow. Someone else had drawn the middle finger. I entered the house consumed with hate and hoping to catch one vandal. Once the door flung open, the house was on fire, burning, and the heat blasted on my face like a warm slap. I could hear the flames sizzling and crackling, and in the nightmare, I thought we had lost our memories in the fire.

Fuck the memories, I lost my family. The words shocked me; they are not words merely written from ignorance or prejudice; I am not a victim. No one was adding insult over injury, I well deserved the insult.

It was pitch black outside the office. I pressed the screen of the electronic clock which said 3:32 a.m. Gary turned in his small bed, and he sat up. I doubt he slept.

"How are you now? You slept for some time, and I kept you here. I thought we better continue directly after you woke up. Jesus, so early." He said in a low voice looking at his wristwatch.

How the fuck was I supposed to feel when my family was dead? Psychopaths would not process emotions appropriately, should I worry about his question?

"I don't know. Let's make coffee. Do you have any here?"

"Yes, but only the instant kind. Do you remember what we talked about?" He sat down across from me.

"Instant is fine. I do," I desired to scream again but had no energy.

"I want you to stop the train of thought when it tells you what happened is not real. Whenever you want to scream, try to replace the frustration with phrases, like, this happened, but I did nothing, or I wasn't myself during the incident. Later on, you can replace the phrase. What we don't want is to refuse the fact and thus the reality."

"Have I ever reached this stage? You know, in our earlier meetings?" I asked, he smiled. "Please tell me."

"Yes. The reason you regress is that you push the knowledge out of reality, so the experience stays somewhere inside and not in contact with the present. The current consciousness kicks the content or *encounter*s out."

I don't get it.

"Difficult to understand, but this compartmentalization is what happens in our brains. The pain is immeasurable. I can't tell you not to feel it, but I can tell you how to manage those painful feelings. Hopefully along the way, the pain will slowly subside. The situation is unimaginable now, but it will become better."

"It's so bad. Oh, man, I didn't even say goodbye." My tears fell again, and I sobbed.

"Be honest. What are you thinking? What is your view on life?" He waited, but I didn't respond, I couldn't. I didn't want to say anything. I didn't want to live without them.

"Do you want to live?" he asked.

He waited for a response that didn't come. "Can you find a reason to live? Do you want to *stop* living?" he asked.

"No. Yes," I sobbed.

"Also understandable, and it's normal to think this way. We have limits as human beings. We can only handle a certain amount of pain. If we're feeling extreme fear, we can lose consciousness once it surpasses our tolerable threshold" He paused. "I want you to find a reason to live. What if you can honor their memories?"

It's not enough. But the words didn't come out.

"What if there is another thing? Something big enough to give you the drive to live. You spend your time fighting with yourself, we need to change this."

"What?" I was hoping to connect with the spiritual world, a gate through dimensions. The best thing was to be with them, hugging them.

"Come and see," he said.

He held a small photo, and I sat next to him. The photo was of our family, but with a boy.

"Who's this boy? I know him from somewhere," I said.

"His name is Mathew. Do you recognize him? Or remember any specific time you spent with him?"

"No. But I have seen him a lot." He could be a neighbor's kids or someone Lea had babysat.

Dr. Thompson showed me another photo. "Look at this one." I was holding that same boy up in the air. He appeared to be about seven or eight years old.

"Wow. That's shocking. I don't recall who he is, but I remember this photo. This is a birthday party, and I am thrilled. No clue about him though." I felt scared. Perhaps Lisa or I had hurt the neighbors' kid. I hoped he wasn't also a victim or collateral damage.

"This is your son, Jason, and this was his birthday party." Dr. Thompson said.

The revelation stunned me, but within a minute, the memories flooded in. I perceived them downloading into my brain as if I were watching a progress bar.

"How could I have forgotten my own son? Where is my boy? Mathew. Is he okay? Oh, God. Please let him be okay."

"We don't know for certain. The police presumed him alive, but they haven't located him yet."

"What do you mean 'presumed alive'? We must go get him, search for him. What did the cops do?"

I was excited but equally worried because many months had passed. "When did he go missing?"

"He's been missing since the incident. The cops did a lot. Let's use this to focus on getting better."

I was pacing the room. I lit another small cigar, even though my hand was shaking.

"Let's call Luke now. Maybe he knows something."

We called Luke, and together they explained further what had happened. In short, someone had kidnapped Mathew, and the chances of finding him were slim, at least they and the police thought so.

CHAPTER

7

PEANUTS OVER WALNUTS

I don't understand why things happened in life. People tell you it is all part of a bigger plan, or God is testing you, or you are paying for your mistakes - karma. I prefer a different idea about purification, basically meaning the same soul kept coming back to Earth to be cleansed by passing through many cycles. The imagination behind this idea is admirable. But, of course, we can't be sure about any elucidation. I tried to be practical, to rationalize my catastrophe and understand the reasons.

Why me? I often asked myself. The spiritual roots were inside me, but they were dried up and dead. I settled for accepting I hadn't done an adequate job of protecting my family, from myself.

My diagnosis was 'crazy, with a possible second insane personality'. Dr. Thompson told me the medical term is dissociative identity disorder. He also mentioned he had taken his time in coming to this diagnosis, as per the most recent criteria.

Within a month, I stabilized to a functional stage, and I enjoyed the facility. The downside was that I had to partake in a sex offenders group. I couldn't fathom being treated for something I didn't have, for what I wasn't, despite *all* evidence.

On many occasions I would decide to leave, fed up with the routine and the treatment, but I was surprised when they told me my stay was court-mandated. Luke said, "You were unfit to stand trial, so they found you not guilty by reason of insanity. However, they sentenced you to go to a mental hospital. You should be thankful you're in this place, where you can do what you want."

"This was what happened when the cops found you drenched in blood while standing over your family's bodies, unable to remember anything. Then they matched your DNA and concluded that... You know. That you were sleeping with your daughter, your own flesh and blood.

Luke explained what would have happened if the ruling had been guilty but mentally ill. It meant I would have had to go through all this and then continue my sentence in prison. Apparently, there is an enormous difference between "guilty but mentally ill" and "not guilty by reason of insanity."

My legal team, which Luke wasn't part of, did an almost impossible job of proving I was insane beyond any reasonable doubt. The rate of accepted insanity defense cases is very low, and after acceptance, you must win them. Only one in ten thousand cases were accepted and won.

Despite my lack of knowledge of the judicial system, Luke tried his best to explain to me what happened. Afterward, I felt ashamed that the entire world joined the choir: *rapist, incest, killer.*

"When do I get out?" I asked Luke, more times than I could remember.

"I don't know. Nothing is certain in such cases. Usually, they release you when you're no longer a threat to yourself or others. They will review your case in six months. Just play along, my friend. Benefit from your stay. Consider the stay an opportunity to heal from the loss." He didn't dare to suggest healing my sexual perversions or wash away my guilt.

I wondered if the staff could sense my despair. Every day, I opened my eyes and felt disappointed to be alive. I spent a lot of time wishing I would die peacefully during the night.

Oh, fuck I'm still here! I'll make some coffee, I would think when I woke up.

I was smoking again. I had only quit for health reasons. I smoked again because I didn't care anymore, despite the improvements in my stamina and the rigorous exercise.

Luke believed someone had framed me, so he helped me as a friend and not as a lawyer. Nobody was as generous with his time as he was.

The state's narrative is that Lea had sent a text to Lisa saying: "Too bad you couldn't keep your man. I'm moving out." Lisa confronted Lea about "our" relationship. Lisa, unable to accept the facts, shot Lea. The detectives found gunpowder residue on her hand.

One bullet hit Lea in the chest and pierced her heart, and the second passed by her as she fell and hit the wall behind her. The shooting angle confirmed the height of the shooter was similar to Lisa's, not to mine. The investigators confirmed in the ballistics report that the shooter equipped the gun with a silencer.

I couldn't get over the fact that Lisa had a gun to begin with. Now I was supposed to believe she'd bought one with a silencer? Had she been planning a perfect crime? The idea was strange and didn't fit the image of the woman I'd idolized for her peaceful approach and respect for others.

"The question isn't whether she kept a gun," Luke told me, "because she could have bought one for personal defense. Remember, you weren't always sleeping in the house. The question is whether she needed a firearm. Intended to use one. Was capable of using one."

I didn't know all the answers, but surely, she could handle a gun. "Why would she buy a silencer? Doesn't that confirm her intent?" I asked.

Luke explained it was a possibility, but sometimes the arms dealer tempted customers to buy both the gun and the silencer as a package or just told inexperienced buyers the silencer was part of the package - we sell them together. So, *she* could have bought the gun with a silencer for protection.

Lisa had discarded the gun into one of the many dumpsters at the back of the neighborhood while on her way to pick Mathew up. The police's theory was that after the crime, she'd wanted to smuggle Mathew out of the country. The cameras confirmed Lisa came alone in her car and picked him up at 2:35 p.m. Afterward, she must have handed him over to someone before coming home to collect clothes and cash.

At 2:10, Lisa had gotten the text from Lea.

At 2:35, Lisa had picked up Mathew from school.

I came home at around 3:15.

Lisa didn't expect me to come home early, but I did. Presumably, I saw Lea's body and flipped out. I confronted her; she admitted it, and I strangled her with one of my belts, but not the one I was wearing. Mathew was not there.

A few hours later, a neighbor knocked on our door to discuss the neighborhood patrol. He saw the scene through the window and called the cops. I had cleaned the bodies and dressed them, prepared dinner, and seated them around the dining room table. The cops said I was speaking for all three of us when they arrived, that I was in a complete trance.

Nobody in the neighborhood had heard the two gunshots.

Still no sign of Mathew's whereabouts.

All the police officers' and private investigators' following leads got nowhere. They didn't leave a stone unturned in the whole country. Luke ran ads across the nation, and he received thousands of hollow calls. He still had an investigator on the case. We wished someone would just hand him over out of the blue. The reward reached one million dollars, with no benefit.

Life inside the facility was comfortable but not thrilling. I floated along without a purpose, counting the days. They offered family therapy, but I didn't have a family anymore, my brother and sister wanted nothing to do with me. They thought I would molest their children. I didn't expect them to come, although I had always supported them when they needed me, but they could have at least called and asked about me.

I never thought of escaping again. Wherever I wanted to go, my destiny was sealed. I was finished on many levels, but I still didn't want to end up in prison.

On one of my walks with Luke, I thanked him sincerely for being there for me. He said, "My friend, I've witnessed a lot during my years of practice, and I learned not to trust what people claim. Even when we're certain of the truth, you can never imagine what's going on inside someone. You're innocent, but you know how the legal system works." I knew he thought I was innocent, but hearing him say it comforted me, despite all the zombifying meds I had ingested. He also mentioned, "I don't believe you had a second personality under which you acted and killed."

They separated us into groups inside the facility, and everyone despised my group. Imagine being an outcast even in a mental institution, as if being in one isn't enough to destroy you. My group included pedophiles and people who had kept child pornography.

I had to pass the time to get out. They said I wasn't making progress in therapy. After many discussions with Luke, he asked, "You aren't sick, so how can they treat you? You must be sick to be treated. Do you get where I'm going?" So, I had to fake sexual perversion, then show progress in my treatment for it. The act was demeaning, but according to their scale, I had made considerable progress in no time.

A month is now considered no time, not valid from my point of view.

A slender, fine-looking woman attended one of my counseling groups, so I had something to look forward to three times a week. The therapists divided us into teams for tasks such as doing puzzles or building bridges. The woman always tried to cross the room and join my team. But when they put us in pairs, she would run away.

She attracted me, but I didn't know if her magnetism was because I hadn't had sex for a year. Like grocery shopping when you're hungry—it's not recommended. I didn't even masturbate during my entire stay. I'd had a few wet dreams, which happens if you don't empty. I wondered if animals got wet dreams too. I intended to look it up online later.

The woman's name was Kelly. I wanted to know more about her. I asked her why she was in the center, and she said, "You take an interest in me, and the first thing you ask is what's wrong with me? Try harder."

I followed her around the compound. Following someone energized me in a gruesome way. I wondered whether I felt this thrilled when I stalked Lisa. I gained little about

Kelly, except that she often shopped at the only two places available in the facility. I gathered she had lived in the drug addiction unit first and later moved to the general population residence, but the information wasn't sure. There was something strange about her case, she also attended sex offenders group sessions.

"If the circumstances were different, I would ask you out," I told her. I used my sexy eyes, but without success. She didn't take her eyes off the block building we were working on. It was a complex, three-dimensional puzzle, and we'd already passed the one-hour mark.

"I said, if we could go out of here, I would have asked you out."

She looked at me and folded her arms, and my confidence went skydiving. I said, "I would treat you well, show you a good time. We'd have fun for a change."

I used to be good at this. Now I've become a joke.

"I can go out. You can't," she said.

Shit, this is harsh.

"Yeah? Really? That's cool." We were silent for some time.

Then she said, "If you help me finish this before the others, maybe I'll consider your offer."

I got to appreciate her more. She was an artist, and she traveled a lot. She didn't tell me what they treated her for, and I didn't ask again. After a few more encounters she became friendly, and after a few more, flirtatious.

"You know you can ask me out here," she said one time.

When I drew closer to her, I watched her body and her breasts when she leaned forward. She smelled of flowers. You had to take a deep breath to catch it.

"Okay, I will see you at seven," she said. "Oh, bring your laptop with you. Mine has a problem. You can show me something interesting if you have any."

The last thing she uttered threw me off. I assumed she thought I might own some twisted pornography. I wasn't interested in going anymore. The rules in the center were not to share electronic devices.

As big a hard-on as she gave me, I decided not to go, to stand her up. I looked at the watch every minute until half past seven. I was sitting in the rec area, and she stormed in.

"Motherfucker. Standing me up. You think you can do this shit with me, you piece of crap? You're nothing, asshole. Fuck you!" she yelled.

I tried to act as if she didn't direct her shouts at me.

"Relax, Kelly. It happens to the best of us. Go get a pretzel," I said calmly.

She left, cursing me.

The next day, she bumped me during breakfast, knocking my tray out of my arms. I caught her smiling as I picked up the items off the floor. Over the day, I kept following her, making it look coincidental. I wished I could follow her to the bathroom while she showered. I was so horny, I couldn't believe it. I imagined bottling my libido and selling it.

Later that day, I saw her while going to the counseling meeting, so I strolled to make sure we met at the corner.

She was wearing low-rise jeans with a wide belt and a sleeveless cotton shirt. She walked faster on purpose, and I missed her. At the end of the hall, we would make a right turn to go into our group meeting room. She surprised me and took a left, so I pursued her. The direction led to the basketball court, typically empty at that time. I pushed the door open, found the court empty, and turned to go back. But as I did, she leaped out and grabbed my throat with her left hand.

I raised my hands gesturing surrender. "Easy, easy. I didn't mean to scare you," I said.

"You don't scare me."

She pressed a shiv against my inner thigh. "Do you want me to cut and spill your balls, or are you going to stop following me around? Speak up, sicko."

Yes, even the best leopards are caught sneaking up on their prey.

"First," I said, "I'm not a sicko. Second, I like you. If you didn't shut me out and try to trick me into using my laptop, I wouldn't be following you. The session has started, let's go. Truce?"

I acted calm, but with one jolt I overturned her, taking the weapon, grabbing her neck from behind and pointing the shiv at her cheek.

Her body was warm and throbbing. I dropped the shiv, relaxed my grip around her neck. I slid my hand down to the front of her body, over a necklace, my fingers smooth and light on her chest, and I rested my hand on her abdomen. Our eyes locked. Her breath was steamy and smelled of cherries. "You're so beautiful. I have been think-ing a lot about this." I kissed her, and she kissed me back as passionately as I imagined it.

A GRAY RAINBOW

The days weren't so bad with Kelly around. She was fun and light. She would impersonate the therapists and some patients. We shared our smoking hideouts. It was exciting to sneak around the guards for a smoke before hanging out in our rooms, like teenagers. After a while we became inseparable. We exercised, ate, and read together, but we didn't sleep together. Two months passed, and we didn't fuck; she had a no access policy and she wasn't willing to explain.

Kelly was of eastern Asian origin; with blonde hair except for the two inches nearest the scalp. She had a southern accent. Her overalls look didn't match how she sounded, but I got used to it. As days went by, I developed feelings for her, and they grew with time.

I searched for her online, but she didn't seem to exist. She never told me why she enrolled in the treatment, although I persisted in asking. She asked me a few times about my past, and I lied. I feared that if she knew my history, she would stop wanting to be around me. I became attached to her and wasn't willing to risk separation. Confidentiality was one of the key selling points of this place. Nobody knew why you were here except for specific therapists. Even the group therapists didn't know.

Gary wasn't doing well, and the treatments came with terrible side effects. He said things were okay on the survival side; however, the treatment became worse than the illness itself. He said he left me a letter, and when the time came I should read it when in need. I hoped that he'd get through.

I fought a lot with Kelly. We were different. One time she pressed me hard about my past and I insisted that I'd told her everything. She kept pressing, and I got defensive. I thought if I told her and we broke up later, she would leak my story. Ironically, when I shouted, she said, "Jason, relax, honey. Everybody knows about you. Your case was on the news all the time. So unless someone here is totally nuts, they know who you are. It's simple. If you hadn't been on TV, then maybe you could have kept your story a secret."

The revelation shocked me. I thought about how confidently I had walked the halls of this place, thinking my past was well-hidden. I spent the next few days alone, avoiding all activities and interactions.

The visiting area was close to the communal area but separate. I passed by regularly to get a glimpse of what the outer world looked like. One time I thought I saw Lisa's father, Deen, so I hid behind the wall and peeked. We were worlds apart, and no way he could visit anyone in the center.

After a few minutes of focused staring, I decided it wasn't him. He resembled Deen, but this guy was thin while Deen wasn't. I walked between the tables, keeping an eye on him, and suddenly he smiled. Not a threatening smile, but not a happy one, either. I thought about the smile. What did it contain? He hit me with a juice bottle, knocked me down, and kicked me. The security guards took him off me. You could imagine the things he said.

After the incident with Deen, I became more insecure and ashamed. People who didn't know about me now knew. I spent more time in my room, and Kelly visited me frequently.

You remember how people made you feel, more than incidents or things, which is how our brains process memory. I was happy with Kelly. She accepted me for what I was. It was as if I had died and gone to heaven, and all was forgiven. She slept with me and I thought it was out of pity.

Therapy progressed well, and my scoring changed to very good. "Spectacular progress," they said.

For me, the relationship remained steady, and I shared great moments with Kelly. It was real for me. I wanted to get out and rent a place together, live a peaceful life. She might help me search for Mathew.

She asked a lot about my past, and she tried some hypnotic stunts with me. She had a deep insight into my condition. I told her about my plans for when we left, and she said, "I'm leaving next week. I have already decided so."

I went mad and then felt broken. I asked her why she hadn't told me before, and she pleaded with me not to be mad. She gave me her real name so I could look her up when I got out. Her first name *was* Kelly, but she had a different surname. Her real name appeared nowhere online, as if it had been erased intentionally.

On the last day, she said she was some kind of doctor and had a relationship with a patient that led to her license being revoked. The turbulent changes devastated her, and she lost her lover. She slipped into a turmoil of sex and drugs, but she refused to give me the details. I burned inside, knowing she might have been passed around in fuck gangs, high and unaware.

"What do you mean sexy and dangerous? How many? For how long?" I repeatedly asked, and she refused to respond. She said it didn't matter if she understood why and could identify the signals to prevent such slip-ups again. Another time she mentioned her past didn't matter because she had feelings for me.

I liked to think she was sincere when she said she had feelings for me, this was something I kept alive in my memory and used it as a constant motivation to push myself to get out of here as soon as possible. I'd thought no one could ever love me, let alone be in a relationship with me.

The last two months were agonizing, boring, and un-eventful. But at last, I was getting out. Searching for my son excited me. Starting a new life and finding the truth. Any-thing was possible, including having Kelly by my side. The only problem was while waiting for my release, I could not be in touch with her in any way, she promised to visit but never did.

Luke found me a new home. I couldn't go to my old house for many reasons, it was smeared and too painful.

On my release date, we expected journalists, but I didn't care. My medicine bag was prepared, my prescription re-newed, my follow-up sessions planned. And all I focused on was Mathew, Kelly, and the truth.

I wanted to call Kelly and say, "Babe, I'm getting out!" But I decided to wait until I was settled in my new place.

PART

2

JERRY

CHAPTER

9

WHO AM I?

I liked to take a panoramic view of my life every now and then. One could call it a sanity check. This time, I wanted an external eye, a fresh opinion, an unbiased assessment of myself and my philosophy.

I contacted a web psychotherapist on a secure website - difficult to find - because I could not walk to a nearby therapist, as it was not secure and traceable. Supposedly, therapists are the best at understanding people. She advised me to get a notebook in which I had to write the important things I discovered, my theories about life, and the exercises she assigned me.

Instead of a paper notebook, I got a new model tablet that the manufacturer advertised as being uncrackable. Encrypted, with joint biometric and password protection. They deliberately designed the tablet not to connect through WiFi. The only way to connect to the Internet was through a cable.

I powered on the tablet and started my first exercise:

Who am I?

I'm Jerry. I'm a human being. A superior one to the flock of the worthless.

I'm in my late twenties, and I'm a hypersexual being. We are all hunters and gatherers, but we descended from a diverse genetic pool, I belong to the elite hunters. In every tribe, in every nation, my ancestors fought savagely to protect their group.

Nowadays, they have no more use for us. They've replaced us with tanks and drones. We're castaways. But the drive remains within us, the few of us left. We have a massive lust, we're hungry to mate and multiply, thirsty for blood.

They hunt us, prosecute us, make an example of us. In the last one hundred years, they've erased thousands of years of savagery and viciousness, and they've transformed societies for nesting robots, gatherers, thinkers, and feeders. The hunter gene, the killer instinct, the raiding elite is endangered; most are unaware of themselves and their potential, and instead, they accept mediocrity. The hunters of yesterday are now teaching Pilates.

How do I live with my nature? I seek pleasure in the dark. I propagate by donating sperm. Shameful. We were once at the head of the flock, and the leaders dreamed of marrying their daughters to us.

We'll endure for now, but in time we shall rise again.

If I could get one message across the world, it would be: "Lady Death is sweet but misunderstood. When she visits you, she is eternally tender and soft. She does not inflict pain. She relieves you from the suffering. Embrace her as if she is your savior."

My phone buzzed to alert me of an incoming message from Vicky.

Vicky: "Hey, babe, how are you? I woke up thinking about you."

The second one: Tongue and kiss emoticons. "Special boy. Wink."

Third: "What are you doing? I miss you."

Me: "Nothing much, working. Miss you too. What's on your mind?"

Vicky: "My friends are talking about loyalty and monogamy, that kind of shit."

And, "Bitches want it all but want their men to stick around. Ughhh. I'm so mad."

And, "They said men cheat more, or at least they have historically."

I didn't understand why she couldn't send all the texts in one message.

"And do you agree that men cheat more?" I replied.

Vicky: "No. Possibly the same."

And, "As long as the couple communicates what they need and how they want it, the relationship will survive." A winking face.

And, "What's your say?"

"I agree. Respect and openness go for both," I replied.

Vicky: An emoticon face with tears of joy. "Allison's face is beet red. LOL."

"Why?" I replied. I loved gossip.

Vicky: "She slept with Becca's boyfriend over the weekend." Devil face. "Becca doesn't know, but she suspects it."

"Allison gave herself away."

"If a fight breaks out, I'll record it for you."

I took a quick note. Familiarize yourself with her friends.

"Shit. What will you do? I thought Allison had a boyfriend," I replied.

Vicky: "Nothing. Not my shit. She does!!!!! And he is hottt. But she does not believe in monogamy."

Vicky: "Will you stay faithful to me?"

I ignored her and returned to my tablet, but a few minutes later the phone buzzed.

Vicky: Middle finger.

Vicky: "Come on, babe." Hearts.

A few more minutes.

Vicky: "Ben. I'm waiting." Three angry faces.

"Hold your horses," I sent, and then, "I told you we can't figure this out now. Too early for us, we haven't cracked the surface yet."

I hoped she got the message. I had been patient enough with her, and couldn't tolerate the situation anymore.

Vicky: "I know." Hands over the face.

"I have a surprise for you. I told you I'm getting ready."

"Give me a minute."

Oh yeah, the wait is over.

I wrote, "I'll always be faithful. I want us to stay close. If I ever want something more, I'll tell you." Kisses.

Three pictures were now downloading. Delicious. They were of her crotch, as she sat on a chair, phone between legs and wearing a skirt. Dark, but I could still see.

Vicky: "Commando. And Shaved!!! As you like it." Tongue emoji.

Vicky: "Words. Tell me."

"Yummy. Fresh. Can't wait. So tonight?" I replied. We hadn't fucked yet, and it was about time. I didn't know how I waited for a month.

Vicky: "Send me yours." Banana emoticon.

"My V is burning, I don't know if it is normal." Fire. Red face.

"I'm not promising, but maybe if you play your cards right." Wink.

"Can't. At work." I replied. I was at home, in my basement, but I didn't want to send her anything. Too risky.

Vicky: "I'm in class!!! Find a way."

"People around. Impossible. What time should I pick you up?" I replied.

Vicky: "Ditching last period. 2 p.m."

"Same thing, underground parking. K?" I replied.

Vicky: "Yeah…" Thumbs up. "No one will see. They can't wait to leave. Nobody stays a minute after classes end."

She was a good girl. Hot, but the anxious type. I wished I had met her a couple of years earlier, but things wouldn't have worked out back then. She was fifteen and still too shy.

I pulled out Ben's details to review them, not that I needed to – I'd made them up – but just in case I had forgotten a small detail.

I transferred Vicky's photos to the laptop and moved them to the encrypted external storage in the closet. I jerked off to them, my second time of the day. The storage capacity in the closet was over 500 terabytes, the many hard disks hooked together were all in organized folders. I also transferred new content from the closet to a primary backup every week. The primary backup was in an apartment ––hidden within many worthless memorabilia items.

I left nothing exposed in my basement. The laptop either traveled with me or was placed in the faux wall. I had a desktop computer serving as camouflage and accounted for my time in network mission games. The drawers had the phones and the tablet, paper, and pen.

I had created an emergency safety measure for the hard disks in the closet by stripping them of their cases and exposing their interiors. I'd placed them all in a reinforced plastic container with sensors, and then I mounted two large flasks of corrosive acid within the container. If anyone tried any password-cracking activities on the laptop or the desktop, or tried to break into the encasing container, or entered the wrong password on either computer a couple of times, a fuse would light and allow the acid into the container. Total time to the expungement was about forty seconds.

Nellie was awake; I heard her rumbling around. She lacked interest in my activities and rarely came down to the basement, especially since I did our laundry.

I received a message on the computer from Dr-Anna45. I messaged back that I didn't want to have a session that day, but I would pay her. She insisted she didn't care about the money and she wanted to learn more about me. She angered me by incorrectly describing me during our last session, so I wasn't sure if I would ever speak to her again, but I hadn't reached a decision yet.

Vicky and I eventually had sex. Unfortunately, I had to use a rubber, which is against my convictions. Let nature take its course and bear my child. The sex was fantastic, except for her labored sounds of enjoyment and her pathetic attempts to hide her pain. *Embrace it.*

A few years ago, I would have skipped the rubber. If she got pregnant, I would have left town. Sadly, running away was no longer an option. We used to move a lot, change houses, start fresh, but Nellie said she wanted to settle and grow in her career. Plus, she had fallen ill with something, not life-threatening, but limited her movement.

I was kind to her, took care of her. She had these frequent spastic episodes, after which she could do nothing for a day. I gave her showers on such days, and she cried from humiliation. She said, "If things take a bad turn for me, I want you to take care of the situation." I asked what she meant, and she said, "Finish it for me." What a fucking cliché. She was asking me to end her life.

What a drama queen. I comforted her during the episode, and the following day she was fine.

INTO THE ABYSS

I slept three hours, as intended, and only as much as the body needed. How useless sleep was when we had so much to accomplish in life. For myself and my kind, saving time became more than necessary—it was fundamental to our survival. If we couldn't live as our nature dictated, we would perish.

I started the day with breathing exercises, to clear the head and make way for planning, and then a jerk off. I stored the semen in the fridge; I would take it with me to the sperm donation center. The chain smoker reception-ist would be surprised at the quantity I came back with from the private room. She would say things like, "Look how much he's packing," and "Honey, have you been sav-ing it all week?" She would stare at my crotch.

I was donating at two centers. At one, my profile said I was your average Joe. For the other, I forged a hell of a profile for a better chance at being highly ranked and selected. Then the center requested certain things from the donor like an audio recording, a temperament test, and genetic sequencing. As per their profiling, I was an idealist slash entertainer; I could pass any test with the right help. I blamed myself for not thinking of this plan earlier and would compensate by donating to as many banks and centers as possible.

I unlocked the tablet, recorded the date, and wrote:

Of Man and Fear

Before man became the human we know today, fear molded him. The signs of fear in our era differ from the old times. Societies are now driven by fear regarding possessions and social image.

The biggest currency that our original fathers had was fear. They instilled it in others and received it on rare occasions. Those who caused terror in their enemies won before the first strike of battle.

Tell me what you fear, and I tell you who you are.

I fear nothing. I loathe weakness; I prey on the frail; I befriend death.

The computer buzzed announcing a message from Dr-Anna45. The chat room on this secure web erased the messages automatically within seconds of being read or within minutes if not yet read. No trail and no history log.

Dr-Anna45: "Hi, Kevin. How are you? Ready?" Smiley face emoji.

"Hi. Good. Yes, but on the condition that you apologize for the descriptions you used last time, and you promise not to use them. I didn't argue my case, and I don't want to hear your science lingo. Save them for your lectures."

Dr-Anna45: "hehehe. Okay. I'M SORRY. Won't happen again, I promise you. I assumed you were fine with the terminology." Folded hands saying please.

"One more thing. You get to ask me questions, but I get to ask you questions as well, and you must be honest. You can omit or replace anything that could reveal your identity. Deal?"

Dr-Anna45: "Deal." Shaking hands emoji.

"Shoot." Flying kiss.

Dr-Anna45: "Is anyone in your family like you? Does anyone have any psychiatric illnesses?"

Infuriating. Keep it together.

"This attraction and activity are normal. Society's current labels are new and inaccurate. They don't match human history. No one in my family told me they were like me, but I'm sure their genes contained hypersexual activity, but they repressed it. No illnesses of such."

Dr-Anna45: "How was masturbation over the past week and during the week we didn't chat?"

"Regular. Four to six times per day. It's a pity you ask about masturbation instead of sex. Assumptions don't speak well of your experience."

Dr-Anna45: "You mean you had something going on in the past two weeks? Do tell. I want to look at each type of sexual activity individually. What material did you use to masturbate?"

"The usual."

Dr-Anna45: "Porn of underage individuals, right? I'm just confirming."

"Yes. Women who have biologically come of age but are labeled children. Other times I used the videos of me and my girlfriend."

Dr-Anna45: "How old is she?"

"Fifteen." Smiley face. Shit, I hadn't meant to share this.

Dr-Anna45: "Declaration: This is not my view, but I'll tell you what science says. You are compulsory masturbator, and it usually accompanies more severe psychiatric disorders."

"No. I disagree. My libido is different than the regular population's. It's an expression of my deep desire to enjoy and multiply. My preference is also different, but I respect and take care of the women I go out with."

Dr-Anna45: "Stop calling them women!!!" Angry face.

We argued over two points, and I knew I didn't convince her, but I made solid, logical arguments no one could refute. First, sleeping exclusively with individuals over 18 years has only recently become the norm. Throughout history, girls became women when they got their period and became fertile. After they became women, they were allowed to have sex and to marry. It didn't matter if they were nine, twelve, or eighteen.

Second, sex with any individual of any age group still happened on a daily basis around the world, in multiple cultures, and even in our country if you were famous and powerful enough to get away with it. Third, my preference was widespread globally. Billions of dollars were spent satisfying these specific desires, and the businesses that satisfied them had all the characteristics necessary to be called an industry. Most importantly, my passion for girls just past the age of puberty burned inside me, dictated by my carefully selected genes over thousands of years. The only thing satisfying my urges was to act on it.

She argued that communities advance and create new laws, and these women were incapable of giving consent. That kind of shit. And she said no matter how intense the urges were, I shouldn't act upon them. "Like killing, it's still wrong. Even if you have urges to do it, you'll face repercussions." We stopped debating at one point. I didn't want to dwell on what killing meant to humanity, how it had evolved in form but never disappeared.

Dr-Anna45: "What do you feel when you masturbate, and afterward? What is the feeling that makes you decide to do it? "

"I get a boner. My body signals to me when it's time. *Mate, I'm ready to mate.* So, I do what's necessary. Better than coffee. Happy, relaxed, and focused."

Dr-Anna45: "No ideas before? No stimulation before? Random boners? Any guilt afterward?"

"No ideas or stimulation at all." Smiley face, flying kisses. "But I used to get them more often at a younger age, and people laughed at my awkward erections. Now I empty before going out, avoiding awkward situations."

Dr-Anna45: "So are you turned on by their physique or the fact they are helpless and don't know any better?"

"It matters that they're at a certain size and form. But for me, I'm in it for the long-term. I love to be around them as they bloom. I have desires to do something to them before puberty, but I keep it platonic. The body changes turn me on wildly. The best part is when the breasts start budding."

She didn't reply for a couple of minutes.

"Why are you getting so worked up? Calm down, honey. Aren't you here to help, supposedly? My turn. Tell me about your wildest sex fantasy."

Dr-Anna45: "So, do you love your GF?"

"I like her. Most of my relationships aren't serious. I might call it quits in a couple of weeks."

She asked me whether spirituality and religion meant something to me, whether or not I practiced. I replied that nothing mattered for me except my urges and constructing my life to make my fantasies come true. I told her we should live to express our inner nature, we didn't live to the fullest unless we unleashed ourselves to follow our desires, even for violence. Greed, fear, and lust in reproduction drove humanity here.

She argued a lot. I gave her the example of putting a group of teenagers on an island. The result would always be mayhem and sex. She didn't agree.

Dr-Anna45: "How is your sex life with your wife? Still non-existent?" Smirking face.

Low blow. Fuck you. I'll kill you, bitch.

"Very slow, but whenever the time comes, I pop a pill to strengthen my fella, I close my eyes, and imagine Vicky."

Shit, another slip. I panicked for a second. Untraceable though. *Never tell her name. Now she has the age and the name.*

Dr-Anna45: "Which school does she go to? Pretty Vicky. She must be head over heels for you."

"Fuck you. We can't work like this. You're still trying to report me. It isn't a slip, I am testing you. Of course, her name isn't Vicky." Middle finger and a spit.

I set my chat status to "unavailable." She sent me a few messages anyway, which I read. She apologized, admitting she had tried to uncover details about my identity in order to report me. I set my status back to "active," and I lied to her and told her I wanted her help, that I had tried many medications and interventions, and nothing worked. I told her to consider me her brother or her child in need of help. She lost me. I no longer tried to convince her of my superiority among the useless billions. At this stage I only wanted to teach her a lesson.

We agreed on goals—her goals. I intended to fake it all. She said we had to make changes to both my behavior and my desire. She asked me to replace what turned me on with more acceptable alternatives.

My motives changed after this session. I wanted to find Dr-Anna45 and fuck her all night; her resistance and disgust turned me. Afterward, I would take her life.

KALEIDOSCOPE

I was so excited I hardly slept that night. Instead of my regular, refreshing three hours, one was more than enough. I was out of bed at 4 am, and I kept looking at my watch. Finally, it showed 7 in the morning. The adrenaline made me quiver.

I knocked on the apartment door. The numbers 326, formed in fading bronze, were nailed to the red door. She should open the door. Through the secret cameras, I saw her preparing for class. Some of her luggage and boxes weren't unpacked yet.

The door squeaked as she opened it: I'd never fixed the hinges. She didn't check the peephole—careless. That was a point for me regarding my excellent tenant selection.

She was more beautiful in reality than in the pictures on her social media. Hazelnut hair, albeit wet, apparently

5'8" or 9", green eyes, not chubby but full. I liked that I could look her straight in the eyes without looking down. Regular jeans and a regular top, nothing revealing there. I couldn't confirm her inclinations, but I was hoping she was her same wild Internet self.

"Good morning. I'm Andy, the maintenance supervisor. I'm here to look into the electrical problem." She was taken aback. Her reaction was prolonged.

I extended my hand to shake hers, putting the tool bag on the floor.

"Hello. Hi." She shook my hand. "What problem? I don't think there's anything wrong." Teenagers of this era were generous with facial gestures. I didn't know why their generation made faces all the time. *What a waste of energy. Useless, worthless shit.*

I took out a copy of the tenancy contract. "Ms. Laurette." I pretended to read her name off the paper. "It's just some burned fuses. Although most of the apartment is lit, some outlets are dead, and a few appliances won't work. Did you check the whole place?"

She shook her head and opened the door a bit more, her hair still wet. "As per your contract, your apartment must be up to code, and we have to do the check on your first or second day. Can't be postponed." I put on a smile. I hoped my plan worked.

"Call me Laurie, please. Yeah, maybe in the afternoon we can go over all of this," she raised her eyebrows. I didn't know what the fuck her facial expression meant, so I smiled.

"If I may enter, I'll quickly show you the affected areas and the box needing repair," I said.

"Yeah, please." She held the door open, and as I passed by her, I inhaled deeply to register her smell.

I went left to the kitchen. The apartment was a small place, and I knew every inch in it. Straight through the front door was the living room, which had a huge window with a view of the street. On the right was one door for the bedroom that had a similar window, and a bathroom with a shower.

"Your microwave won't work," I said. Afterward, I pressed on its buttons, unplugged it and plugged it back in. "No life in it." This appliance was essential to students—it was like their mother. Some might have starved if it broke down.

"Oh."

Back to the living. "The router is working fine, but the signal booster here in the corner isn't working," I said, picking up the device for demonstration. "No blinking. The other one blinks. If you use the web in the bedroom or work there, you might have interruptions." All of them ate, worked, and shit in the bed, which was made for *sleeping*.

Worthless shits.

Internet was a necessary thing for millennials, like a clean water source. Many asked me about speed details, so I printed out a paper with the details and hung over the kitchen counter to avoid discussion. Actually, the signal booster was for me. Without it, I wouldn't be able to watch the live broadcast from across the street.

"You mean the Internet?" she giggled. Of course, she didn't know I said the web on purpose.

I preferred to let people think I was dumb.

You do not fear what you do not see.

"Yup, the one and only," I said and smiled, fatherly. "This will take about three hours all in all. Then we'll do a test of all appliances and the network."

"Ok, sounds good. This afternoon then? Please. I can't be late, its orientation day," she said.

"Oh no. Can't do afternoon, I leave the area on time, otherwise will have to wait for the late-night bus." I said.

"Can you do the work while I'm away? Please. Just leave the papers for me on the coffee table, and I'll sign them when I get back." She did something with her eyes and shoulders that resembled seduction, but which youngsters used when for asking for favors or trying to be cute.

"Oh no, that won't work. I can't be alone here with your stuff. I've been in this neighborhood for eight years and worked maintenance without complaints, but I learned this way. And we have to do the testing together."

Take the bait, take the bait.

"But I can't stay with you. You don't want me to miss orientation. Come on, Andy." She prolonged the A in my name; I found it very annoying when they thought playfulness could work. She read the response off my face. "Wait for me, then. In the afternoon we'll sort things out."

"Okay, how about you lock your valuables in your closet or the safe, and I'll begin the work while you're in class?" I suggested. She was happy and made a silly small jump.

When I had first started interacting with tenants, I'd suggested they lock their rooms to keep their belongings safe, but that wouldn't be practical for what I had planned. So, I had convinced Mrs. Sharbadian that mounting a safe in the closet would be a nice feature and give her an edge in the competition for tenants. She had three apartments in the block, and I oversaw everything, including payments. She only had to interview the tenants, whom *I* recommended most of the time. Laurie was unique, though. She hadn't gotten this place by responding to one of my ads; she knew the property owner. Fate.

"Your da best, man. You saved me," she rushed to the bedroom, and I stayed in my place.

I took a breath to raise my voice. "Miss, anything else you want me to do: hang some things? How's the shower?"

She leaned in from the connecting door, head and shoulders visible but tilted. "Really? You would do that?" She was surprised.

"Usually I fix problems, but nothing prevents me from doing some upgrades. By the way, we didn't agree on the meeting time today. I should finish before four. What time will you be back?"

I heard a lock snap. Tasty, this will be fun. *Can't wait, can't wait.*

"That's great," she said. "I finish around three. I should be home afterward."

She came back eager holding a box. "Please, can you hang these, a clock and a poster?" She held one up in each hand, and I nodded. "Clock above the TV, and the poster on the wall facing the bed."

"Consider it done," I said. People trust a deeper voice, which I reminded myself of, so I repeated what I'd said in a different tone. "Consider it done. Anything else?"

"The water flow in the shower is weak, and the shower head is leaking. I need more flow. You know—stronger. Can you fix it?"

I always put an old, leaking shower head on for new tenants, with these tricks I'd build initial trust.

"I'll install a new one. No charge, of course."

"Okay, great." She came out of the bedroom with her handbag, from which a laptop protruded, and a generously sized phone or perhaps a tablet in hand.

"How are you going, miss? By car or foot?" I asked.

The question surprised her, but I already knew the answer. "I'm walking. It's very close. Right?" Oh man, what a generation. Equipped with all the zebibytes in the world, and they still trusted word-of-mouth. This was beyond self-doubt, this was stupidity.

"Yeah, just stay on main streets. Don't go into alleyways," I used my deep voice; I sounded like Batman.

She grabbed the doorknob. "Sure. See ya later."

"Do you have your key?" I asked. She checked the inside pocket of her handbag.

"Yes," she said, taking out the key not on a keychain.

"I have your second key in case you want to give someone a copy. Take this one with the key chain and give me yours," I said. The keychain was a triangle made of rigid plastic but the corners were movable, so it was also a toy. I played with it, and we made the exchange.

"I know no one yet, but I feel lucky," she said and winked at me. I disregarded it, remaining professional. But I couldn't wait to know if she was attracted to men or women, or both. There was no way of knowing nowadays. I put her down as straight, but she probably hadn't experienced her full sexual potential.

The extra key I gave her had a live satellite GPS tracking chip in the key chain. The battery could not last forever but enough to provide me with a head start.

"Wait, miss, take my cellular phone number," No one used this term anymore, but once you said it, people assumed you were of a particular age and belonged to a specific era. This stereotype was what I aimed for.

"Hit me," she said. She was shaking her head, secretly laughing.

I gave her the number. The timing was important. I took out my flip phone, and the sight of the device amazed her.

"Wow, gosh." She chuckled, and it became laughter. She covered her gaping mouth with her left hand. Oh goodness, the energy that young people had. "You own one of those? I gotta take a selfie with this shit," she said.

She was an adolescent transitioning to adulthood, and I was fascinated how she reacted to trivial things. *Small things matter.*

Her laughter was my cue to start my act. I looked down at the floor and frowned as if I felt hurt and disrespected.

"Shit. Sorry, I didn't mean anything by it. But really, this shit is swag."

My phone vibrated. I showed her, and she confirmed her number. "And do you have your landlord's number?" I asked.

"Yes," she answered. I turned around and entered the kitchen as she uttered the word, but I saw she had blushed. She was embarrassed for having hurt me.

I heard the door close, and I began to work. In an hour, I finished everything: seven planted secret cameras switched on and streaming live to my house, plus new cameras in the entrance light, kitchen fire alarm, living room ceiling light, a receiver under the TV, fire alarm over the bed, plastic plant on the bookshelf facing the bed, and last but not least, the bathroom. Full views from every corner.

For $3,200, one could order the spy cameras online, and they would arrive at your doorstep, or you could do what I did to avoid leaving an electronic trail. I drove 500 miles to buy them in cash, undetected and untraceable. The drive wasn't so bad. I'd taken Nellie with me. She thought the breeze helped her.

I remembered when I'd started with one camera. I used to worry less about the risk of exposure. Silly me—it didn't matter if they caught you with one or fifty cameras, the punishment was the same. Now the manufacturers tested the secret cameras by seeing if members of the public could find where they were hidden. Market research was part of the sales pitch.

I replaced the shower head with the semi-new one I'd brought with me.

I set everything and including the clock and the poster, but before I left, I copied her class schedule and looked in the safe. (I had a spare key for every lock in this apartment, including the safe.) A few hundred-dollar bills, one debit card, one credit card, and a passport. I took photos of the documents, might need them in the future.

Afterward, another part of the hunt began with the drawers. Pandora's box. I applied extra care in this task because everything had to go back in place and look untouched. The dresser gave me nothing major, but I enjoyed going through the panties and bras. A few were worn out, and I smelled them just in case, but they were all clean, fresh from the laundry. I had big hopes for Laurie. We would achieve a lot together.

The closet contained the regular variety of what a woman owned, but I noted two more handbags.

Now the bedside drawers. My heart was racing. *What could be in there?* Jackpot! There was a sex toy. A two-headed device with multiple vibration options. Did owning the device mean she wasn't a virgin? Seemingly, but I couldn't be sure. I registered the toy's exact location, took the dildo out with a napkin, and smelled it. Although clean, it still had a faint smell of her wet endeavors. It was important that she owned one—it meant we didn't have to wait for her to get a boyfriend to get some action.

Not all people masturbated. About a third of women and a fifth of men don't partake at all, whereas only a tenth of all women and a quarter of all men masturbated frequently. *Worthless people, void of the drive.*

I couldn't wait; the possibilities were endless.

I'd saved the best for last: the laundry basket. *Yippee!* We all had a mammalian instinct to smell one other, but societies had condemned it over the years. And we ended up void of any pheromones and incapable of olfactory-based attraction. What a waste. I could barely resist taking one pair of panties for my collection—a white pair with pink flamingos on it. I kept it with me in my pocket and would put it back before I left the apartment. I rubbed it on a piece of cloth to pass along the smell so I could take it with me.

My alarm sounded at half past ten. I made a quick trip to the convenience store to get her some consumables, bonding items, and some of my plan accessories, to see what she would choose.

I came back and stocked the fridge with fresh juice, water, and fruit. Mango, an aphrodisiac. On the counter, I placed a coffee blend, mixed nuts, pre-made pizza, bread, and ready-to-cook noodles.

On the coffee table, I put four used books: a famous erotic novel made into a movie that critics claimed was good and pretty rough, a self-help book about exploring one's potential, a romance novel with adventures involving time travel and aliens, and a prominent psychologist's biography. I wanted to know her preference.

In the second empty dresser drawer, I placed a joint in a sealed plastic bag with a note that read, "Hey there, from the old tenant to you, an offering. Left it sealed in the bag for freshness. Enjoy." Smiley face.

I finished my sandwich and stretched out on the sofa, thinking about possible future plans for Laurie once we got the basics out of the way. I took out my electronic notepad and started drafting, I wanted to create some fresh ideas. If everything failed, then I would not have a choice but to use the roofies.

Laurie - apartment 326 - ideas:

Fear:

1. Is she afraid of ghosts and what is her fear limit? Make the place haunted?
2. Make her feel someone is following her and wants to kill her?
3. Hackers steal her identity: Post on her Instagram account pictures of places she went but different food. Funny.
4. What will her entertainment be when I cut her Internet? Old but gold.
5. A secret admirer: gifts and notes and a meetup plan.
6. Tasks: will she do weird errands for money?
7. Laxatives? Dull. No.
8. Bankruptcy? Take all her money and see what she does.
9. Drugs?

Suddenly I couldn't think straight again. The bitch psychotherapist was getting into my mind. She'd once said, "Spying is a form of attack. You're hurting people. Would you want someone doing this to you?"

My breathing had become tense, and my rage had started building. "Well, fuck you," I'd written back. "A prey not protecting itself deserves anything that happens to it. Banks do shit every day to millions. If anyone can spy on me, then they're welcome to. Or at least they're welcome to try."

I whistled to calm myself down. I imagined myself finding out her address and going there to choke her, seeing her last breath come out. I hated the bitch so much I dreamed of sitting next to her body as it got cold. "Yeah, FUCK YOU!"

Shit, I'd shouted.

I checked the GPS signal on my phone. Laurie was in class. Soon, I'd be on her tail, seeing where she went and what she bought, whom she interacted with. I hoped she was exactly as she was on the Internet, a non-monogamist. Otherwise, I must force her out of the apartment and get someone else in.

I went back to my basement. Nellie was half asleep on the couch, and I could smell the old wine stench on her. She was in this state most of the time, drunk and high on her pills. Sometimes a day passed without us speaking to each other, and then when we did speak, it was nasty.

We were in a situation where each of us wanted the other to move out, but no one would admit it. I wanted her out of here, where my setup was. I kept crushing sleeping pills and putting them into her bottles of wine. I just bought bottles with screw caps instead of corks. She got irritable and sometimes aggressive when she wasn't high.

I wanted to find someone like me, with my drive and passion for life. Laurie might be that person. The hunts would be more fun. I realized that even if the other person's drive wasn't like mine, at least having someone who believed in me could make us inseparable.

I took the cloth out of my pocket, smelled it, and jerked.

Watching from a distance still had the same excitement as before. Even if I was watching something I'd seen earlier in one way or another, seeing a new, different person gave me endless thoughts. How confident was she about herself? How frequently did she look at the mirror? Did she roam naked in her house? How and where did she eat? Did she jiggle her tits to see how they moved? How often did she masturbate? How and who did she fuck?

Like a fierce predator, I didn't have to attack and kill every time I stalked someone. The joy came from the journey of hunting, even without the final act. Even a failed attack had its joys.

Every passing hour seemed longer than the one before it, but finally, it was almost time, almost. One more hour and she would be coming. I would go to meet her. Then I would retreat to my laptop to view her life. I was growing sick of Vicky, and I wanted to give Laurie all my time.

THE ONE

I was well-rested after my three hours of sleep, but little time had passed. It seemed like years had passed from dawn until seven, and Laurie was still asleep. I reorganized my folders, cleared some clutter, cleared my gonads, and stored my jizz. Instead of waiting another hour for her to wake up, I made a quick trip to her building and made construction noise in front of her apartment.

The disturbance woke her up.

Afterward, I went back and positioned myself in front of my monitors, observing her. I was falling for this woman. The two weeks since she had moved in had been stunning. She'd had ten guys up to her place, and masturbated another ten times, all over the apartment. Gladly she had allowed no one to sleep over; we wanted no creeps coming between us.

I snuck in a lot, to smell her sheets and her clothes. The resemblance between us was incredible. I'd seen nothing like it. She was the one for me. She wasn't like the worthless ones before her who spent their time on video games, knitting, and cooking.

I found her.

She was annoyed and grumpy; she shuffled to the kitchen to make her coffee. She slept only with panties on, and sometimes without them, but she put on a cotton shirt immediately after waking up. The shirt was three or four sizes too large, probably left behind by a zealous boyfriend.

I jumped into my seat, startled by the music she'd turned on. I took out my notepad to make an important and long overdue addition to my notes that had lurked in my mind.

Of Man and Noise

Man has created a wide range of sounds and instruments throughout history, and they proved crucial for our tribe's survival. Warriors used one variety in war, another for terrorizing their enemies, and the elite used some for stirring up sexual desire in dormant souls.

Those sounds became useless noises occupying our lives, no taste, and no end goal. Just waste, a byproduct of the worthless who roam the earth.

She took a quick shower, shaved a few hairs here and there on her arm, sniffed a bra which she ended up wearing, and off she went. I had to think of ways to keep her in the apartment. I had enjoyed following her initially, but not so much now.

I broke up with Vicky. She became too needy and attached. I'd told her I had an assignment across the state, she'd cried, and I'd comforted her by promising I would be back in two or three months. I couldn't let go of the way we'd met and how much time it had taken for me to convince her we could have a relationship. She wanted a friend to speak to about her insecurities and what she wanted to do in life. I didn't have time for that, but I endured to get where we were. Then the relationship slowed down and became more talking than anything else.

I put on my community guard vest. I hated how the yellow glowed in the light. I knew the whole neighborhood, who lived where and what they did, where there were street cameras, police patrols... I kept records of who moved in and out. You could never be too sure. I avoided the street where Vicky lived but didn't worry about the school because no students would be around when I patrolled there.

I imagined coming up to Laurie, asking her out for coffee, and telling her we were alike and how compatible we are. She was one of a kind, and I believed we could have a great relationship. Soon I would confess to her. I wished she were three years younger. No, seven years younger. That would have been a dream.

She was in class and no point in waiting for her. I went to her apartment, provided a "free" subscription to the best porn channel with video on demand.

I couldn't wait 'til she turned the porn channel on. Perhaps this would decrease the number of visitors. I approved of her active sex life, but not of the people she selected—worthless beings. The fact of her getting pregnant by one of the scumbags frightened me.

In her mailbox, I put a magazine article that related two models talking about morning masturbation and its benefits. I'd had to search a while for them. What could I do next week? Plant microphones in her handbags? I didn't know, so I waited to see how things played out.

Laurie was so much better than the prior, worthless tenants who'd had to start with the "benefits of sex," "accept your sexuality," and "embrace your body" bullshit. I went into Laurie's bedroom. I wanted to lie in her bed and relieve myself. I imagined her walking in on me, catching me in the act. But, come to think of it again, that would end badly—for her.

Before I could finish, I heard the keys jingling.

Is this happening?

Then I heard the giggling coming from the hallway and the key turning. Shit! I hadn't checked the GPS for the last half an hour, and she'd come back. I thought of hiding in the bathroom, but this was a common mistake made in movies. Eventually, people would go into the bathroom. I hid under the bed.

Steamy kissing. A bag dropped on the floor. A man grunted. Laurie said, "I want you right now. Give me your best." They entered the room. Their feet looked like those of amateurs in their first dance class. He sat on the bed, and she remained standing. I'd never felt jealous of the men she brought over, but at that moment, I was boiling. Maybe because I was physically in the room, and my elite genes were firing for action.

In the old warrior days, I would have jumped out from under the bed and taken his life with my bare hands. And she would have been fascinated and turned on. And we would have made love over the ruins of war. These days, I had to burn and suffer.

She remained standing, and her pants dropped. I was about to faint. I was extremely horny, and I could have killed someone. She knelt down, her knees two inches away from me. I wanted to join in. Later I would see it, as many times as I desired. But at the moment how could I see them? I heard her gulping and spitting. I remembered my phones in my pocket; I checked and set both on silent mode. I opened the smartphone and logged into the streaming feed. Almost there, loading, and live.

Fuck. Mr. Frekampt. *Really?* They called him Mr. Freak or Mr. Freakish. He was a sad, fat, old man with a huge beer belly. Worthless. *You would sleep with him? Bad choice, Laurie.*

What the hell was she doing with her English teacher? Did she like him or did she need the grade? Fuck. I opened my zipper slowly.

They were both on the bed, and the supporting wood below struggled and bounced with their movement. He tried to get on top of her, a 250-pound shit barrel with hair all over his back. She didn't allow it. She pushed him down and got on top of him.

She was loud. Too loud. She sounded fake compared to how she usually sounded. It seemed like the three of us had a synchronized orgasm, but I didn't think so. He and I finished, and I doubted she did. Her moaning and his grunting hid my heavy breathing, but I was worried they would discover me under the bed.

He put on his clothes and mumbled, "Wow," too many times, and she said, "Yeah, this was excellent." His face was still so red. She made up an excuse, and he left. She turned on the shower and dialed a number. I was anxious she would look under the bed. If she caught me, I would either have to kill her, or we could start a friendship. I could explain to her my fascination with all that she did, and she would admire my effort. Could happen. And hey, such an encounter might be better than coffee.

"Yeah, I did it," Laurie said. "No, you're a slut. Hahaha."

I guessed she was speaking to Manuela—Manny—a close friend in a nearby city. They talked every two days.

"How do you think it went?... No, I didn't come. How could I? He's a fat pig." She said. "Yeah, yeah." She added. "Yeah. Why wouldn't I? Like another bad Tinder date, but at least I benefited from it. Uh-huh.... Yeah, average size. Or no, actually, big but he couldn't get it up all the way.... Yeah, right? Next time I'll tell him, Please, sir, take your pill before you hump." She laughed.

Now I must put microphones in her handbags. Apparently, I was missing out on action outside the apartment. I wanted to know what she thought.

"Doesn't matter, bitch. Now I don't even have to go to his class.... Yeah, love you too. Byeee." She hung up.

I was sure she was the one.

A few minutes after the call, she entered the bathroom. I heard the sound of the water change when she stepped under it.

I got out from under the bed. I stood with my back to the wall next to the bathroom door and peeked in; she was rinsing her hair. That was the closest I had been to her. I wanted to hold her.

An idea occurred to me.

I made a noise in the living room, left the place in a hurry, and left the door open.

"Hello? Anyone there?" Laurie shouted. "Get out before I call the cops!"

I hope it works. Come on, come on.

My phone rang. I was so happy to see her name on the screen, and I assured her I'd be there right away and that her security was of the utmost importance. I searched the apartment looking for the perpetrator. "All clear!" and returned to the room. She told me what happened, and I explained to her it could have been one of a few scenarios.

It could have been a disgruntled boyfriend who copied her key and wanted to sneak in on her. She said she didn't have a boyfriend, but we both knew I meant the many people who slept over. Or maybe she'd forgotten to shut the door, and someone had heard the shower and seen an opportunity to look at a naked neighbor. She agreed it was possible. I told her she could blame no one because she was a very attractive woman and she had left the door open.

We agreed that she should secure the door with the chain whenever she was home. I told her she should contact me anytime if something scared her, even at night. I made her promise, and I left feeling satisfied.

COURAGE

Her words stuck with me: "Give me your best." I wanted to give her my best. Although against my protocols, I created an online dating profile to search for her. Maybe we would match up. I didn't approve of the worldwide web communication in any form, on any platform, because of security concerns. Even when I worked on the dark web, I had to discern where I conducted my business.

I wondered what I would do next—invite her in or ask her out. I struggled to write a description of myself and ended up writing about exercise, watching movies, loving animals... Most of it I copied from other people's profiles. *Running on the beach, the sand tickling my feet. Worthless shits.*

I kept scrolling and swiping, and ultimately, I found her. No action yet. I must learn how this platform worked before taking any action. How we described ourselves and how we were in real life were often very different. Her profile spoke truthfully about her. She wrote a few sentences about what she wanted:

I'm all about the fun, about the fun. Not serious.

I want the party and the Netflix chill. Down for all.

Think twice about your opener and leave me alone when I ask you to. Pllllleasssseeee.

After some time, although still early in the morning, I swiped to match and waited. She had to do the same for me and then we could talk. I could strike up a conversation before she swiped, but I might seem too desperate.

A few hours passed with nothing from her. I kept checking to see if she went online. A green dot appeared next to her image when she did. She stayed for an hour, went off, then came back on for an hour. And nothing for me. She came home again around lunchtime.

I sent her a super like, and after an hour I bought more and sent her a couple. Still, nothing. I waited in anger. She made a couple of calls—irrelevant. She phoned her mom to tell her she wasn't coming home this weekend; she had midterms. There were no midterms at this time.

The bitch had snubbed me. I was mad, so mad I could've punched her if I'd seen her. My watch showed 5 p.m., and still nothing.

She was texting someone, and she got mad gradually, afterward she threw the phone and yelled into her pillow. She paced the room and made another call.

"Jenny. Don't lie to me. Please don't lie," she said. "Is Chris going out with someone?... I know I wanted our relationship to be like this, but still, he's ditching me! He said he won't come over tonight, he has a party. And he didn't even ask me to come with him."

Chris was a regular, possibly a semi-boyfriend.

"I won't go. I don't want to run into him, like, alone. It's too desperate. Are you going?... Look for him and text me. If he's alone, I'll come... Love you, too."

I put on a yellow shirt. I looked good in yellow. I wished there was a way to hear all her conversations and see all her text messages. I felt optimistic about her possible breakup with Chris, so I decided to start a conversation.

I typed: "Hey there, gorgeous. I always wonder what you're up to. Let's binge on movies or chemicals tonight." And send.

I buttoned up my shirt, thinking of a response like, "Anytime is okay with me. You want to hook up now?"

I checked the cameras. She had put on a porn movie and gave herself a go with the vibrator on the couch. A few stains already ruined the couch.

I looked at the phone; she'd seen my message. She finished and muttered, "Fuck you, Chris. Don't need your ass."

I typed a new message: "A coffee would do. We can chat as well."

A few minutes passed. She saw the message and still didn't reply. I was furious. I sent another one. "Whatever you want. I promise you we'd have a wonderful time."

This time I caught her reaction as she read it: she rolled her eyes.

I was crouching on the stairs to her apartment. I had an urge to enter and slap her face. I wondered why she would treat me like this.

After an hour I decided to get two to-go coffees and knock on her door. Yeah, fuck it. Luck favors the bold. I had seen her coming four times in a day, alone sometimes, other times with two different guys. So, I wouldn't be a burden. I couldn't let a person with a drive like me get away. She was one of a kind, and I loved her.

She opened the door while chewing on a slice of cold pizza. She was wearing the same cotton shirt I'd seen on the video stream, and she hadn't bothered to put on some pants or shorts. I didn't need to wonder what was under the shirt. Thanks to the cameras, I knew she was wearing a thong. Her nipples protruded out without the restraint of a bra.

"If you won't go for coffee, the coffee will come to you," I smiled. "Can I come in?"

She looked cleaner on the screen. I hated acting on impulse, but love made me blind.

"I saw your messages. You know, you should give people some time to answer."

"Let's chat." I gestured my hand to enter, and she agreed. I felt so much lust for her; I could have jumped on her.

She muted the TV. She'd been watching reruns. "Okay, but like, *this* is your chance. Show me what you've got, Mr.

Handy Man. Here goes your date." She sighed and rested on the couch.

I laughed, but I sounded fake. I cleared my throat to use my deep voice.

"Well," I said, "we are different, but different works. I feel like I know you. Actually, understand you is more accurate. You're wild and hyperactive, and you have big dreams."

"Not bad," she said. "Go on."

She truly was a bitch.

"You don't want to be tied up at this stage of your life—not that you'd mind a naughty tying up once in a while. You must stay a free bird. All I want is to spend some good times with you. Keep it casual."

"Won't work between us," she said. She took her phone out and leaned back on the couch, sighing. She was showing me her disinterest. She was probably texting Jenny or whoever to tell them *Guess what the creepy handyman just did. Lol omg.*

"Why? Hmm?" I asked.

"You're the clingy type, and you do this with every girl who moves in."

"I'm not the clingy type," I told her. "And no, I've never done this. But you've got this energy in you—it radiates. You're brilliant, but as well as you take care of your mind, you take care of your body even better. The body has its needs. Its... maintenance, right?"

"I don't know. Maybe. Thanks for the coffee, though," she said.

I didn't have much time left. She might have heard all of that before. I needed to change my approach.

"If we were in a club, and we'd just had a couple vodkas, and you saw me, you'd be attracted to me, right? No doubt, I'm physically your type. And I can teach you one or two things. You're someone who isn't shy about saying I need a dick today, out loud or to someone. And you want to look back later in life and say, 'I slept with all kinds of men,' and have no regrets. And I'm that kinda man, not your sixty-year-old pig."

I'd heard her say she wanted a dick on a specific night or she would die. But the pig example was too close to Mr. Frekampt.

She said nothing. I thought she was on the verge of kicking me out. Her face didn't change.

I said, "Okay, I and my nine inches will be waiting if you ever need me. Text me." I stood up, game over. What a cheap thing to say. And by the way, my penis isn't anything near nine inches, but you know.

I wondered whether I should offer her some money, or a break on her rent. Worth the risk, but after standing for a couple of seconds, I moved toward the door.

"Nine inches? Bullshit. Show me."

I turned. "Really?" I said.

"Come on, don't be shy. Let the snake out." She flailed her hands.

"I'll show you if you show me." I unzipped.

"We'll see," she said as I moved closer to the couch. "Oh, that is nice. Hard. I'll blow you, no sex. I'll need dinner before that."

Laurie was a great gal. I obsessed over her. I respected how open and comfortable she was with her drive. Even *I,* wasn't this active at her age.

I texted her and called her many times, but she didn't reply. Over the next three weeks, nothing changed in her routine. I was getting crazier over her by the day. When I followed her, I waited outside classrooms like some lonely loser.

She invited many guys up in her place, and I was so jealous. One time I pressed the fire alarm, and they evacuated the building, and afterward, she returned with him as if nothing had happened.

I entered the apartment a few times when she was asleep, just to see her. I stood in front of the couch where we'd had a good time. Too bad. We could have had something sweet.

I was lost. I wanted to win her over so badly. Otherwise, I'd have to leave, or she'd have to leave.

I ain't going nowhere.

I could potentially take her against her will.

ENKIDU

I suffered because of Laurie, and I couldn't wrap my head around the fact of her snubbing me as she did and throwing herself into the hands of worthless men. Did she not know what kind of people she was meeting online? And as much as I admired her body, she took a lot of pictures, and she posted more than I liked her to. I bet she also had no clue about identity theft.

Dr-Anna45 thought we had become friends. She accepted my flaws and had faith I could change. Along the way, she said I was changing. She said, "We can be friends," and I wanted to take advantage of her change of heart to get my revenge soon.

I woke up before dawn, as usual, reorganized my folders and watched some great moments. Some were mine, and friends on the dark web had shared others. I made a quick trip to the apartment where I kept the main backup storage and added the new recordings.

As I drove back home, the sun came out, and a brilliant light filled the skies. The cold breeze coming in through the window bumped me better than any coffee could. I decided to tell Dr-Anna45 about my first relationship. She would think the story was part of the changing process, but my first relationship stood as a point of pride for me because of my young age, something that should be normal for humans but sadly not the case.

In the basement, I checked up on my friends. Safe and secure in the fridge.

I sat back down at my laptop, logged in, and waited for her.

Incoming sound. A message from Dr-Anna45: "Morning."

"Hi. What took you so long?" I replied.

Dr-Anna45: "I just opened my eyes, and I'm still having my coffee. What about you?"

"I have been up for few hours, had some errands to run. You know, the hard drives, the 48-hour updates." Yeah, I had told her that. No harm in it.

Dr-Anna45: "What time is it now?"

"I can't tell you the time. Duhhh," I said. Sharing the time might help her locate me. *Trying to outsmart me, you devil.*

Dr-Anna45: "I thought we were past that, but anyhow your call." A weird and new smiling face emoji. "Have you considered the offer?"

"Yeah, I know, but still, old habits die hard. Anyway, I have some juice for you." The offer was mainly that if I shared my early relationship experiences, she would share something of equal value, not yet determined.

Dr-Anna45: "Cool, spill it. But I haven't decided what I'll tell you in return. Maybe when you're done, I'll know what to share."

"Okay. So, I was eleven and about to turn twelve in a few months, and I hooked up with a neighbor on the corner of the block called Ms. Margaret." I could see her typing before I finished the sentence.

Dr-Anna45: "Age, marital status, living alone, description?" With a nerd emoji.

"She was in her forties, single and living alone." I hit send and continued. "I remember she was very kind, and beautiful. A bit busty, and full, with the deep voice of a heavy smoker. She used to wear a long skirt with a tucked-in shirt with a few open buttons. And she always wore a wool or cotton fleece on top."

Dr-Anna45: "What did she do for a living and how did you meet her?"

"I don't remember her work exactly, possibly something like a librarian or a bookstore clerk. I remember she punched the clock from eight to two."

Dr-Anna45: "How did you meet? Do you think she targeted you for a particular reason?"

"Chill. Why do you always want to label things?" I sent an angry face. "I'm sharing with you something intimate, my first one, so enjoy the story for once without having to analyze it."

Dr-Anna45: "Sorry. Old habits..."

"One time on my way back from school during the springtime, the weather was nice, and she was standing outside on the lawn watering the plants. She said 'Young man, are you interested in earning some money for hard but simple work?' And I said sure. She asked me to return in a couple hours if my mom agreed that I could help her move some boxes and clean some rooms."

Dr-Anna45: "I'm with you. Continue at your pace."

"So I came back. We moved some boxes and cleaned some rooms, and I earned eight dollars, a good amount back then. Before I left, she said I could come by on Saturday at noon because she'd be arranging the kitchen."

Dr-Anna45: "And your mom okay with you going? And nothing happened in those early visits?"

"Mom had different priorities because of the situation with my dad. I'll tell you later. In brief, I don't think she minded anyone taking me off her hands. And Ms. Margaret was a well-respected person in the neighborhood, so no problems." I hit send.

"Nothing happened during the first visit, but I stared at her boobs a lot. With a few shirt buttons open, the sight was pleasant for me. She said 'Young man, you stare at my breasts a lot. I worry you'll grab them.'"

Dr-Anna45: "What did you do or say to her?"

"Nothing. I stared at the floor and waited for the right moment, when she kneeled down, to get a good look. I used to have an erection for hours. A bit painful. I would kill for such erections now."

Dr-Anna45: "What happened on Saturday?"

"I knocked on her door, and when she opened it, she was wearing an old bra over her pajama pants. And the bra was a horrendous old one, looked like a vest. But for me, back in the days, this was action, hot action. I remember how I jolted when she opened the door, and I couldn't stop my-self from saying, 'Wow.' To HER FACE." I sent that part to Dr-Anna45 with multiple tear-rolling, laughing faces.

Dr-Anna45: "Hehehhehe."

"I followed her in, and she said 'You have an attitude of a man but you ain't a man yet, boy.' And I replied to her, 'I'm a man, Ms. Margaret. My mustache has grown in.' My mustache was basically twelve hairs. And she said, 'We'll see about that.'"

Dr-Anna45: "Mr. Know-It-All."

"Thinking about her excited me. I got accustomed to her smell—perfume, smoke, and sweat. As we finished the kitchen, I wondered what I could do to get her attention, how I could get to kiss her. And if she agreed, how would I kiss her given she was much taller than I was. I surrendered not knowing what to do, I planned to sneak a peek under her skirt the next time she wore one."

A minute passed, and I didn't type a word. I traveled back in memories of how gracious of her to it was to con-sider me, to select me from among all the boys.

Dr-Anna45: "Where are you? Still on?"

"Yes. Flashbacks. I drifted."

Dr-Anna45: "So what happened? Was she in the bra the whole time?"

"She asked me to follow her to the living room. No, she put on a cotton shirt. She lay down and put her feet up, and she asked me to rub her feet." Sent.

"I didn't particularly know how to massage feet, but she gave me instructions along the way. After some time, she took off the bra from under the cotton shirt, and I went ballistic inside. Bells and fireworks. The bra resembled one of my mom's, I wanted to examine its details as it rested next to me on the floor. 'Focus boy!' she yelled a few times, and her deep voice filled the room.

"She lit up one of her cigarettes and put a plastic filter on it. I just couldn't take my eyes off her breasts, each one hanging toward a side on her body, and the nipples protruding through the shirt."

Dr-Anna45: "What was the time? Did you have a curfew?"

"Lunchtime, around two or three. I remember it very well because I was starving. No, not really. I usually spent Saturdays with the neighborhood kids, and we were on the street 'til it got dark."

Dr-Anna45: "So what happened after that?"

"She took off her pajamas and asked me to do the same as I was doing to her feet on her inner thighs. She even got me a chair and placed it facing the sofa. She wore blue cotton underwear.

"After some time, she asked me what I knew about that area, and whether I wanted to become a man. It sounded so absurd to hear her say *become a man*.

"I told her what I knew. A man and a woman kiss and afterward the man sees the boobs and kisses them, and then they hug, and people call this sex. And she broke into laughter. She laughed so hard she coughed, and her face turned red." I sent a laughing face.

Dr-Anna45: "LOL."

"She told me to keep rubbing her thighs, and later we'd do that. After a few minutes, she instructed me to go up to her crotch, and I did. One friend at school had told me the area was important, but I didn't believe him. For a long while, I thought some men preferred either the boobs or the vagina.

"She instructed me to rub her as if I was scratching an itch but not with my fingernails, but with my fingertips. On top of her underwear."

Dr-Anna45: "How did you feel?"

"Well, I liked the experience; I am happy and proud I got involved physically with someone at such an early age."

Dr-Anna45: "No. How did you feel at the moment?"

"I don't know what you want exactly. I felt nothing. If this answer satisfies you."

Dr-Anna45: "You must have felt something. Did you enjoy the act? Did it mean something to you?"

Dr-Anna45: "Was it okay for you to do something without knowing what it was?"

Fuck that, again with the diagnoses. She wanted to say *abuse, molestation*. I decided to lie to her, I would even tell her Ms. Margaret hurt me, deeply.

"We expect too much from the people. This happened over twenty years ago. She didn't know any better, and her love and admiration drove her to set up the relationship."

"By the way, I didn't finish. I'd appreciate it if you would wait 'til the end. Afterward, we can discuss what the relationship meant and whatnot."

Dr-Anna45: "K."

"I felt her panties getting wet, and she took them off. She pointed at the area where I should focus on. The hairy pubic area smelled a little like fish. I continued, and after some time she shivered and made sounds."

"I didn't know back then what an orgasm was. While coming, she grabbed my wrist and squeezed causing me some pain. She shouted, 'Go in circles! Circles, you dumb boy.'"

"I broke into tears. Suddenly she stopped and adjusted the way she was sitting. She consoled me and asked me what was wrong. I told her I hated the hair on her vagina, the fish smell, and that she squeezed my wrist. She promised the next time she would clean up the area, but right then I had to continue the rub. Otherwise, her tutu would be sore."

Dr-Anna45: "Tutu. A cute name. Hehehe."

"We started again, and when we finished, my hand was all wet and smelly. *Disgusting*. I thought I would leave and never come back. But she put on her panties and kissed me, and she took my hand and placed it on her breasts. This was my first time touching breasts, and they were such big ones, too. Amazing. 'Your turn,' she said, and she took off my pants."

Dr-Anna45: "Wow." With a surprised emoji.

"Once she saw my penis and my pubic hair, she chuckled. She said it would grow soon and the hair would change. She started doing things with her mouth to my penis, and she sat me on the couch. She licked and sucked 'til I also quivered and shot something out of my dick. The ejaculate was a transparent liquid. I asked her if it was pee, and she explained everything about intercourse, pleasuring the partner, semen..."

Dr-Anna45: "And did you leave?"

"She told me not to tell anyone because she had a lover living abroad and it would make a problem for her. And she said I was her secret young lover here.

"I told her she officially is my girlfriend."

Dr-Anna45: "Well. I'm speechless. How long did this go on for?"

"Three years, give or take. She taught me how to treat a lady, intercourse, and many other things. Later she gave me alcoholic drinks, sometimes pills, and she would let me try her cigarettes. She gave me a nickname, Bliss Giver."

Dr-Anna45: "I'M SPEECHLESS. Fuck." Angry face.

"What? You want to call her a pedophile as well?"

Dr-Anna45: "One sec. What were the pills for?"

"I don't know. We used to take so many kinds. Some to make us feel better, some to strengthen my penis, and others were for her only."

Dr-Anna45: "I can't accept her. I accept you, because you have been through a lot, and you're reaching out. But not her. I know you, and I don't know her. Hell, no."

Dr-Anna45: "I'm not afraid to say she is a pedophile. And a nasty one. And I think you are what you are because of your past, specifically this childhood experience with her."

Dr-Anna45: "She is the reason you have your preferences, and you do what you do. If you must be mad at someone, be mad at HER. A fucking PEDO."

Again with the insults. I barely kept myself together, but this bitch didn't make it any easier.

"Why can't you say or admit she loved me? Why not? Can't you consider the possibility? From my point of view, this was a relationship like any other. Like when you see a twenty-year-old man with a sixty-year-old woman.

"Maybe she is the reason. We can't be sure."

A minute or two passed before she sent something.

Dr-Anna45: "Let's agree to disagree...."

"Anna, again, this thing called pedophilia is a new concept, not even a hundred years old. We expect teenagers to sleep with each other, but we can't accept they sleep with adults. Simply idiotic."

She sent a neutral face emoji.

"Your turn. There's no benefit in arguing."

Dr-Anna45: "I lost my virginity at sixteen years old. We had been dating for six months, and we had done a lot of stuff and had beautiful orgasms, but not intercourse."

Dr-Anna45: "He was a year older than me, and we had a lot of fun as a couple. I remember a lot of laughter. Then we picked a weekend to have sex."

Dr-Anna45: "We slept together, we came in less than four minutes. The rest of the weekend was amazing. THAT is a relationship."

"Are you trying to insinuate something? Comparing my experience to normalcy?

"You're obsessed with normalcy and social order."

Dr-Anna45: "Well, only sharing the truth. No insinuation. This is my experience and my history."

"By the way. Your story is not juicy, but good enough."

Is she telling the truth? Anna might deceive me.

"I feel like I'm being labeled a victim, and I don't believe I am one. You want me to be a victim."

Dr-Anna45: "Well, I didn't label you. You just did."

Yeah, fuck you. I set my status to "Unavailable," knowing that would make her angry. *Control freak.*

A few minutes and a message alert went off. Dr-Anna45. "Listen, I'm sorry. I will respect your perspective. Come back on."

I reset my status after five minutes.

"Anna, you're single-minded, and you think on one level only. Guess what? I am testing you. I made up the whole story."

"I knew that you'd assume it was the reason for how I am."

"I am what I am because of my genes and my destiny, like many other millions who were hunters and killers over tens of thousands of years."

No response after a couple of minutes.

"We've reduced seventy or eighty thousand years of killing, of marrying and fucking at any age, to the norms we've only had for the last eighty years. THAT is absurd, not the other way around. Your whole doctrine of science differed back then, and now it labels the warriors like me, who helped shape society into its current state."

No response. Wow. Either she was seeing the truth for the first time, or she was fuming. I continued.

"This civilization has had warriors since we were in tribes. We waged their wars and made their enemies shit their pants with fear. And now civilization is trying to retire us.

"If I'd told you I lost my virginity at thirty or thirty-five, you would have said the reason behind my sexual preference is caused by the repression of not having lost my virginity earlier."

I saw her typing, finally.

Dr-Anna45: "I understand, but we progressed. There's no more need for violence and wars. I want to point out that before I argue with you the relevance of rape and sexual relationships with underage girls."

Fuck you, bitch. I'll talk to you in your language then. "I see your point, but I'm sure the current way we live is un-sustainable."

Dr-Anna45: "What if I said you can stop, and you can change, and you can love someone with whom you can age and grow old?"

"Let's see. We can discuss face to face, it will be different. Trust me." A laughing face emoji. "Got to go, speak to you later. I'll teach you about the elderly in our society."

I had to return to my business. So much going on. She finally opened up, I knew sharing my stories would change her opinion about me. Soon we would meet, and I would have my revenge.

BOREDOM

I was still bored. There wasn't much to do. My interest in the cameras stagnated, and I wasn't getting my way with the tenants. I wanted to barge in, collect their stuff, and throw it all away. Kick them the fuck out. The fuckers weren't acting how they should have been!

I put on a new outfit. Each item costing a few dollars, intended for onetime use, and bought in cash. I prepared my backpack. And by noontime, I took in deep breaths and headed out on foot.

Moving briskly, I covered three blocks in no time. After a few attempts, I found an open car with the keys hidden in the sun visor. What weak, self-loathing person left their car unlocked with the keys inside? I knew who it was, *someone unworthy of living, unworthy of breathing.*

I headed back to an alley next to the university campus. The foot traffic in this place was slow, but I hoped a nice piece of prey would get caught in the trap. I placed three cameras at different angles, front, back, and sideways. These were of the type used to record an accident or an interaction with law enforcement.

I parked the car close to the wall, a few yards away from the dumpster, and at a reasonable distance from the road. I could start the car and drive out of the place in less than a minute. I'd probably return the car before the fuckers woke up. Cap and sun shades on, I put the car seat backward and took out a magazine.

I unzipped and pulled down my jeans, folded my shirt back to expose my belly. I was already erect from the rush, and the memories were turning me on as well. A decade ago, I used to do this a few times a week. However, I evolved into a different man now. I had been blessed by the knowledge of my superiority.

I waited for some time. A couple of delivery guys on motorcycles passed by, then an old lady. I pulled my clothes up when they passed. My frustration grew, and I hit the steering wheel to flush out some of my anger.

What if today was a vacation for the university? Like Presidents' Day, or a break. *Don't doubt. Doubt is the enemy.* I hid the cameras; the cash was ready, and no windows overlooked the car... *Breathe.* I undid my clothes and returned to my ready state.

The profile of the girl I waited for was an under-achieving student with a cheap regard for life, no class, and low self-esteem. And she must be beautiful. In the past, anyone would do. I looked for the reaction; I longed for a giggle. Now I wanted the perfect prey. I wanted society's deviant to jump in next to me and do a quick one. Like mammals who were so activated by the sight of sex, they started copulation.

Someone was approaching. She seemed beautiful, a bit too mature for my taste. I placed the magazine on my thigh and started with some lubrication. Silly me, I used to ejaculate alone; now, I know better.

"Hi, there, pretty boy. You shouldn't waste that." She placed her hands on the car door. "I can help you finish for thirty. All the way is fifty."

A prostitute, really? This is a new low, Jerry.

She was also looking for prey, but of an inferior class. I wanted to kill myself.

"No, ma'am. It's not like that. I just finished my shift, and my girl complains if I finish too quickly. Premature, they call it." I tidied myself up and turned the car on. "So I pop one out before heading home. I don't want her to look for pleasure elsewhere." I took out my wallet. "Here's a fifty for your trouble."

"Yeah, I've seen that. Best pals be like jaybirds." She laughed. "Make it a hundred, and I'll forget it all. You won't get mistaken for some loose nut job."

I complied.

She walked away, and I pretended to leave. The premature ejaculation excuse I'd given her was a product of trial and error, not a quick reaction. I passed through a lot, fleeing the scene before the cops arrived.

I took out my phone, logged into a secure network, and texted Anna from the web-based chat application. "Remind me to tell you my views on prostitutes."

Within a couple seconds, Anna wrote back, "Go ahead."

"Can't do now, I'm busy." I kept my eyes on the road, waiting.

Dr-Anna45: "Are you doing something bad? How is the wagon?" A lame inside joke, about being off the wagon.

"No, hun. It's just work errands. All under control. Following your advice, but the urges are intense. Managing with pain. Hope to see you, I want to thank you in person."

As expected, I frightened her. As intended, she left me in peace.

Another passerby fitting the profile. Would she help me? Report me? Would she be disgusted or turned on? A feminist? *Oh god, please not a feminist.*

Fuck it. She was really old, a dried tomato. I packed up my things and fled. I needed a pristine source of entertainment, a new way to ignite the fire inside me, and I wished to pursue an unfamiliar type of pleasure.

I drove around until darkness filled the sky, I parked the car, not even moonlight. I tried to relax by breathing. I saw an old woman walking. She had an obvious hip problem. I knew the street very well, no CCTV, no overlooking windows, and unusual foot traffic. I put on my ski mask and hid in the bushes.

When she drew closer, I jumped out and hit her on the head. Once she fell down, I dislocated her shoulder. *Fuck you.*

I knew what Dr-Anna45 would say, that I had become violent because Laurie had shut me out, and this made me angrier. I wanted to go home, relax my body, and think about what I wanted. I couldn't keep going like this.

I reached home and wrote:

On Men and Aging

When I'm of the age that crawls and yawns, that moans and cries, please kill me. Our race is in a moral decline because we have many old people among us. They are using our resources, and sometimes our women. We should do something about them to make space for the young.

We can start by ending their right to vote, then limiting their movement within society during nighttime, and later during the daytime.

NOTHINGNESS

A few days ago, I read some disturbing things about the difference between pedophilia and child abuse, the former defined as only the urges, and the latter delineated acting upon urges, stimulation, grooming, exposure, and exploitation. A saddening realization hit me. Other hunters, part of the premium breed, were afraid to act upon their desires. *What a waste.* As if we chose our desires and preferences.

I wished to reach out to all the hunters and move someplace where we would be respected and admired. I dreamed of a haven, Hunters Paradise. Unfortunately, our kind lived in an extremely hostile era, and making the dream into reality was possible but required a blood sacrifice.

The wall watch showed 6 a.m. I slept for a refreshing couple hours, and was then ready to go. I checked on my cameras:

- Apartment 326: Laurie still asleep
- Apartment 433: Mandy and Alan still asleep.
- House on the corner: Brenda ineffective in waking up the children.

Melanie and Sylvie left town to visit a distant relative, and they wouldn't be back for a few days. Their parting frustrated me, I badly missed Sylvie.

I reviewed the recorded hours, and they were useless, so I deleted them to save memory space. I thought about drones, peeping toms in chairs outside windows, sauna lurkers. *How silly, unprofessional, and unsustainable. Why do something that will get you caught?*

The hunt lost the early thrill: interview, watch, follow, see whom they hook up with, what they eat, how often they shower... I couldn't wait 'til I owned a hotel, I would build an ultramodern establishment, people check in and check out at a fast pace. *I'll call it 'Warriors' Relief'.* However, thinking more about spying on women and grownups, I gathered that now it no longer scratched my itch. The camera business was only for fun or maintenance, but definitely not the real deal. Sylvie must come back now.

I couldn't figure out my next step. The whole cycle became boring and repetitive. I wanted someone fresh to fill the void in my heart. I acted on impulse and went out, I might meet someone worthy.

Message from Dr-Anna45: "Hi. How are you today?"

Then, "You told me you're a hunter. What does that mean?"

"Hi. Great. Following your instructions."

Dr-Anna45: "Great. Keep it up." Forearm biceps.

"Being a hunter means during the lunch breaks I go around to special places like supermarkets and restaurants, and people leave their name tags on. So I can easily track where they live and what they do for a living. But I'm no longer hunting."

Dr-Anna45: "That's it? I thought you followed or attacked people." Face with eyebrows up.

"I also use **the gaze**. I imagine myself gathering a wave of energy that starts down in my gonads, goes up to my arms and shoulders, and then concentrates back down. Afterward, all the energy is ready for disposal from my waist to the target, and I can direct it at any woman I want. I just focus and unleash the wave."

Dr-Anna45: "And does it work? I mean, do you have a success rate?" Face with eyes looking up.

"The gaze works, but no problem if it didn't. Don't think of it as a net that catches fish; instead imagine a special magnet specifically for catching the fertile, the hungry, and sometimes also the weak. The energy beam of the gaze is very similar to food, always present, but you eat only if you're hungry."

Dr-Anna45: "Will the gaze work if it's sent from a woman to a man?"

"No, definitely not. I'm surprised by your questions."

Dr-Anna45: The faces with open eyes. "Why wouldn't I ask about this? Don't you think men and women are equal?"

"I won't answer."

Dr-Anna45: "WE ARE EQUAL. In IQ and emotional intelligence. And actually, in all aspects except muscle power. And if we train the same way or take hormones, women can develop strength equal to that of any man of any size." Red, angry face.

Calm down. Tell her what she wants to hear. Easier said than done.

Dr-Anna45: "Answer. Don't bail." Three angry red faces.

"Does what *I* say matter? Really? We have a history of at least seventy or eighty thousand years that prove men and women not equal.

"And currently, over three-quarters of the world says so. The majority in leadership positions are men... I don't want to argue about it."

Dr-Anna45: "...I'm disappointed in you."

Lie, man. Lie.

"Don't be, please. You always get me wrong. I mean that I don't know. I treat them equally, but scientifically, you must educate me."

Yeah right. As if some scientific test and a following article would change my mind. If women were really equal then why hadn't they changed the course of history? I didn't want to argue with her, though. It surely wouldn't lead anywhere.

Dr-Anna45: "I see. We'll discuss this later. I'm pissed off."

"No. Stay, please. I enrolled in community service, and I'm volunteering at a support group for families of drug addicts."

I didn't tell her I had hunted in the addiction help centers for the last couple of years.

Dr-Anna45: "Proud of you. Well done. Sorry, but I'm not in the mood to continue the conversation."

Should I tell her I met someone? Of course, I shouldn't share that I was after the daughter.

"I know how to get us in the mood. Some wine and jazz." Winking face.

Dr-Anna45: "Hehehehe. It's not even 7 a.m. What else?"

"I don't know, strip poker? Or maybe smoke something funny? Skinny dipping? Depends on how wild you're feeling."

Dr-Anna45: "I meant about NA."

"I liked someone in the meeting, and I want to start something normal and healthy. However, you know it's difficult for me."

Dr-Anna45: "You can cross the barrier and ask her out, if she's in recovery. Not early in the journey."

"I know that. I also have us to worry about. I feel we share something special. What about us? Can we meet?"

Dr-Anna45: "There is no us." Face with tears.

TURBULENCE

Melanie volunteered to accompany another member to an awareness event conducted by a foundation in firms eager to educate their staff. The event included a presentation, testimonial about recovery, and a discussion. An unnecessary exposure and risk for me, but I went with her anyway.

I hated being unprepared. Many people about whom I knew nothing about filled the room. The morning kickoff scared me as I transitioned from displeased to distressed. However, during the day, I noticed a beautiful woman. She stood out from among the hundred in the room. I longed for the times of warriors and emperors when you could point your finger, and the men would carry her to you.

After the break, I changed places and sat behind her. I leaned forward to smell her; I registered her fruity scent.

Hazelnut hair, bright brown eyes, slender body, no makeup, and no hair on her face or arms.

She had tattoos between a few of her fingers, and watermelon-sized slices on her wrist and ankle. She wore a white dress covered in big yellow leaves, with opened buttons in front from the thigh down, and she tightened a belt of the same fabric at the thinnest area of her waist. When she bent forward to retrieve a small chocolate from her bag, I could see her bra through the sleeveless dress—black. I glimpsed the tip of a tattoo flashed ending at her armpit.

I wanted to rip off her dress, send buttons flying. Her tears would pour, and afterward, I would kiss every tattoo, and end up having beautiful makeup sex. I smiled.

She took out a lip balm, and I couldn't wait. I had to masturbate, or else I'd jump on her. I hated to leave my place, and I had nothing I could use to store my sperm. I also panicked about spy cams in the bathroom, but I settled on relieving myself. I fantasized about asking her about her tattoos, how she would say they were her erogenous zones.

I could dump Melanie in a second to seek the fabulous lady, but then I wouldn't see Sylvie again. I compared the two women. Drugs have worn out my -decade older than me- girlfriend, and the thick makeup didn't hide her hideousness. *Uggghhh. Disgusting.*

I decided to stalk this lady soon. I eavesdropped to learn her name—Mona, like the painting. Name and work enough to find her home address. I would put a camera in her place and replicate this moment. I would do exactly as I imagined.

I was so disgusted with Melanie that by lunchtime I was giving her the cold shoulder. Soon I would get rid of her, for good. I wanted her to disappear, so I buried my face in my phone. Anna was texting.

Dr-Anna45: "How are you holding up?"

"Great, on a personal level. And you?"

Dr-Anna45: "Can't complain. What other levels are there?" Lifted eyebrow face.

"You!!!"

Dr-Anna45: "??? Oh, come on. You know I can't. I told you." Frowning face.

"It hurts. We're this close and understand each other so well, and yet we're apart and can't meet."

Dr-Anna45: "I know, but you know I'm married. Can't." Hands over face emoji.

"We can still meet."

Dr-Anna45: "Tough. Please forget it." Gun to the head.

"Anna, we can keep on talking. But I'm afraid of what my future will be."

Dr-Anna45: "What do you mean?"

"You've got my heart, and I can't build a normal relationship now. I'll go back to doing my old stuff, and I can't live with myself, so I'm doomed."

Dr-Anna45: "What?? Don't say that. You'll meet someone."

"I'll kill myself if I slip into my addiction again, or fall in love with a young woman girl."

Dr-Anna45: "OHHH."

She was typing, but I continued. "We can meet as friends."

Maybe she's afraid, or she can see through me. Push more.

Dr-Anna45: "Let me think about it."

"Okay." Kisses. "Don't forget to send me a couple of photos when you can."

Yesss. Finally. I can't wait to strangle the bitch.

I decided to get rid of Melanie as soon as we reached home, although I was enjoying the pace with which I progressed with Sylvie. Things had to move faster because our talks, how we slept together, and her whole speech about being healed, sickened me.

A few days ago, I bought a bag of heroin from one dealer who stood on the corner, Melanie said she used to buy from him. Once we got back to Melanie's house from the workshop, I placed the bag next to a pasta carton in the food cabinet. She did not cook and rarely opened this cabinet, if she opened the cabinet and found drugs she shouldn't be surprised. She might think she forgot the bag back in the days, or one of her friends kept it there. *I hope.*

I wasn't living there, but I kept the essentials if I slept over. Most of the time I left at midnight to go to my place, take care of my stuff, catch some shuteye in my basement, and return by dawn.

"Mel, I'll go pick up Sylvie. Can you boil some pasta? I'll get the chicken on the way." She nodded. *I hope the bag will prove irresistible.*

She asked to drink some wine. I agreed but said we couldn't get wasted because I planned a movie night with popcorn and games. "I'll tell Sylvie she can hang out with us for the movie and games, but not dinner. Dinner is for two only, moi and toi. AAANND I brought a deck of cards for later." We played strip poker, Twister... games to get me going with her, along with the pill.

Most likely she wouldn't be able to resist the temptation. Otherwise, I'd be stuck with her for a romantic evening. *What if my plan fails? I can blame no one but myself. Too soon.*

"Bye, love." *Uggghh*. Pick up Sylvie from soccer practice, stop for chicken and wine, and lastly, make the call.

Sylvie got in the car, as usual, cheerful and full of life. She was sweaty but still smelled nice. I kept looking down at her thighs, her skin reddish from all the running.

I had once heard her friend say I was "fit" and "a hot piece of ass." Sylvie had blushed and said to her, "Shut up, bitch."

We'd become friends over the past two months. I'd bought her a tablet, topped up her phone balance, listened to her, and driven her around. The girl was lonely; no doubt she felt ashamed of her addict mom.

She always looked away when I took my shirt off, so once I had asked her to hold my feet while I did crunches. Not that I needed any help, but I was dying to see her reaction. I told her couples kiss when the person doing the crunches reaches the top. She giggled, and I said, "But none for you, miss," and her excitement disappeared.

I teased her. I said things like she is too young to know or to understand, or experience is paramount, but I also exposed her to adult matters. I'd once left the door open while having sex with Mel, and I took my time, so Sylvie passed by and saw us. Our heads were at the bottom of the bed, and I could see the door but Mel couldn't, and I caught Sylvie taking a peek.

I resisted the urge to put cameras in her room, or to sneak into her bathroom while showering. I deserve an award for my restraint.

One time, she'd heard Mel moaning *like a pig*, and afterward, when I went down for a cup of water, Sylvie had her head buried in her phone. I asked her, "Sylvie, are we friends? Real friends, close?"

She said yes, and that I didn't need to worry she had heard us. "But noise-canceling headphones can be sweet, and they would solve both our problems." And I said she would have them in the morning.

On the way back from soccer practice, I took my phone out to call, but I already had received a text from Mel. "Babe. I got this severe headache out of the blue, I'll sleep it off. Kisses."

Amazing. She is high. Phase one accomplished.

I acted sad and disappointed after I got the text, and Sylvie asked me what was wrong a couple times. I told her Mel had been acting funny, and her behavior worried me.

Once we reached the house, Sylvie headed upstairs to take a shower, and I headed to the kitchen to set up the table. Candle in the middle, two wine glasses, the chicken heated, the pasta ready. I placed the deck of cards and

Twister on the coffee table and sunk in the couch. And I waited.

I heard her footsteps, always filled with energy. She wore a cotton t-shirt with jogging shorts, and her wet hair stained the t-shirt.

She'd turned thirteen a few months before, and she was a brilliant lady. Took care of her duties and was fun to be around. Her breasts were small, still budding, exquisite like passion fruit. That night she didn't wear a bra. Initially, she'd had one on whenever I visited, and if I came in and she wasn't wearing one, she'd hold on to a cushion to hide her protruding nipples. Now she became more comfortable around me.

She sat next to me on the couch with her heels up beneath her butt. I felt an electric current pass through me. I prayed her feet would cramp so I could massage them. I imagined ways I could get my hands on her without being too forward.

"Where's Mom? I thought you guys are dining alone. You know," she said, turning her head away. She blushed, knowing that meant sex.

"Well, she has a terrible headache. You know," I said folding my hands. "Bad. Awful." I shook my head.

"What do you mean? Where is she?" Sylvie asked.

"She's upstairs. Fuck it. Listen, Sylvie, I want to treat you as a friend, and as a mature person. She's back on drugs. I tried my best, I swear, I don't know what happened. I'm so hurt that after all I've done for her, she slips back."

Sylvie gasped. "Oh, my god. That bitch. Sorry." Such a polite girl. Tears fell. "That selfish bitch. I knew it wouldn't last. I wish she'd died. Couldn't she wait two years 'til I left?"

I drifted closer to her and put my arm around her. I kissed her head. *Fuck, too fatherly, I shouldn't have.* "It's not your fault, doll," I said.

She turned and looked at me, her eyes red. "You know, you look a lot like her, but younger and much more beautiful. She hasn't taken care of herself."

Sylvie put her head on my shoulder, and I hugged her tight. I could have kissed her, but I didn't. Not yet. *We can do better.*

I moved back to my seat, and she eyed me weirdly. *Fuck me.* I'd ruined the moment. I said, "You wanted to move out. That's interesting. Why not for a couple of years?"

"I don't know," she said. "I'll be old enough. Have a job, maybe."

"Let's eat," I said. "Come."

We went to the table, and she asked for wine. I refused and said she'd like it, and then she'd be drinking to get drunk, and she shouldn't do that. I promised to let her taste it later.

"I'm underdressed, and you look good." She said and giggled.

"No worries. I know I can do better." She kicked my ass, and I ran after her but didn't catch her. We ate in peace afterward.

We talked about how a person should live up to their potential and not throw their lives away by being lazy or being restrained by social norms. We joked. We had inside jokes. I used to wink when Mel searched for a mysterious antiseptic. We both knew she was looking for a forgotten baggie.

We moved to the couch, and I poured my third drink. I knew I shouldn't get wasted because I must remain focused, but I wanted to celebrate getting the fuck away from Melanie.

"I blame myself," I said, "because I saw the signs, and I thought she was just having cravings. Cravings can be normal. Recently she was searching every corner for drugs."

Sylvie extended her legs on the couch.

"Fuck her," Sylvie said. "Sorry. Like, don't worry about her. You deserve better."

"You know what? I'll ask you something, but be honest. If I broke up with her, would we still be friends? Still talk like we do?" I asked.

"Please don't," she said. "Please. Pretty please." She looked at me weirdly, giving me what they call doe's eyes. For me, it could be a doe, a squirrel, a cow... *I don't see a fucking difference.*

"I've waited a long time," I said. "I feel like she failed me, but I also failed her in many ways. And then there's you... and... and she says hurtful things. And she jeopardizes my work in the group... and on top of all of that—never mind. You won't understand."

"Such a great friend. Omg. Don't make me angry," she pointed a finger at me.

"You don't even know," I said. *Almost there.*

She grabbed her mobile and held it up like a knife. "Say it or else."

"You know. *Sex.* You've never done it, so you don't know. Have you even gotten your period yet?"

She turned red. Being a blonde, it showed more on her. She jumped on the couch. "You killed me. Oh, oh. To the heart." She cleared her throat. "I'm proud to tell you, yes, I got it. And No, never has sex before."

"Oh. So it doesn't matter if I tell you."

"Sam." She stood, went behind the couch, and locked my head in her arms. I could feel her breath. "Say it."

"The sex," I said. "It doesn't happen much, and when it does, it's terrible... I'm not a cheater, but damn, how fucked up is it to wait and then be rejected. I endure all that.... and jerk off a lot. I feel like I'm a teenager with her."

Sylvie broke into laughter.

"Oh, man, this wine is great," I said.

"Let me taste it," she said. "You promised."

"Come." She sat next to me. "How can I make sure you won't drink it all?"

"I won't. Cross my heart."

"No. I'll hold it while you sip," I said.

We ended up with four hands on the glass, and we laughed during multiple attempts at getting the glass to her mouth. I tried to lean away, and she put her leg on mine. She sipped. Our eyes were close, they kept jumping down to the other's lips and back up. I could have kissed her.

Kiss her, you fool!

Don't be greedy!

She's the one!

I cleared my throat and said, "Syl. Your turn to answer a tough one. Have you ever masturbated? You know, had an orgasm?"

Her eyes were open. She pursed her lips. She took the cushion and yelled into it, jokingly. Then she said, "I tried, but it didn't work!"

"You know what I wish?" I said and looked away, dead serious. "That you were older. I'm just so unlucky."

She jumped into my lap and hugged me. Happiness filled my heart, I could have flown. We kissed passionately.

"We don't have to wait for me to be older. Do me."

"No. You should do it with someone you love," I said, holding her shoulders.

"Oh, I love you. A lot," she said. More kisses. "I've loved you since I first saw you. I love you, I love you, I love you."

We kissed for a few minutes, and I said, "No sex, but I'll make you orgasm. Give you oral and teach you how to give it." She nodded.

Wow. I am proud. I waited so long, and she is worth the wait.

PART

3

JASON

A FREE BIRD

I got a new place. I couldn't go back to the old one because it had so many memories, and it would drain me. Luke told me starting in a new place was better for my recovery.

Before the incident, I had been greedy. I'd wanted everything, and my priorities had revolved around materialistic goals. Those priorities didn't matter now; I had lost the most important things - Lea, Lisa, Mathew.

The new house was good enough. It had two levels with the bedrooms and office upstairs and the kitchen and living area downstairs. It had old wallpaper and old furniture, but not antique. It smelled funny—dusty and musky. I replaced the sofa – I wanted something more comfortable – but otherwise, I kept everything the same.

I moved all our possessions from our old place to the new house, which made it feel crowded with the stuff that was already there. Decluttering and throwing things away kept me busy.

Still, the first few days were awkward. Where the fuck do I start? What do I do? What is normal?

Luke said, '"Get a healthy start. Go to the grocery shop, play a basketball game or watch a movie. Keep it light, bro."

The first minute after I woke up each day was the only decent one. I'd stretch my hands and smile, excited to get up and see my family, to plan a super-productive day. Then I would remember, and I'd become instantly devastated. That summed up my days.

I wanted to call Kelly. I resisted for the first three days I was in the house. I played scenarios out in my mind: "Babe, I'm out!" or "Guess what?" or "Guess who's out and ready to mingle?"

In the end, I decided to text her, "Hi Kelly. This is Jason. How are you? I miss you. Can't wait 'til we meet. Where are you? What does your calendar look like?" Pretty lame, but I went with a low-risk approach.

A couple of hours passed by, and she didn't text back. I got worried. I sent another text, "?? All okay?"

Incoming message. "Hiii. Very happy you're out. I'm fine, all is well. How are you adjusting? Sorry we can't meet. Please move on. I wish you all the best and I wish you well. TC."

Another one, "PS: I know you're innocent. Wish I could help but I can't. Forgive me." Kisses.

I read it a few times, and it didn't make sense. Although we hadn't discussed catching up and meeting, I thought it was a given based on earlier conversations.

I called her, and she picked up on the fifth ring. "Hi," she said, her voice distant and low.

"Hi, Kelly. What's wrong? I've missed you." She didn't respond, but I could hear her breathing.

I broke the silence, "You know my feelings are real. Did I do something wrong? You know, other than what I was accused of?"

Once I said it, I felt bad. It wasn't funny at all. I really missed my family.

"Nothing is wrong," she said, "I know. Uhhh. I know. And me too, honestly. But things aren't the same." She sighed. "Major changes have happened, and I can't be with you anymore."

My jaw tensed, and I ground my teeth. "Why? Did someone threaten you or tell you not to see me?" I asked.

"No, no. Nothing like that. I haven't been honest with you." She sighed again. "Oh, gosh, this is tough. Forgive me, Jason. I'm married. I was married and then we separated, and I started using and then got admitted to the facility. My husband went to court and got full custody of our daughter. But since I've been out, things have changed. We're now living together, for our daughter's sake."

"That doesn't make sense," I said. "You could have told me. Wow. That's huge."

After several moments of silence, I said, "Listen, leave him. I mean, consider leaving him and taking your daughter, and come live with me."

As if her husband would say, Yeah, take my daughter to live with a murderer.

"It's not that simple. Actually impossible." She chuckled. "Oh, honey. I'm sorry. You don't need this, and you deserve better. Sorry. You're adorable. Bye."

She hung up before I could say a thing.

The next day was boring. I did some chores, walked around, and watched a couple of movies. By evening, I was wondering what to do next and how would I sustain myself over a longer time period.

I wasn't supposed to, but I had a drink. Nothing heavy, just a glass of wine, but two hours later I poured the last of the bottle. I put on a comedy. I knew I couldn't laugh, but I needed something light to pass the time.

I closed my eyes, and I could hear them. Lisa, Lea, and Mathew. I squinted, and I could see shadows, which I decided were them.

I drifted into the memories. We listened to a song at home, and we started dancing... Our bodies were close. Suddenly I felt my shoulder grow wet. Lisa was crying.

"What's wrong, babe?"

"Don't laugh at me. I have an unshakable hunch that you're going to die. It's irrational, but this feeling is constantly inside of me." She sobbed, then started laughing.

"Don't say that," I told her. "We're healthy. We take good care of ourselves."

I left the living room and went into the kitchen. I wondered if she thought I was unstable. I thought of the last time I'd had such an intense desire to leave this life. Nothing that I'd acted on, but a sense of emptiness and darkness, a wish to just vanish. The peak was maybe a decade ago, around the time I'd graduated.

During that period, I talked a lot to myself. I'd decided to keep going in life, even knowing how much energy it took to continue doing so.

After I'd had a family, the feeling came and went. Nothing scary, although some days were very bleak. I just had to wait for them to pass.

I sobbed in the living room, emptying the glass of wine. "Oh, babe. I'm so sorry." Look how silly life is. You are dead, and I'm alive. You loved life, and I'm indifferent.

I jolted and became alert. Dr. Thompson had warned me about spiraling into negative thoughts. He said drinking with my medication might have detrimental effects. I'd said that "detrimental" was a fancy word. He'd said that would help me remember it, and I should call him if I had any suicidal thoughts. I chuckled to myself and wondered what I would do if I were always suicidal.

CHAPTER

19

GO ON

Having decided that my current life was unbearable, I finally convinced Luke to help me take on a new business venture. I chose a local pub to turn around. I had to admit that I wasn't in the best shape, and I needed to keep better track of my medication and stop drinking. I promised to check in with one of the doctors on Dr. Thompson's team on a daily basis.

Looking at the numbers was calming, and acquiring a business had its own thrills. We thought the place could be profitable. Three weeks passed quickly, and we reopened the pub. We named it the Diamond Ace. Luke asked me not to spend all my time in the pub, I didn't want to upset him, so I let it go. I knew he didn't want me to drink.

We hired new staff and the recruitment was fun: Andrea, a bartender and manager; Stephanie, a waitress; and

George, our all-in-one guy. He could work the bar, wait tables, and break up fights. George was a young college graduate who soon would transition into corporate life but wanted a year or two before he became a *slave*, as he called it. He was a bulky guy with piercing eyes. I trusted him.

Stephanie was the money-maker. She knew what the customers wanted, and she had groups ordering specialty shots. She was tanned with dark eyes and blonde hair. They didn't go together, but she pulled it off. She had curves that she was proud of. I liked her. I guess I was attracted to her.

Luke saw that I was starting to resemble my old self, so he got me the files for the case against me. Reading was depressing and painful. I requested my family's phones and laptops, but he resisted a bit, saying, "Bro, really, it would be too painful. Please, no." Then, he gave in.

I bought a whiteboard sized more than two yards long. He said that once I'd finished going through everything, he would put me in touch with the private investigator we had on payroll.

He said, "They are professional and know what they are doing."

I said, "Ok."

Luke said, "Let me know when you're ready, I will put you in contact with Danny Miller, our private investigator."

Kelly called me a couple of times. Once to check on me, to find out what I was doing and whether there was anything new happening in the investigation.

The other time she called, she was really upset because her husband had found out that she was practicing online without a license, and they didn't need the money. She said she had to have her own income so she could set some aside in case they broke up or she needed to run away. She told me how much she missed me, and I missed her, too. I needed her, and truthfully I was disappointed that we were apart.

I had my doubts about her being married and having a daughter. I still couldn't find any details about her online, so I asked her for her address. She didn't want to give it up, so I asked her to meet up for coffee.

She agreed, and we met. We exchanged pleasantries, and then she told me that she still had feelings for me. I told her the feeling was mutual. She showed me photos of her family. We hugged, we kissed, and she left.

I shouldn't have done it, but I followed her to where she lived. When she parked she rested her head on the wheel, and I could see she was crying. She entered the house, a regular suburban place. I couldn't resist following her inside. It was noon, and her daughter and so-called husband shouldn't have been around.

I opened the door and walked slowly inside. She had nice furniture, but too many rugs.

"Kelly? Kelly! It's Jason!"

I went up a few more steps, and she jumped out in front of me holding the largest knife I had ever seen.

She screamed, "Get out! Get Out! What the fuck are you doing here, Jason? Get out!"

I took two more steps and hugged her. She dropped the knife.

"I swear I'll get a restraining order if I see you in this neighborhood again," she said.

I could see the kitchen from where we were standing, and I saw a large calendar and drawings. I kept hugging her. She was sobbing. I said, "You're amazing. I wish you well."

"Jason, don't do creepy things." She sniffled. "I know you're paranoid and it is normal after what you've been through, but I am married."

I hugged her from behind and pushed my body against hers. I whispered, "I want you."

I pulled her blouse up a little and unhooked her bra. We moved a few steps, and I pushed her against the wall.

"JASON," she yelled.

I froze.

"I said NO. NO. What is wrong with you?"

This wasn't me. I didn't recognize myself.

Oh fuck, I'm crazy.

I hadn't heard her say no.

I swear, you have to believe me.

"I'm so sorry. I'm leaving," I said, holding my hands up.

I apologized and promised her never to come to her house again.

I wondered what had gotten into me. I had never obsessed over sex and never imagined I would miss a signal from a woman, let alone a NO.

CHAPTER

20

GUARDIAN ANGEL

I was visiting the pub much less often, at first, the ownership or the challenge of turning the business around stirred me. But now the pub generated enough income to cover most of the costs and would soon make profits, I had to accept that the excitement had passed.

I reached the pub at 3 p.m., and Andrea stood behind the bar drying some glasses, the lights were dimmed. We no longer opened early to offer the scum of the Earth their daylight drink. When we had opened early, the customers who came for happy hour at six crossed paths with the wasted noon drunks, and we learned the mismatch proved harmful for the business.

"Hi. Glad you still remember how to find the place," she said sarcastically.

The place is mine, I can come and go as I want, You can fuck off.

"Hey, yourself. Come on, if I could, I'd stay here twenty-four seven."

My lies are always convincing.

She was wearing a sleeveless black denim shirt over low-rise blue jeans.

Who the hell still wears this retro outfit? I hated myself when I judged people, but at least I was aware of it, so I stopped myself before analyzing her further.

"Here, I have the box of ornaments you requested," I said.

Thirty minutes tops and I'll be out of here. Must continue working on the case.

I walked over to the bar and handed her the box. Holding it, she turned and squatted down with her back to me so she could put it on the floor. When she bent down, I could see her lower back skin, and then a gray thong appeared. While in a full squat, the thong rose out of her jeans by an inch or two.

Soo sexy and provocative. The sight turned me on. Given my recent emotional history, I was taken aback by the fact that anything could move me. A few moments later, I became worried about my erection and my rapid sexual arousal.

How long has it been? Four months. No, five months.

She stood and pivoted. She caught me staring.

"What?" she said.

"What *what?*" I knew exactly what.

"Relax, hon." She said. I hated the word *hon*. "You liked what you were seeing. Normal."

I smirked at her, unamused.

She took a couple of steps around the end of the bar and toward me. A few inches separated us, her breath gently caressed my cheek, and we locked eyes.

I liked her short hair, and the shaven part on one side was so funky, albeit out of fashion. The few pink tips showed nicely when she wore her hair in a ponytail. She was really tall, and her face was pretty. Despite her radiating the power of an independent woman, her eyes conveyed a certain kindness.

Say something, dammit.

"Don't worry, I can take off the thong before the customers come in," she said in a flirtatious tone.

Is it flirtatious? I can't be sure. I might be imagining sexual signs.

Did she mean she would literally take them off, or she would take them off and something would happen between us?

"Free country. Take them off, leave'm on. Your call, *hon*."

After a minute I added, "you don't want customers to hit on you or anything. But they look nice, hot."

What the hell!

I could laugh at myself. "Sexy, I mean. I would... pfffff. Sorry."

I could feel how warm my ears were, which meant my face was red from embarrassment. The best thing to do was to flee the scene.

"Listen," Andrea said. "How about I make you a nice cocktail, and we can have an honest, hearty chat, just until you finish the drink?"

My story interested everyone and anyone - a broken man, a murderer, a molester, a rapist... People's motives differed between uncovering the truth, getting famous, or simply being curious.

"Sounds fine, Andrea," I said.

Within a couple minutes, she served me a Rum and coke, and I took a sip. It had been some time since I'd sipped so politely. I preferred gulps and clean bottoms. She drank hers in one shot.

"Jason," she said, "we all deserve a chance in life, at whatever endeavor we take on. Sometimes we deserve a second chance."

Oh my god, was she one of those find Jesus freaks? Was she going to start with the forgiveness talk now?

She sensed my dismay and changed strategies. She took off her sleeveless denim top, revealing more of her body. Her bra showed through her white undershirt. Very hot, but cheap.

"Stephanie. Don't ask her out." She folded her arms, and I wasn't pleased with the conversation. "I overheard her on the phone, and she isn't who you think she is. She is only pretending to like you."

I replied with a cliché. "We all have a past." Mine is a bloody one. "And she's allowed to have one, too."

"She's a fucking journalist. An undercover, investigative journalist," Andrea said.

I became concerned. Was Andrea lying or was Stephanie really a journalist?

"Listen, Andrea, I shouldn't be talking about this," I said. I was bluffing. "We can't be sure she's a journalist. But thanks for letting me know, anyway."

"Let me show you something. Follow me," she said and walked ahead of me to my office.

She walked behind the desk and took my seat, so I sat down on the leather two-seater. She took out a bag from one of the cabinets and came to sit on the arm of the couch. She smelled nice, nothing fancy, probably a body cream and not a perfume.

She opened the bag. "Look. This is what I found in her locker." A laminated press pass ID and an old smartphone.

"Her true name is Rosa Dempsey, and she has written a book on missing children. If you search for online, you will recognize her face despite the changes."

I tried not to react, but I was fuming. "And here's a photo of her going into the newspaper office," Andrea said. "I followed her."

I carefully prepared my words, "We all have a job to do, and hers happens to be this," I said.

She fooled me. She didn't like me—it was all an act!

"What?" Andrea asked angrily. "Seriously? You know she's getting close to you just to find out where you *buried* your son."

Her words brought a lump in my throat, words escaped me, and I could only nod. I didn't bury my son; I didn't kill my son. I miss my son, I would do anything to get him back.

She threw her bag on the desk and paced the room. "First," she said, "get the bitch out of here. Second, let's work on your case together."

I thought back on all my conversations and texts with Stephanie. In retrospect, her admiration had been too good to be true. I had hoped to ask her out and start a proper relationship. I'd have to get accustomed to calling her Rosa.

What a fucking fool.

Andrea sat back down on the couch arm. She took my face in her hands and turned it toward hers, tilting closer to me.

"I've been reading about your case since you hired me here. I believe something went very wrong, and I believe you're innocent."

She kissed me. I barely moved my lips. I was scared of breaking down again, fearful of what Rosa could have discovered. Was I afraid because I was guilty? I couldn't focus. Andrea was still trying to kiss me.

We sat in silence for a few minutes. "I'll fire her ass," I stood up. "Tonight. Fuck her." I hugged Andrea and thanked her.

AND ACTION

I'd spent all my time reading my case files, and since day one I'd been reading the Internet coverage and people's speculations.

The time came to meet our long-retained private investigator. A car pulled into my driveway, and a short woman got out. I ran downstairs to greet her before she knocked. We exchanged pleasantries, and I offered her coffee, which she said was much needed. I watched her grimace as she entered the living room, and I wondered if she reacted to the old smell or a new one.

She sniffled a lot, probably because of allergies to the dust, or from the smoke of my cigarettes. I never asked anyone if I could smoke inside—people were free to leave if they didn't like it.

"I'll bring you up to speed regarding the work done so far," Danny said. "I must be straight with you about the fact that the first six months were intense and very different from how it's been this past year. But with you here, we can think together, we can do things differently—detailed, comprehensive."

It seemed as though she had rehearsed this part.

"I want you to tell me everything from your perspective," she said. "Every detail is important."

For her winning was getting proof of who the killer was, whether it was me or someone else, so she intended to invade my space and memories.

"No worries," I said. "I understand. Whatever's necessary."

She nodded and cleared the table, pulled out folders from her bag, and I excused myself to refill my coffee. I took mine Irish, half and half. I was a bit worried she would smell the liquor on me; I drank quite a bit those days; I called it the noon to the moon buzz.

After I shared my side of the story and what I remembered, she said, "The reward for finding Mathew brought in countless useless and misleading information, but we had to attend to each tip. Did you go over the case files?" she said.

I nodded. She picked up the first folder.

"The most important part of any investigation is the crime scene. I'll spare you the details, but you should know that in your house there was no physical evidence whatsoever: DNA, body fluids, hair, tissue, prints, tire marks, or even shoe traces." She waited for me to say something.

"Go on, please."

"Here are some things we know regarding Lea's and Lisa's murder. The belt used to strangle your wife didn't give us any information, and there were no signs of a struggle. They recovered two 9mm bullets." She cleared her throat. "But they found no gun. No witnesses."

"Okay."

"Nothing else led us anywhere. Now, let's discuss the other important locations relevant to the case," she grabbed another folder. "The school, both cars, your other office. The new one and Lea's studio."

"I remember the studio, I rented it for her as a birthday gift. She didn't have space at home for drawing."

"Okay, that's a relief," Danny chuckled, still sniffling. "I was worried you might not remember."

I smiled politely.

"So," Danny sighed, "there were two working theories."

"Okay," I said, drinking my coffee faster. *Oh god, this really hurts.*

"Our theory is that the killer is a middle-aged male who hated Lisa, and while strangling her, Lea interrupted him, so he shot her. Or…"

"Or my second personality is responsible," I interrupted.

"The second personality is the police's theory, and it's all over the press—that you're the killer and your split personality is responsible. Either you killed them both, or you were in love with your daughter, and you killed your wife after she discovered the relationship and killed Lea. Notably, you didn't have gunshot residue on your hands whereas your late wife did. That's why they went with the split personality theory."

"So what are you doing with these theories? The second personality one doesn't concern me—let them say what they want. But what are you doing to find Mathew? "

"Luke provided me with a list of people who dislike you and your family. None of them fit the profile, and most had solid alibis. What would help is if you could make your own list of enemies." She said.

"I will soon," I said. I felt the anxious sweat beads forming, but the whiskey comforted me.

"Email me. Go back to your school days if you can."

"Okay. Next." I said.

"You know your wife was having an affair, and we checked the guy out after the police did. Jeb. He didn't have a solid alibi, but he and your wife weren't particularly close, neither of them was in love. In brief, the police eliminated him as a suspect. Which takes us to the next part." She took out a third folder.

"Next is the digital evidence. Nothing of use in the phones and laptops and we didn't get much from the cell phone tower signals. All the times checked out, and nothing seemed odd. Your wife and Jeb didn't meet much, they didn't chat regularly. He had no motive. The guy was having marital troubles, but a week prior to the murder, he returned to his wife."

"But doesn't that give him the motive to hurt Lisa? To make sure she didn't mess things up with his wife?" I asked, and I lost my breath, I couldn't handle long sentences.

"Not really. His wife was his alibi, and she said she knew about Lisa and because they were separated, she looked past his infidelity. Text messages prove he told his wife about Lisa before they got back together."

"The wife? Could she be the killer?" I asked.

"No. she doesn't fit the profile," Danny said.

Fuck you. Don't say 'fit the profile.' Investigate! Do your damn job!

"I'm sorry, but I don't agree," I said. "You should investigate her."

"Actually, she was sick at the time, Mr. Stankovic. Too weak to commit the act. I don't even know if she's still alive. Her husband returned home when she started treatment."

"Oh. Okay."

"We looked at all Lea's friends, the police didn't think there was enough motive. The peculiar thing is that Lea had a boyfriend, and no one knew anything about him, not even her closest friends. One of them mentioned he had sent roses to Lea several times over the last few months, but I could not trace who sent them. The texts from the mysterious boyfriend on Lea's phone were sent from a burner phone, and we can retrieve nothing."

"What did you do about it?" I interrupted.

"We covered all of her 800-something social media friends, and none of them admitted to being her boyfriend. This is a knot we couldn't untie."

"But this is very important," I said. "This is what we've been looking for. We must find this boyfriend."

I got excited. Finally, we had what I had hoped for—a lead.

"This is where I must be frank with you Mr. Stankovic. People assume you're the person behind the messages. Especially because the only images on her phone are of the two of you." She paused for ten seconds. "And your history of planning dinner dates didn't work against this assumption." She said with assertiveness in her voice–she could have bluntly said *you are the boyfriend, so please knock it off.*

Not so much for hope. I was glad I hadn't mentioned the roses I sent Lea. If Danny knew I'd sent them, she might not investigate this further.

"I feel terrible," I said. "I really don't remember a burner. And I assure you nothing was going on between my daughter and me. for god's sake."

"Lastly, we have the interviews with the people surrounding you—neighbors, colleagues, friends, and even family members. Nothing there. They all mentioned how good you and Lisa were to each other and said they thought what you were going through was only a rough patch." She took out a small pad from her pocket and flipped through it.

"Okay, so what do we do?" I asked. "Isn't there anything to be done about the burner, like a new technology or something?"

"Unfortunately, no. Even if we found it now, let's say by a miracle, it's like a used notebook. We won't know who used it."

"But I sent Lea messages from my personal phone. Why would I also send them from a burner?" I asked.

"The police suggested your other personality sent the messages, provoked by the drugs you were taking."

"Okay," I said. Coffee was over. I wanted her to leave.

"Anyway, let's move forward. I want you to send me your list of enemies and to look at the recordings, maybe you recognize someone familiar or something odd we may have missed."

"And I want you to look again at her friends, her teachers, and Jeb's wife, even if she is dead," I sputtered.

Danny didn't reply, but her grimace gave away her thoughts. She pursed her lips and nodded.

"If you don't want the job," I said, "let me know. I can hire someone else."

"No, no. Not like that. I—"

I interrupted. "I know. Chances are low. Extremely low. And a 99% chance it was me. Just forget the chances and concentrate on the task at hand. And what can we do about finding Mathew? Are there any new leads?"

"Each time we run ads for the reward, we get hundreds of tips. I also want to be direct with you, ultimately, every open investigation reaches a dead end where there are no more leads to pursue. Even the major national bureaus disband large task forces when investigations reach a block. People die, move on, leave the country... no question about our intentions and efforts, but a matter of *what else* can we do. We won't stop looking for him. I'll put together a report about our search's progress and come up with some new recommendations. We have to stay hopeful."

"We have to. Hope is all I have."

"One more thing," she said. "We want your handwriting for analysis. There was a Post-it note in Lea's studio on which someone had written, *I love you, babe. Kisses.* Maybe we can analyze the handwriting to find out if you wrote the note. Mind you, even if it isn't a match, experts say other personalities can have their distinct handwriting."

My eyes filled with tears as I wrote the words for the handwriting sample, but I held them until Danny left. I wished I could hug Lea and whisper the words into her ears. I so badly wanted to find the person who had done this to us and to find my son. I believed he was alive; I chose to believe that. People on the Internet accused me of killing and burying him because I couldn't face having killed his mother and sister.

I refilled my coffee mug, another day of hard liquor and no medication.

CHAPTER

22

SO WHAT?

The night after Danny left became the starting point for looking into what had happened, ground zero. I didn't watch the recordings, but I organized them, so the next day I only needed to press play. Being relatively drunk, I would not remember what I saw, postponing to the following day made sense.

I woke up with a hangover and my head buzzing; I tried to vomit, but nothing came out. I downed a strong black coffee and studied the whiteboard:

1. Male. Middle age. Hate? A sick loon? A burglar (less likely). Lea's boyfriend.
2. With Danny: enemies list, watch recordings, hand-writing test, check devices.

3. Alone: burner phone? Friends, Lisa's work, my work + Lisa's boyfriend and his wife.
4. Mathew... with the killer? Alive.

I tilted my head, smoked a cigarette, and waited for the Aha! Moment, but it never came. I thought I could move again and start fresh. Argentina? Or someplace where I could live on the beach and drink myself to death. *Yeah, right.*

I circled the boyfriend and the wife. I underlined "Alive" three times.

I became less energetic and more hammered, maybe because I had missed my meds. I drifted, and my vision blurred. If someone spoke to me, is my speech coherent? I didn't want to be paranoid about what others thought. So what if they saw me drifting away or drunk or sleepy? But I could avoid going out and talking to anyone.

Don't be paranoid.

Alcohol withdrawal could also explain my physical state, so I decided to eat something and afterward have a beer to see if I improve.

As I opened a second bottle, I wondered if my lack of sleep might explain my state of mind. I slept less, just a few hours now, and sometimes only a couple of hours. I decided to try some sleeping pills in the upcoming days.

The next forty-eight hours were all tears and alcohol. We didn't have enemies, and the recordings contained nothing in them except everyone in the area walking down streets and entering buildings. Checking the phones and laptops was too painful—my heart ached, I had spells of intense crying. At one point I kissed the screens, hugged the computer, and screamed at the top of my voice. Surely the neighbors heard, called me crazy, and ignored me.

Danny called. "Do you have the list?"

I said yes, and she asked me to email it to her. I told her I'd gotten nothing from the recordings, and she said that Lea's boyfriend had been to the studio, but no one had been able to ID him. She asked me to watch it again. Maybe someone wearing a cap or sunglasses would catch my attention.

I read Lea's messages to the guy again. I wanted to check the building security footage for a person in a cap and shades.

2:23: Lea: "Can you come over? My place."

2:25: Him: "Hi, babe. Missed you a lot. Sure. I am thinking about you. You're really something."

2:30: Lea: "Okay."

2:31: Him: "Be there in 15. Can't wait."

I jumped to the computer and scrolled to the day and the time of the message.

And there he was, entering the building.

I hope the police had checked this initially.

I put on running shoes, shorts, and a cotton t-shirt. Once outside, I realized my attire wasn't weather-appropriate. I didn't want to go back in and change, but the way I dressed wouldn't serve me as far as appearing sane and stable went.

After a fifteen minutes walk from home, I arrived at the studio building. I waited for the doorman in the entrance. People were going in and out, eyeing me weirdly. At least I thought they were, but I could have been wrong. Could just be paranoid.

Finally, the doorman came over to me. "Hello, Mr. Stankovic. It's been a long time. How have you been?"

He remembered me. I used to pay him well for extra security.

"Good. How are you? All is well?"

Finish the casual talk. No need to attend to his pity or engage with him.

I showed him a video still of the man in the cap and sunglasses. He looked at the image and at me, a few times, once taking a step back to look at my posture. The asshole thought the man in the photo was me in disguise.

He said he didn't recognize the guy, but he remembered him because he'd found it strange that someone kept wearing the ball cap and sunglasses inside. He also said he shared the same observation with the detectives in the early few weeks of the investigation. "In the beginning, I thought he had an eye infection or was hiding bad hair. But he dressed like that every time he came here, so I knew he did it to disguise himself when he came to visit Ms. Lea—may her soul rest in peace." The corner of his mouth moved slightly down in a micro-expression of contempt and displeasure. The asshole was confident I was the boyfriend, and that I had killed my wife.

I went home, looked at the security footage, and recorded every day and time the guy had visited Lea's studio. If I could prove that the man in the footage wasn't me, then I could discredit the theory that I had been in love with Lea. The whole case would fall apart. Surely no one else had done this, who cared about proving my innocence anyway?

I failed. The problem was I hadn't gone into my office for three months, and so I couldn't alibi myself. I made up every meeting and appointment I had put in my calendar. Even if I found something on the calendar to show conflict between the visits and my whereabouts, no one would consider it substantial evidence to prove I was not Lea's *boyfriend*.

For a reason I can't explain, walking back home, I sensed I was being followed. I couldn't be sure because my senses were numb, so I glanced back every few seconds. Someone behind me took the same turns I took! But suddenly the individual disappeared.

Shit, am I hallucinating?

INSPECTION

Time passed smoothly, but I didn't catch my break-through in the case. The sleeping pills helped me sleep but didn't improve my energy. Luke said my depression caused the lethargy, and that I should take my medication. I didn't mind taking the pills, but on the other hand, they caused apathy. So I chose the inactivity over the indifference.

"Are you? Jason? Are you taking your pills?" he asked.

And I said, "I'm disappointed you're asking me that. Of course I'm taking them. I need the help, any kind."

I will not overmedicate myself, the meds make me accept the tragedy.

"If you get in trouble, things will end up badly for you."

"Understood, let's meet soon for a beer," I said.

"I'll go but on the condition you don't drink, not even a single beer," Luke said.

"Sure, not one. Say tomorrow, at 8 p.m.?"

Fuck you. I am not going.

"Okay," he said. "I'll call you tomorrow to pick a place."

After I hung up, I went to the home of Lisa's boyfriend, Jeb.

What kind of name is Jeb?

His wife was sound and healthy, and nothing had stopped her from laughing, talking, and enjoying her life. I parked about a hundred yards away in a rental car with dark windows. I would have preferred tinted windows, but I was afraid of getting pulled over by the cops.

I would have taken that chance, though, if it proved valuable to finding Mathew. When the time was right, I would jump Jeb and force the truth out of him.

If he is the killer, then he is keeping Mathew somewhere.

Sometimes killers return to the scenes of their crimes out of guilt or for pleasure. The sick ones returned to masturbate, replaying the exercise of power. I turned the car on and drove to my old house, the family place. I staked it out, hoping the fucker might return while I was there.

I slept a bit and woke up at dawn. I hadn't seen any suspicious movement during the night. *Shit.* It hit me that people might think I was the killer because I returned to the crime scene.

My frustration grew, and the way I was missing essential links put me down, anger blazed through, and I acted on impulse, I headed back to Jeb's house.

As I drove back to Jeb's house, I felt like I was being followed. A dark sedan moved slowly behind me, but at a distance. I was an unreliable judge, though. I ignored the feeling.

Luckily, Jeb's wife and daughter had left before him. He stepped outside and waved at them. *Happy fucking family.*

I walked carefully to stand with my back against the side of the house. If he intended to walk to the car, he would pass without spotting me. Half an hour later, I got cold. I lit a cigarette at the risk of being seen.

Another half an hour and another cigarette later, Jeb walked to his car with a briefcase. I jumped him, and he stumbled, but he straightened up quickly and ran toward his car. I chased him, and we were both silent.

He mumbled, "No. I swear no. Wait. Let's talk like men."

I chased him around the house, and he tripped and fell to the ground. I used my knee to pin his arms to his back. I pulled his hair, and he screamed in pain.

"Keep it down," I said. "And now speak up. What the fuck did you do to my family, you sick bastard?"

He swore and kept on swearing.

"I'll cut off your balls and feed them to you. No, I'll cut everything I can cut from your body. Where is Mathew? Where is Mathew?"

He gave away nothing. I pulled on his ears until I felt they might detach. I amped up the pressure on his left arm, and he started sobbing. So I stopped and sat down next to him to think of my next move.

Useless shit face.

Nothing came to mind. I decided to head home for some soothing wine, something light. I thought I ought to eat soon and probably shower today. Tomorrow at the latest. I spotted the dark sedan that had followed me earlier, and this time I memorized the plate number, make, and model. Next time I'd know for sure whether I was being followed or I was being paranoid.

"What the fuck do you think you're doing?" Luke yelled on the phone.

"Whipping some scrambled eggs. Join me," I said before chugging a beer. I'd already had two glasses of wine, and it wasn't even noon.

"Stop messing around, Jason. This is serious. I'll pull the plug on you. Jeb's lawyer called, they can fuck us up. He threatened to press charges." Luke screamed louder.

"The next time won't just be a beating," I said. "I'll take his eyes out and crack his neck." I paced the house, anger filling me.

"We want none of that," Luke said. "Please stop. I convinced him not to do anything, I actually pleaded. And I fucking hate that, I never do that. For anyone."

"How about we release a statement? Not about them or to reply. To say that I'm sorry and that I'm also a victim."

"That's a bad idea, and it was among the options we considered early on. I'll tell you more later when we meet. 8 p.m., right?"

"Eight is good. The Ace," I said and hung up. He actually thought I would go.

CHAPTER

24

PLANS OF HOPE

My head hurt terribly, and I felt every heartbeat at my temples. I took some painkillers, but I guessed nothing would work. Presumably cocaine withdrawal. I tightened a belt around my head.

"I gotta keep going," I said to myself. I was about to solve something, or at least, was getting close to something. Luke and Andrea thought I imagined things, and Andrea wanted nothing to do with me anymore, but I went with my hunches.

Someone *broke* into my home!

Someone *followed* me!

I felt it, despite the lack of any proof. I had heard people talk about the power of the gaze, and scientists had studied it. They tested on a group of people whether they could feel that someone in a crowd was looking at them... and they felt correct. People stared, subjects felt; people didn't stare, subjects felt nothing.

I attached a spycam to my backpack—eyes in my back. I walked around the block for a couple days without checking the footage. I would review all the recording once. I didn't want to obsess about them. *Yeah, right.*

My guard was never down. Although I could now potentially view who was following me, that didn't mean that I would leave my back unattended. Every few seconds I turned to have a look, and I walked with the lights or sun behind me so I could see the shadows. If someone were creeping on me or getting too close, I would have a heads-up. Other than that, I acted normal, kept to my routine.

I texted Luke, "Asshole. I have an ongoing plan. I'm not asking you to believe me, I'm asking you to wait. Hang around please. You're all that's left for me."

He disappointed me. If there was even a one percent chance that whoever was following me knew something about Mathew, then I had to do this. I had to try, as crazy that sounded.

During the walk, I thought about what I could do at home. If I put security cameras up and locked everything, the intruder would be reluctant to break in. Most security systems would automatically alert the company and subsequently the police, and they quickly identify and apprehend the intruder. But that would not give me back my son.

I decided to lure him or her in. I would go out on the front porch and act wasted, a bottle in my hand, cursing, shouting, and falling off the stairs, then passing out in a slump. An invitation. I hadn't decided what to do if I caught the intruder, but I might crush his every bone in revenge.

I must have been damaged to be considering something so extreme before even being sure this person had anything to do with my family. It could be another stalker, a burglar, or even a nosy journalist.

I took my walks in the early morning, afternoon, and at night. I wished I had a dog with me to make me feel safer.

I couldn't claim I had seen anyone, but my hunch said someone lurked around. I couldn't wait to have a look at the footage after a day and a half. So, I connected the camera to the TV, lit up a cigarette, and poured myself a bourbon, the noon buzz. There he was, a man in a hoodie and sunglasses, always keeping back a distance of fifty to one hundred yards. *Motherfucker*. The picture got blurry if I tried to zoom in on the face. I wondered if any agency had image enhancement software, or if that was something they only did on TV.

I wanted to tell Luke, but for what? *So he could mock me*? I went with my plan instead. In a few hours, I could put on my act and invite my enemy inside. I had to watch out not to kill him. Or her. The only problem was that I really got drunk, so I spent the next few hours doing push-ups and cardio exercises, trying to flush some of the poison out.

At eight in the evening, I walked to the liquor store and bought a bottle of whiskey in a brown paper bag. Then I drank, walked, and sang a few things. I thought I did an excellent job. I fell on the stairs, stumbled inside, made a loud crash with the bottle. Then I hid under the dining table, moving the cloth to cover me. I had left the door open four inches.

I waited for twenty minutes, but my legs started to cramp, and I craved a cigarette. I heard footsteps. My heart jumped. I didn't think this through; I didn't even have something in hand with which to hit him. I breathed shallowly and waited as he entered the room, drifting steadily. He came close to the table, and I waited until he turned around to jump out and hit him.

Suddenly, he kicked me, and his knee landed on my neck, as if he knew exactly where I was hiding!

"I'll rip your throat out, motherfucker!" I screamed as I staggered to my feet. Another kick. I felt my head jolt sideways, and I fell down. I was losing consciousness. I saw him kneeling, but I closed my eyes without having seen his face.

He put his hands on my cheeks and pressed, lifting my head up off the ground. I felt his breath. He whispered, "Worthless shit."

I gathered all the energy left inside of me and said, "where is Mathew?" and then I passed out.

I called Luke and told him what had happened. He said, "Didn't you know he could have killed you? Reckless, man, reckless. This is... unbelievable."

Other than that, he wasn't helpful, and he urged me to stop this and get a security system. He said, "So you acted very drunk and then entered your home, leaving the door open. Anyone could have seen you and seized the opportunity and entered to steal something."

I explained that if the man had been a burglar, then why didn't he steal anything, and he couldn't answer. I got fed up with Luke. *I am on my own.*

How had he known where I was hiding? I thought about it as I pressed a bag of frozen peas against my face. After some time, I wondered if maybe he had cameras installed inside my house. *Unreasonable*, I said to myself. *Don't obsess.* I decided to dedicate a few hours to searching the place.

I looked in appliances and smoke detectors and found nothing. After a couple of bourbons, I examined the air conditioning system. I removed a vent and found wires. I pulled the wires and found that they went through the wall down to the electrical outlet. He must have removed the camera before he left, or else someone left this from before I rented the place.

Another hour passed, and I kept thinking and drinking. When I went online to search for places someone could hide spycams, I felt old.

The search results helped. I went to the DVR, one place people hid cameras. I didn't find a camera, but the warranty void sticker on the screws showed that someone tampered with the device.

I got you, motherfucker. I bought that when I moved in!

This had to be recent. Although the sticker was carefully placed back in its place, one of the edges was elevated as if someone previously peeled it.

Did I do this?

Damn it. I terribly wanted to remember. Am I taunting myself? Am I the monster or the victim?

Call Luke again? The clock showed 2 a.m. No. Bourbon and a good night's sleep, the beating had worn me out. I locked my bedroom door and closed my eyes. I wished I had a dog. I felt lonely.

The next day I called a private detective to search the place, Danny would most probably mock my paranoia and afterward inform Luke. He did a mediocre job looking for cameras, but he had a device to scan for bugs. We didn't find anything. He told me that although there wasn't anything there now, bugs were easy to plant.

I wanted to find the person, get him under my mercy, question him. I eventually packed a bag and went to a motel.

I asked for two rooms, one was along the balcony, and the other was just at the corner over-viewing the first, both overlooking the parking lot. I moved all my bags into one and stayed in the second. The location was optimal. I could see the road, the room across, and the walk along the balcony. The first hour went by quickly. I kept scanning the area, assuming he had followed me. I stared at the bushes and waited for them to move.

During the second hour of waiting, I began doubting myself. *Do I imagine things? Am I crazy?* Indeed, I wasn't normal or stable, at this point in my life. Was it possible I had another personality who was tormenting me?

Don't doubt yourself. I smoked a lot as I sat there with no lights on, not moving.

I remembered what Andrea had said "You aren't letting go. You're addicted to your pain. You feel guilty if you let yourself be happy for a second. You're like a gambler hooked on losing."

I hadn't replied, but I'd felt the corners of my mouth drooping downward.

"You'll die," she'd said. "You always punish yourself."

We had sat for some time, not talking, and then she picked up her bag, kissed me, and told me to call when I was better.

I was hurting inside. I felt so lonely. I hummed softly, and it helped. From an external perspective, I was a loose cannon who had booked a room and sat in it, smoking, for the last four hours.

Motherfucker, where are you?

What if I fell asleep and he killed me? These doors couldn't take a small kick.

As time passed, my anticipation turned to agitation. Every time a guest arrived or left, I got quiet, then irritable. I wanted to smash the room and leave. *To go to where?* Maybe I'd check into a five-star hotel, run myself a bath.

I dozed off and woke up to a car pulling up outside. Its headlights were off.

Why are they off?

Was it him? The car parked on the street and not in the parking lot, and the driver disappeared.

A gun. *Fuck me.* I hadn't even thought about getting one. I thought my bodybuilding and cardio exercises were enough to defend myself, but not when I was wasted, and not against this person.

He had vanished. I scanned the landscape three times, looking for any movement in the bushes. I swore I could have heard them if they'd even rustled.

He suddenly emerged on the walking path. He moved smoothly and swiftly in the shadow patches. He went to the first room, peeking in the window.

He opened the door and turned on a flashlight he was carrying for two seconds. He closed the door and moved toward my room. Apparently, the $200 I had given to the receptionist were worth nothing. He was coming for me.

I hid behind the door, a glass bottle in my hand. First, a strike to the head to knock him down, and when it was broken, I'd make a shallow, non-fatal wound in his belly. I held my breath.

The door opened, the flashlight shone. He took one step in. I moved to my left and swung with all my strength. He whirled and stepped behind me, kicking the back of my knee. I screamed and went down. He put me in a headlock and we fell to the floor.

"Listen, this is your final warning," His voice was deep and breathy. "I will tell you this only once - "

"Who are you?" I interrupted. Saliva was drooling out of my mouth. "I'll kill you. You hurt my family. Where is Mathew?"

"I didn't do a thing to your family. I'm with the CBB. We bugged your apartment without a warrant to see if you'd confess to your lawyer or a friend. If you had, then the Bureau would have come after you. But there was no reason to spend taxpayer's money on your sorry ass."

The CBB was the national intelligence agency; they were well known for their shady ways including spying on citizens and labeling every unlawful arrest as an act to protect the interests of national security. In short, they were dangerous, ominous, and not to be fucked with.

I put my left arm under his leg and wiggled my right hand around his neck to use his weight against him and flip him over.

He kept me in the headlock while hitting me twice in the abdomen and gonads. He was merciless. I saw bright stars from the pain.

"I knew you were coming here. I'll let you go now, and you'll never see us again. We did nothing to you. We don't need to harm you."

He pulled my hair back, but I still couldn't see him. "I could break your fucking neck now. I could knock you out and stick a needle of heroin in your arm. Nobody would even ask about you, you worthless shit. I'm saying the CBB will leave you alone. But you must keep your fucking mouth shut and stop acting nuts."

Two more punches to the abdomen and I lay flat on the floor, and he delivered a powerful kick to my chest. He flashed the light in my eyes. "Don't follow me," he said and left.

Helpless. Broken. In blood and tears. Were they allowed to do this? Was it really the CBB? I didn't know, but they sure had an odd way of conducting their affairs.

I felt like I was losing my son again. I couldn't tell Luke. I want to stay down and never wake up.

I failed you.

DANCING WITH A LADY

Empty bottles were everywhere on the floor. I rearranged them to make a walking path. The majority were beer bottles, then wine, and whiskey. Time became meaningless, purposeless and dark. I watched family videos around the clock. I felt they were with me. I laughed and cried continuously. I missed them so much.

I had nothing else to do, no plan. Maybe Danny was right. We could do nothing else at some point, no more leads to pursue.

What bothered me most was that I had to accept it and move on, without getting my revenge. Even worse, I had to admit it was my fault and my doing. Essentially, I had to live with the fact that I *AM* a criminal.

Unless I don't live at all.

I ran away from home, from the past, where I heard them and saw them. Oh, beautiful ladies and my sweet Mathew. Forgive me, forgive my blindness, forgive my ignorance, forgive my stupidity.

I took the car and roamed around, slept in hotels and motels. I hung around pubs from the time they opened 'til they closed, sometimes 'til they asked me to leave. I went by other names, Jerry and Jim. Pretending to be someone else lulled me, and for a brief time, I forgot my tragedy.

I did drugs. At one point someone offered me heroin, but I refused. Using heroin meant the end of the road, no coming back. *Is this the end?* Maybe, but heroin addiction wasn't the way to go.

Every person knew when they should surrender, when they couldn't fathom the fighting of what is real and what is not. Sometimes I felt a bit better, but then I'd hear a song or remember morning breakfasts, and it all began again. Some of my internal thoughts tormented me as though I fostered monsters inside. *Smile, take the exit. It's enough, you must pay.*

I knew it was over for me, that I would die soon. I couldn't keep going on like this. I couldn't spend a day without drinking, and it made me weaker and weaker. Some people are afraid to admit they are suicidal, even to themselves, although the behaviors creeped in: distancing people who cared, alcohol, drugs and meaningless sex. The same things happened, but I showered more.

I tried reaching out to Will and Wanda. I had high expectations for my siblings who never called. After a few *I'll get back to you, in a meeting* messages, I got ahold of Will. He said if we ever happened to be in the same city, we could meet. So, I said I traveled to his city on a business trip.

Let me see what you'll say, asshole.

He said they had planned a vacation for the family and he hadn't told me so to avoid upsetting me. It was understandable: they didn't want me near their children.

I drove the car at high speed and closed my eyes for a few seconds. Then I tried closing my eyes for half a minute. I wanted to see if I could go off the road. I thought it resembled Russian roulette. I renamed it dancing with Lady Death.

Luke had called over the past month, but I never picked up. I had nothing to offer him and nothing to promise. He called again.

A text buzzed at 8:17: "Pick up. Thompson is dead and he left you a letter. Join me for the funeral."

My suit looked ridiculous on me, it could have fit someone who weighed 70 pounds heavier. It rained, so a hat also hid my identity.

The letter contained a lot of good wishes and many instructions for staying sane. Importantly, Thompson wrote about how he thought I was innocent because I didn't fit the profile of someone who would engage in a sexual relationship with his daughter, and that I didn't have a second personality. He believed I hadn't even been present in the house at the time of the murders and he recommended I focus on the healing progress, wait for a change in the investigation, even if that took years.

The letter meant a lot to me, it gave me hope, even if I had to wait a decade until I am reunited with Mathew. Dr. Thompson's death upset me, and I felt terrible; I barely spoke to him. At least I expressed my gratitude at one point.

I cleaned the house a bit. I brought the board into the living room. I crossed out the word "hate" and underlined the words "sick loon." I wrote something down and contemplated it:

1. <u>Male. Middle age. Hate? A sick loon? A burglar (less likely). He has my semen. How the fuck did he get my semen?</u>

This was never a question the police or the private investigator had asked, but now I had to ask. If someone else had killed my family, then how did the sick bastard get my sperm? Could he be a garbage man who took a condom I used? I did a quick search and learned not all condoms on the market had a spermicide. A long shot, surely, but it could be a crucial lead.

SIN

I was on a mission to find a sick person. He might be someone close to us, whether through my work or Lisa's, one of Lea's classmates or friends, or someone from the neighborhood. The murder could not have been a fluke, a random act by a sick villain, or so I chose to believe. Someone targeted our family, planned the murder and was careful enough to leave a clean crime scene behind.

This person could also be Lea's boyfriend.

I ran background checks of people we had known to see if their names were worth passing on to Danny Miller. So far, I'd found nothing. No one we knew had a violent past or a record of deviant sexual behavior, just a few traffic violations.

"You're a hard man to reach, Mr. Stankovic. I've been calling you repeatedly," Danny Miller said.

"Sorry about that, the pub preoccupied me," I said, and we exchanged pleasantries. I wondered whether people still exchanged so many pleasantries.

"The handwriting from the note doesn't match yours. However, as I mentioned before, it isn't valuable."

She tested the handwriting to prove I was the boyfriend and not the other way around.

"What about Mathew? Any updates?" I asked.

"We ran a new sign, and we're still offering a big reward. I've gotten leads, but they check out. If someone took him outside the country, it might be worth the money for me to fly down south and check with people at the borders, maybe get in touch with the top smugglers. We might get lucky."

In other countries, P.I.s could not do that, but it was possible and affordable here, so I told her to go ahead.

She had nothing else to report. The burner phone was a bust, and the enemy list didn't even exist.

I went back to my notes and folders, and I came across old team photos from my firm and Cynthia's eyes were all over me. We'd had an affair for about a year which we ended when Lisa intervened. I used to call Cynthia 'My Sin'.

If you'd asked ten people, not all of them would agree that Cynthia was beautiful, but all of them would say she was an attractive and seductive woman. I thought she had a beautiful face, and I liked features other people didn't ap-preciate—the too-small nose, the too-white face, and the too-big, light green eyes. Her silky long black hair covered part of her slender and toned body, and I had urged her to wear it in a way to expose her figure. She knew her strengths and her seductive powers. Heels with everything, even jeans. I used to joke that she wore heels on the treadmill.

People knew about us at work. When a guy asked her out and she politely declined. He told me, to my face, that he wondered why married men went out with women who were less attractive than their spouses. I told him to ask the HR if the question bothered him so much.

Cynthia loved to come over in the mornings after Lisa left home, and she caused problems. One day Lisa got angry when she discovered someone cut up her shoes with scissors, a few pairs. She knew I always had something going on, and she wasn't proud of it, but she didn't stop me. I said the cleaners must have done it, some disgruntled employee. I promised to let the company know, get us a refund, and never allow this person in our house again.

Lisa said, "Are you sure the cleaning people are responsible? What about Bigfoot? Aliens?" I didn't want to fire her up anymore. That evening, she gave me the talk: "Don't fall in love and ruin our family." She said I could have minor affairs as long as she didn't know about them and as long as no one got hurt. "...and please be safe. Don't bring scum into our life." I promised her. Nothing serious, only sex.

I spoke with Cynthia, and she said she was so jealous of Lisa and her life with me. She was angry at how I never stayed over and she wanted to enjoy falling asleep and waking up next to me. She promised she would pay us back for the shoes, as if we needed the money. I let her know I wasn't happy at all, and I stayed away for a few weeks.

Then I made the same mistake and allowed Cynthia to visit, even to sleep over when Lisa and the kids were away. One day I got home, and Lisa waited for me at the dining table with an empty glass and a bottle of whiskey.

"Jason, please come sit down. This is for you. We need to talk." She said in a firm voice.

Shit, what did I do this time? I admired my wife a lot. She was one of a kind, a leader with high self-awareness. She knew what she wanted, how to reach her goals, made the right compromises, and had her priorities straight.

"Sure. What can I get you?" I said.

"I am good. Sit." She sighed. "I found this note in my drawer. My *panty* drawer."

She slowly pushed the note across the table with two fingers, looking at me.

I read it: "Hey. From one woman to another, your husband is cheating on you. If I'd known he is married, I would have never come here with him. You seem to have a beautiful family, but honestly, you can do better than this. You deserve better."

I sighed. "I... I don't know."

"Yeah, right. Is it someone new or the same one from work?" she asked.

I didn't answer. "Oh, please, Jason. Cynthia! Come on. Cynthia, right?"

"Yes," I said. "I'm sorry, babe. I shouldn't have brought her here. I'm sorry."

"She's in love with you. She wants me to leave you. Do you love her?"

"No. I love no one but you. You know that." I answered sincerely. No one could match what we had. I would die without her; she kept me going. "You know that, no doubt."

"But *she* loves you, and this is not what we agreed. I want an immediate solution. Do you hear me, Jason?" She was not joking. "Listen well, asshole, I will leave you and take the children with me." I pursed my lips and looked down. "And probably break your legs before I leave or maybe choke you in your sleep."

"Don't say that," I told her. "I love you and you love me, and what we have is irreplaceable. You're angry. Tomorrow I'll make us breakfast with the kids, and we'll go back to our normal life. I'll take care of this immediately. Whether or not she loves me, I don't care. She knows our agreement was sex only."

"Clean this shit up. You have a week." Tears surfaced in her eyes, but her voice was unaffected. "If you had met her before me, you might have ended up with her, right? You rarely stick to one woman, but this has been ongoing for a year or longer." She fell silent for a second. "Answer me, Goddammit!" she shouted.

"I guess so," I said. "I'll take care of it. I'm sorry." I wanted to hold her hand, but when I reached out, she pulled hers away.

"Tonight. Go and end things with her tonight. Keep in mind that if I find out you're still seeing her, I'm gone."

She left the table without me agreeing to do that, but at that stage in our marriage, we just skipped straight to the implementation part.

I called Cynthia and went to her place that same evening. I explained what had happened, and I blamed her for the note. I told her we couldn't meet any more and that it was for the best. I felt dreadful to end our relationship, but things had to be rectified for the sake of my family. Although personally, I knew my heart could hold more than one woman. I could be just as good to one as to the other, but my family needed my undivided attention.

Cynthia said she loved me so much and that she'd probably never be able to love anyone this much again. I told her we all have those thoughts, that they were normal, but she'd pick herself up again. She said she was going to quit her job because it would be too painful to see me at the office every day. I disagreed and said I would be the one to leave. At that stage, I rented a private office. At first, I only intended to work on a personal project for some time but then I grew comfortable doing what I loved, so I never went back.

Cynthia cried some more, and we slept together for the last time. She asked me if I wanted to leave Lisa and be with her. I clarified my feelings for her, them not being the marry-you-and-start-another-family kind. "Yes, they're intense," I admitted, but I added that leaving Lisa wasn't an option. She eventually said she was happy to have known me, wished me the best and said there would always be a special place for me in her heart.

I thought twice before giving her a call after. She might have said I was a sick person, and that she didn't want anything to do with me. She might have even said she had a boyfriend or got married. I had to think of myself. I couldn't meet someone new, and I needed to be loved. She was really a great person, and I still cherished the memories of her.

I called.

GARBAGE BINS

"Hi. Who is this?" Cynthia answered my phone call.

Really? Now you don't remember me? I didn't change my phone number.

"This is Jason. How are you doing? Remember me?"

"Oh, hiii! I'm good. How are *you?* How is everything? Of course I remember you, new phone. Oh my god, long time. When did you get out?" I felt genuine sympathy in her voice.

"A few months ago. I'm good, ups and downs. The downs are pretty tough." I was glad I could share this with someone. Even telling Luke proved hard. "It's difficult, Cyn, you know. It crushed me. I still don't know how to be normal. To top it off, I can't find my child. Awful."

"Oh, dear. I'm so sorry to hear that. Why didn't you reach out to me earlier?" she asked in her trademark croaky voice.

"I don't know, I was afraid, embarrassed. I'm just so happy to hear your voice. I want to see you. Can I?"

She didn't respond.

"Hello, are you still there?" I asked.

"Yeah. Nothing. I'm emotional to hear you in this much pain, hon." Her voice was brittle. She was crying, I guessed. "Pick me up at seven-thirty tonight. I have a new address. Got a pen?"

Finally, something to look forward to. She was one of a kind: smart, hot, and athletic. I'd never thought about it before, but I'd wanted Lea to be like her when she grew up.

I spent the day organizing the garbage man hunt, or not necessarily a garbage man but a man who went through our garbage. I called Danny up and told her to get me a list of people who worked in the neighborhood and to repeat the check on all my neighbors using a much larger radius. I instructed her to look at pedophiles.

When I went to pick Cynthia up, she said she wasn't ready and asked me to come up. She was manipulative and smart, so the delay either meant that she didn't want us to go out at all or she wanted me to see her place.

I had dressed casually so I could enter any place and wouldn't look too fancy if we ended up at a bar. She opened the door wearing a long gray towel pinned under her armpits, and she put her hair up, the way I liked it. Knowing her, she had groomed herself to see me. She stepped out of the apartment and hugged me.

"Oh, god," she said. "You poor thing. Oh god, oh god. I'm so sorry for your loss." I hugged her back and fought the urge to cry. I thought to myself that no one had ever expressed remorse or talked about my loss. Everyone looked at me as a criminal. I cherished the moment.

"Thanks, Cyn. Thanks," I said. My voice was cracking, I held my tears. "Let's go inside. You're in your towel, and you don't want the neighbors to see you like this."

We entered her awesome place—rustic meets modern. Every other item was wood, iron or bronze, and she had a large TV and a superb view. I put my hands in my pockets and heard the door close.

She hugged me from behind. "You're not a big bear anymore. You've lost a lot of weight. Do you like the place?"

"You still have a great body. Yeah, I did. Unfortunately, I haven't exercised these past two years." I smiled in a silly way and held her hands against my abdomen. "The place is fantastic. Please tell me it's not a rental."

"No, I bought it. Two bedrooms. I'll put on some clothes and we can head out."

While dressing, she peeked out from behind the door while only wearing a bra. "Pour yourself a drink."

"Thanks." I wondered whether I should say I wasn't supposed to drink, but I would have one wherever we were going.

She came back in a hot skin-tight black dress with a slit up to her mid-thigh and an open back. I didn't know how her body could have possibly become better. Her breasts had always been a bit too big for her body, but she still fell into the super sexy category and not the vulgar one.

As we were about to leave, I checked her ass for the indentation of a thong, and she caught me. "I'm not wearing anything underneath, but don't get any ideas. I have a boyfriend. It is serious."

"I wasn't asking," I said. Her remark pissed me off.

"I know. I'm just here for you as a close friend." She kissed me on the cheek.

The numerous guys who eyed Cynthia didn't ruin the pleasant evening, for once I was happy that people weren't looking at me. I had to think if they knew who I was.

Our discussion flowed smoothly. She told me about her progress at work and how everybody had reacted to my news. Most of them were nice, she said. They knew me well, and they knew I had nothing going on with Lea and could have never killed Lisa. It felt nice.

For an hour, I forgot my tragedy as we shared updates and news, discussed work and global economics. I admired her sharp intellect.

Then, we discussed the existence of psychopaths among the population. I argued that the government should have a plan to flush them out and abolish them, to prevent them from spreading and populating. She argued that people should know how to protect themselves, and that made things awkward for a bit.

We took a cab back to her apartment. She got out and blew me a kiss after we agreed to meet as much as possible, starting the following day with a jog.

Danny got back to me with a long list based on my request, and she waited for more instructions. I asked her to check their alibis, and she argued that it would take a lot of time and she didn't have the manpower. She didn't understand why I was doing this, but for her, the money kept coming in. I told her to add as many people on her team as she needed because I wanted her to deliver everything in one month and produce a short list of names.

I also gave her the names of a few people from work and asked her to check their alibis, just in case. I included Cynthia's name. It made sense as she was an ex-girlfriend with whom I'd had an affair. Despite her being a woman and not fitting the profile, I suspected everyone; the police looked into the alibis of Cynthia and other colleagues, but there was no harm in checking again.

I initiated a healthy routine with Cynthia. We jogged frequently; we played squash and even went out a few more times. I told her about the last conversation I'd had with Lisa, about how she asked if I had met Cynthia before her. I had never shared that before. She confessed something that made me happy: she didn't have a boyfriend. She just hadn't liked the idea that I wanted her because I had no other choice.

A month passed quickly, and we became really close. Every night one of us slept over, and most of the time it was me. It felt like a vacation to be out of my place and away from the whiteboard and the recordings.

Sex had always been great with Cynthia. She pushed my limits and was a perfectionist who never overlooked a single detail. Every now and then, she liked to try new things. When we'd been having the affair, she had wanted to bring in another person, or go on an adventure. I said no to both. Those were things Lisa wouldn't even consider.

Cynthia helped me get a rescue dog, Buddy, a mixed breed who had nightmares when he slept. He probably had a painful past like mine. I told her about an email that Lisa had sent to me a month before the murders in which she had called me selfish and grandiose and said I only focused on my own needs and dreams. Cynthia told me about a relationship she'd had where she'd cheated on her boyfriend, and he left her. He'd been very upset.

I upset Danny with my frequent phone calls, but she didn't have long to produce the list. It was a long shot, I knew that, but I had to try. I would keep trying 'til I got my son back.

The list contained six names, along with the name of a garbage man. Danny was pissed off that one of them had tried to attack her during their interview. She said she didn't have any leads from the border smugglers, but one of them had mentioned an awkward situation where a man and his boy wanted to get across the border illegally when they could have easily crossed the border legally. She suspected the boy might have been Mathew.

I asked her if they could describe the man or identify Mathew in pictures. She said they'd tried, and it was a dead end. I instructed her to send an agent across the country and advertise the reward locally along the border.

As for the six names, I asked her to confront them with photos and see who flinched when they saw pictures of Lisa and Lea. I also asked her to keep an eye on each one of them and get the hacker to find some dirt on them.

PART

4

JERRY

OUT OF THE COCOON

Nobody knows where they're going in life or how things can change. How a small stone on a mountain biker's path can change his life. Mine was a chat.

While having a crisis of boredom, I started to chat with strangers. One thing led to another, and then the truth manifested itself in front of my eyes.

After a few clicks, passing by ads for fake passports, I accessed a special chatroom on the dark web. I entered a username, quest_for_rush.

I typed: "I have seen it all. I have done it all. I have searched the depths inside and outside of myself. I'm bored. Nothing else to do, now that I've become perfect in what I have done.

"Help. Suggest."

The cursor blinked, talking to me: "What next?" Sick of it, I hit enter.

I received many useless answers, but one stood out: "The thrill of giving life and taking life never ceases. The pleasure of controlling lives is monumental." Sender's name was Xeris_Light2323.

The profound reply captivated me, so I initiated a private chat, and we discussed our deeds. He was a straight shooter. He said I claimed to be a warrior but had never taken a life, that I operated in the shadows, and that my hunts took a long time. We argued a few times, but he was right. I should stop the mediocre activities and go for what moves me most. He said I behaved like a drug addict who hopelessly tried to take the edge off with a cigarette, and that was pitiful.

"Take what is yours. Live your philosophy, and if you're caught, then fuck it. You tried your best and lived as you wanted," he said. He explained that he meant I could commit suicide if the police ever caught me. At other times, he told me I should try boys as well—as long as they were under twelve. That was a strict rule, because otherwise boys wouldn't be as good. I said I'd try, but I never saw any potential in it. He said I could kidnap one and keep him for experimentation. "You can't dislike what you haven't tried," he said.

Xeris_Light2323 and I messaged for about a week. Then he said he would close this chat and move to another place. He left me one piece of advice before going. He said I should be in the game for the long run and that I could have my own children. *Idiot!* I was swearing at my stupidity. I'd never thought of it. I could breed my own! I could start a small community if I wanted to.

Now that I evolved as a man, confidence filled my heart, and I transformed into a soldier on a mission.

My manifesto was almost ready, and I couldn't wait to show it to the world—a truth, screamed loud. I took my tablet, looked at previous notes, and wrote:

Manifesto outline:

Revive the golden age: embrace our biological nature

Make way for youth: make space for a productive generation (eliminate the worthless shits)

Respect the elite: new leaders of the world

Other: man and fear, man and music, man and order, the aging man

I hoped to get an interview request in the near future. I wanted to go big, to share my vision with the world, speaking words everyone must hear, for their benefit, for the benefit of our race! Things must be in their place.

Life owed me, and as an evolved hunter, I claimed what was mine without fear. I knew who I sought and where to find them. I surveyed single moms who might potentially give me their trust. I looked into their financials, family, habits... and surely a daughter at the right age was the grand prize.

I no longer worried about getting old, about the day when I could no longer hunt. What I'd filmed and saved over the years was sufficient for three decades.

My relationship with Laurie was on the right track. She wasn't willing in the beginning, but we resolved our differences. She adored me, and she couldn't wait to bear my child, but I had to give my time equally to everyone. I visited her once every two or three days. My heart went to Sylvie. She was the light, and through her I would be reborn.

I cleaned up my act. I convinced the landlord we should rent the apartments out to single mothers or single dads, to help their children benefit from a close community. She resisted in the beginning, saying that there wouldn't be enough demand, but I swayed her by saying parenthood wasn't a must, we should just consider it a factor. She agreed, on the condition that I wouldn't let any apartment sit empty for longer than a month.

NEW TIMES

Around 7 a.m., the tenants were waking up; I needed more turnover to match my libido, so I'd been renting the apartments to groups that required apartments for a brief stay. A fun fact—people mated more often when they traveled. Something about the vacation mood made them cheerful and welcoming.

Renting to groups, as frequently as I did, took more of my time than I wanted, but in the end, I knew I'd look back and be proud that I'd had that many things going. They partied, and I had to stay awake longer than usual, sometimes sleeping for only an hour when necessary.

I expected a new group over at noon, two couples staying for a week in apartment 401. One was engaged, and the other was dating. They visited the town for tourism.

The dating couple arrived first. I gave them the keys and showed them around the apartment. They were middle-aged, and still uncomfortable around each other. They measured their words, and neither of them wanted to fuck it up with the other. I thought their hookup had probably been arranged, and they dealt with pressure from their families.

They should get married. If they don't, there's something wrong with them.

They unpacked. She sighed, and he sat on the bed edge. I raised the volume of the microphone input so high, I could hear her steps on the wooden floor. She undressed piece by piece, glancing at him over her shoulder as she unhooked her bra. She moved toward him and put her hand on his crotch.

"Nothing," she said. "Why? It's been a month, and I've tried everything. Do you like me? Do you even like women?"

He got angry, and he defended himself. He said he needed something special, and she pleaded for him to show her. He stood up, took off his belt, gave it to her, and told her to hit him. Reluctantly, she stroked him a couple times. He said, "Harder!"

She was whipping him aggressively on the ass, and I could see her tears.

"Come and see," he said.

She felt him and smiled. They started kissing, but while he undressed, the doorbell rang.

I enlarged the window that showed the feed from the front door camera; the second couple arrived. I zoomed in and saw their rings. They rang again and again. The woman inside drifted to the peephole. She looked through and returned to the bedroom. I was surprised she hadn't opened the door for them. She sat on the bed next to her boyfriend, and he asked who rang the bell and why she hadn't let them in. She said she wanted to have time alone with him. I guessed she didn't want to be hitting him while the other couple was in the next room.

Her phone buzzed, once then twice, and then his phone. The couple waiting at the front door got irritated. They hustled the big bags back to the elevator. She looked through the peephole again and, once they left, called her friend. She said they were out and would be back in thirty minutes. I couldn't hear the conversation on the other end.

Once she got back in the room, they kissed, but I would describe it as passionate. After a while, she slapped him a few times, and he enjoyed it. Afterward, she hit him with the belt.

"You're a naughty boy, and I'll punish you." She hit him harder, and he moaned in pain. "Is it working? Shall I go harder?"

He told her to stop. He said he wasn't comfortable with the fact that she hadn't opened the door for her best friend, because she was the one who had introduced them to each other. The woman shouted and she cried—she threatened him. She said that whatever the stakes were, she wouldn't stay with him unless he resolved his arousal problems. She gave him until the end of this trip. "Pop a pill if you need to."

She called her friend, and once the engaged couple came back, a fiasco of shouting filled the apartment. One accused the other of lying, and the other stood firm that they had been out for coffee and just gotten back. The men sat in awkward silence, looking at each other and pursing their lips. They tried to calm the women down, but it didn't work, and a slammed door announced a time out. I had fun watching this, and live, too! I wondered what would happen next.

The fiancée stayed in the room with the guys. She complained that her friend had changed and wasn't aware of her behavior. The woman inside heard her and came storming out with tears in her eyes. She shouted that her friend couldn't imagine what she went through. The boyfriend appeared concerned that she might tell the other couple about their struggles in the bedroom, so he offered to take the fiancée out for a coffee at a nearby place to chat a bit.

The woman stayed behind with the fiancé. She curled up on the couch, and he tried to comfort her. He asked multiple times about her work and family. He told her she should be happy that she met someone her family approved of.

I wondered what that meant. Was she the only heiress to a big fortune and her family wanted her with someone smart and worthy? Or was she unstable, and they wanted someone to take care of her? She said he was the problem. The fiancé asked how, and she said she would show him.

She sprang to the apartment door, locked it with the chain, wiped her tears and quickly fixed her hair. It didn't help much. She stood in front of the fiancé and said, "I'll show you, just bear with me. Don't misunderstand me."

She unbuttoned her shirt slowly as she said, "You always told me I am an attractive woman and that any guy would be lucky to have me. However, you've never truly seen me."

She removed her shirt, then her jeans.

He protested. "What are you doing? Don't. This isn't right."

She said, "I'm not trying to sleep with you. Just wait."

His face turned red. She took his hand and placed it on her breast. I could have sworn his hand was shaking. She kissed him and unhooked her bra. She stood up as he shook his head.

"Don't say a word," she told him.

She grabbed his arm and made him stand, though he resisted. She put her hand on him and said, "See, you've got something. Brendon has nothing. He's gay, or he could be gay. Melissa is unforgiving, she's a controlling bitch. She thinks just because he works with her and is her friend, it should work out between us, but I've had enough of her judgment and condescension."

She got dressed, and he didn't say a word.

"I hate her, Jack. I can't stand it anymore. He's a lying bastard. He spins every situation to his benefit. It's been more than a month, and we haven't slept together, he pleasures me with his hand."

"I don't know what to say," Jack replied.

"Don't say a thing, Jack. With all that's happened, everything I do now is under a microscope. I don't care if you call me crazy. Melissa wants me to get married, so she doesn't have to worry about you and me. I bet you that right now she's paranoid and wondering if we've fucked. She knows that if we had met before you'd met her, she would not stand a chance. Right? You would've picked me over her any time of day, not because I'm hotter but because we have so much in common. I'm not a controlling bitch. I wouldn't give you headaches." She sat on the couch, still straightening her clothes.

"Don't say that," Jack said. "Why do we have to get into that? Relax, let it pass."

"Let what pass? Today he handed me a belt and told me to whip him so he could get a boner. I knew this was a mistake. *He* is a mistake. Melissa just had to get us all to go on a vacation, under the same roof."

"I know," Jack said.

She stood up and hugged him. She said, "I wish I were with you. You're everything I've dreamed of."

"I wish that, too," he said, "but that's not possible. Let's just make the most of this trip." He gently removed her hands, then went into his room and unpacked.

Shit, that is amazing. I felt terrible I hadn't prepared well. I didn't even know her background.

I must pass by Laurie's place, then pick Sylvie up from school, and be at her place 'til evening. I decided to watch the recording from apartment 402 at a speed of 1.30X to compensate. I'd slow down for the relevant parts.

On my way to pick Sylvie up, I thought about the boyfriend, Brendon, and how worthless he was. I would write about that in my manifesto. I'd write a dedicated chapter on the worthlessness and the shapes they came in. While waiting for Sylvie at the school, I took out my tablet and added to the outline.

Manifesto outline:

Abolish the worthless: Be wary—they come in many shapes

I saw Sylvie strolling and waving. She was happy to see me, and I was even more thrilled. She was the one for me. I reminded her not to hug or kiss me in the car because people were watching. She didn't protest, but once we moved she put her hand over mine on the gearshift. She giggled.

I enjoyed the rides with her. She told me about her day, and I loved the gossip. I could tell where society headed based on how the young ones behaved. Suddenly, her mood shifted, and she cried. She said she felt bad for thinking it, but she wished her mother was dead or would somehow disappear.

Tell me about it, I thought.

I didn't say a thing, but Sylvie knew I felt the same way.

Then she said she also felt guilty because she wanted her mom to have one of her *headaches* that night so we could spend the evening together. I said I also felt bad because life wasn't fair to us. In an ideal world, we could be together and even get married when we wanted. She giggled and said, "Mrs. Sam Lyndon."

She reached for my pants. I asked her what she was doing, and she said this was what she'd seen couples do at the movies. I stopped her because it wasn't safe while driving. The truth was different. I had already come four times that day: in the morning, then twice while watching the new tenants, then with Laurie.

Melanie thought she was a functioning addict. She spent mornings at her business, and then she faked being sick half the time during the afternoon. She went on unannounced trips, sometimes coming back after midnight. I had to know her whereabouts at all times, so I put a GPS tracker in her shoes. I couldn't use her purse because addicts forgot their stuff all the time. I just hoped that she never came home without her shoes. Then she'd catch us in the act.

She thought she hid her addiction well, and we played along. It didn't matter to us, so we didn't need to intervene. It didn't take much time to convince Sylvie that we should leave Melanie alone. She benefited anyway.

The stupid bitch thought her money covered her drug use, and then she can quit again and things would go back to normal. I got a message every time she withdrew money from my account, and always topped her balance using ATMs, but without showing my face. If things went south, no one could identify me. I didn't worry she might bankrupt me—I was loaded enough. I was more worried that she would overdose because her death would be early and might ruin my plan. Her time hadn't come. Yet.

We got home, but Melanie wasn't herself. She seemed to do well. She prepared dinner and put on some music. We ate and watched TV. I told her I couldn't sleep over because I had work. Sylvie acted neurotic. She gave her mom attitude and was pissed off that Melanie didn't leave us alone. I was annoyed as well. I wanted this time alone with Sylvie. I wondered whether Melanie suspected anything about my relationship with Sylvie. I couldn't be certain.

We went to bed. We hadn't slept together for two weeks, ever since she'd started using. She wanted to keep me happy; she said she was afraid I would cheat on her to get laid.

After we slept together, she went into the bathroom, and I knew she was using. She could barely walk back to bed, and then she said she needed to rest. Stupid woman—she thought I couldn't tell. I wanted to rest, too, so I stayed in bed. My phone buzzed a few times: Sylvie asking me to come downstairs. Then the door moved slowly, and she walked to the bed and shook me a few times. She grunted and left. A few minutes later, I went down.

Sylvie got very jealous of any affection between her mom and me, so knowing that we fucked a few hours ago made her nuts.

"I wasn't asleep," I said.

"Do you enjoy doing that to me? You know I don't like it when you stay in that room with her." She lowered her voice. "You should sleep next to me."

"Stop it," I said.

She cried. "I'll tell her we are together. She can go fuck herself!" I looked at her, and she continued. "You know, maybe I should tell the entire world we're together."

Anger took over me. I slapped her and pulled her hair. She sobbed and sniffled.

"Are you threatening me? Is this what love is for you? Don't be stupid. They'll put me in prison! You're all I ever wanted, baby. You're so special—more than you know."

"I love you, too," she said. "But why do you make me feel like this? Leave her! Let's go away and have a normal relationship. I want to go to dinner with you and meet your friends."

What friends? I thought.

"Then stop being afraid and let's run together, run from this shithole," I said. "We'll have an amazing time. We'll be great, special. Nothing can separate us."

"Okay," she said, wiping away her tears. "But promise me you'll never hit me again."

"I won't. But never threaten to do something that could separate us."

We kissed passionately, and I then left for my place.

ALPHA

I drove home around 10 p.m. I was excited to know more about the couples on vacation. I thought I should stop by the apartment before they left and have a drink with them or intervene in a way that would stir up more shit. I still blamed myself for not having prepared better. They seemed very interesting.

I turned on the live feeds, texted Sylvie good night, and prepared the missed recording that I wanted to watch.

The couples were having dinner. They didn't chat much, and it didn't feel like they were friends. Brendon sat with his back straight. Jack and the lady whose name I didn't remember were stealing looks at each other every now and then. Melissa was eating elegantly as if she was at an emperor's ball.

They finished. Melissa and Brendon took their wine and sat on the couch, chatting about work. Melissa wore a long skirt and low heels, which looked good on her tall body although they might not have been the best choice for a relaxing vacation. She'd dyed her hair bright red and wore it down to her shoulders.

I could tell a strong woman like her controlled the people around her. She led the conversation with Brendon, and she got the best of him by arguing with everything he said. Her demeanor was definite: *This is the end of this point. Let's move to the next one.*

"Jess, come help me with the dishes," Jack said.

That's her name. I remembered that she'd introduced herself when I gave her the key. I suspected she was a laid-back woman based on how she spoke, dressed, and sat, and she smiled a lot. She was almost flat-chested and had big brown eyes, brown curled hair, and a petite figure that one might call a bit too thin.

"I can help if you want," Melissa said, setting her wine down and standing.

"It's okay," Jack said. "I want to have a chat with Jess." He then whispered to Jess, "See? Not so bad."

"It is!" she hissed. "Believe *me*—it is." She winked at him. "Jack, help me with this apron, please. Can you tie it around my waist?" She intentionally raised her voice.

"Leave her alone, I beg you. She'll fuck up our mood." He wrapped the apron strings around her twice, pass his hands an extra time around her thin waist.

"I want to show you the real Melissa," Jess told him. "The Melissa you don't know."

"Yeah, right," Jack said. "I know Melissa."

They worked in silence over the sink.

"Oh, my god. That's so funny!" Jess laughed, and it didn't seem fake.

What did I miss?

"I didn't say anything, you bitch," Jack replied, laughing a bit.

Melissa gulped the last of her wine and then moved toward the open kitchen. She handed her glass to Jack and asked what was so funny, folding her arms like a school principal who'd caught two mischievous students.

After a moment of silence, Jack saved the situation by saying, "I'm telling Jess about a dream." He giggled. "I woke up still fighting."

"Hmm." Melissa started walking away.

"She probably thought we were talking about her," Jess stage whispered.

"I heard that," Melissa said.

"I don't give two fucks, babe," Jess said. "We were having fun and laughing. Jack is funny and not boring as some people might say." Jess put down a plate she dried and turned around.

"I never said he was boring," Melissa said. "You're lying."

"True," Jess replied. "You never said it, but you think about it. You aren't ashamed of thinking it, and that's something I respect about you. You hold to your principles."

Jack was rinsing glasses. He murmured. "Please stop." Nobody heard him, so he shouted, "Enough! This is becoming a feud."

"It's fine, babe," Melissa said. "I won't sink to such a low level. Don't worry."

"Oh I'm sure you have a level, and it's the lowest among them all," Jess said. "Let's see if this is the bottom or not. I think - and mind you, this is only my opinion - but I think you're with Jack because of his body and you spend time with Brendon because of his brains. It's an ideal situation for you, given what a perfectionist and obsessive person you are. I bet you that you had planned all along to keep Brendon nearby." Jess stayed as calm as if she were discussing the weather.

Melissa's face became redder than her hair. Brendon excused himself to go to bed. Jess's declaration didn't surprise Jack, I thought he might protest. He had broad shoulders and a muscular build, black eyes, black hair styled to the side with a brightening cream, strong jaws, and he was always chewing gum.

"Oh, honey," Melissa said. "I was feeling so sorry for you, but now I'm not sure I should even care about you. Come to think of it, they should have committed you when they had the chance."

Jack interrupted her. "Hey, hey! I said enough. There's no need to say hurtful things to each other."

Jess smiled at Melissa. They were looking at each other like they were eternal enemies.

Melissa continued anyway, "or maybe, if you weren't such a failure, you could have succeeded in taking your own life."

Jess laughed, "and *ta daaaa*! That is the Melissa I know. You hide it really well, but I know you better than you know yourself. Thank you, thank you, thank you. Thank you for showing Jack who you truly are."

"I'm going to bed," Melissa said. "Tomorrow I want to have a blast. Jack, come with me, babe. Leave the sad little mouse alone." Melissa started walking toward her room.

"Go ahead," Jack told her. "I'll join you in a bit."

When they were alone in the living room, Jack apologized for what Melissa had said, and Jess said it was all right. He surprised her with a joint, and she said that Melissa would go nuts if she knew they were going to smoke. He agreed. They smoked anyway. They laughed, she kicked him and he tickled her. They weren't making much sense, but I thought they were cute together.

Suddenly, a door opened violently. "We are trying to get some sleep," Melissa said. "Have some sense, Jess. Jack, let's go. Come to bed."

Jess folded her hands and put one leg over the over, as if to say, *I'm going to enjoy seeing how this unfolds.*

"I don't want to go to bed," Jack said. "I'm on vacation. I'm having fun, for god's sake!"

"Fun to you is smoking weed like teenagers? The room stinks. I'm so disappointed in you." Melissa went back into her bedroom, and she wasn't gentle with the door.

"*I'm so disappointed in you*," Jess repeated, and they broke into hysterical laughter.

"See, you should leave her," Jess said. "This isn't you. I never imagined that *you* would be with someone who treats you like that."

"Let's go for a walk," Jack said. "I don't want Brendon to get annoyed with us, too."

"First, I'd be happy for him if he came out. Second, he's a potato, so don't worry. Third, we are in our PJs." Jess said, he took her hand, and they went out.

I jumped out of my seat, phone in my hand, and went after them. The apartment was only a few minutes away from my place, and luckily, I caught up with them before they wandered off.

They walked for an hour and what a shame, I couldn't hear what they were saying. I kept my distance because there weren't many people walking the streets at 2 a.m. on a weeknight. Jess was cold, so Jack put an arm around her.

They kept walking until they found an open place, where they bought juice. They talked, she cried, and he kissed her. They kissed for some time.

I checked the live feed on my phone. Back in the apartment, Melissa was calling Jack—I guessed it was Jack. Who else would she call? She paced the living room and then she sat down and called him. She must have felt something in the couch, because she reached between the cushions and pulled out a phone. She started crying.

Brendon woke up and went to listen at the door. He came into the living room when he heard her crying. They spoke, but I couldn't listen while I was on the street. She seemed to feel better as he consoled her.

Maybe I should learn to read lips.

Jess and Jack were back at the apartment. I didn't know why, but each of them went to bed with the person they'd come with. I predicted that a storm would probably erupt in the morning.

They woke up and prepared breakfast in silence, Jack and Jess exchanged looks, and they smiled at each other. When Brendon and Melissa weren't looking, Jess held up her small boobs and blew Jack a kiss. He laughed.

As they sat around the table, Melissa cleared her throat. "I want to talk about last night." She paused dramatically. "Some of the things said are not acceptable." She pointed with her index finger, thumb pressed to her middle finger at Jess. I wondered if she really worked as a school principal. Jack looked concerned, Jess indifferent, and Brendon stared at his plate.

"That is not who we are, and I apologize for what I said, but I won't tolerate attacks directed at me, or else..." They looked at her. "Or else I'll pack my things and leave." She paused. "I'm very disappointed at Jess's hurtful words. Jess, I thought you'd be more grateful. After what you went through, you should be grateful to have people supporting you. I've done all I could for you these past ten years. I've helped you find work multiple times, I've stood up to your family for you, and I've set you up with great people. I want you to treat me – and the people you meet through me – with respect."

Silence grew. Jess chewed her food as if nothing had been said. Brendon sighed.

"Oh. You want me to say something? Sure, sure. Let me start." Jess swallowed. "First of all, bitch *please*, and second of all, fuck you. Now let me tell you why. You're another problem in my life. My family compares me to you. You wish you were their daughter, and so do they. All three of you are fucked up. I removed them from my life, and I should remove you from my life."

Melissa's face became red. Jack smiled, and said to Jess, "It's okay. Let it all out. Don't hold back. Continue. Either we fix this, or we let it break badly."

"Thanks, love," Jess said. She put her hand over his, then removed it. She looked back at Melissa. "You're an evil bitch. You're selfish, and you're always scheming to get what you want. Why don't you tell Jack about your cheating? Tell him how many times and with whom. Most importantly, tell him why."

"Fuck you—stop lying." Melissa blurted out.

"You know I'm not." Jess took her phone out of the small pocket in her shorts. "Let me tell you everything, Jack. You deserve to know." She unlocked the phone.

"It isn't what you think, babe," Melissa told Jack defensively. "You have to believe me. None of them meant anything to me. One time when you were traveling, and another time this guy from work took advantage of me while I was drunk."

Jack smiled and nodded continuously. "Let her continue." He put his fingers to his lips to shush her.

"Super. Thanks for the help," Jess said. "I didn't know for sure that you cheated, but you're the type. I'm sure Brendon can confirm that you slept with someone from work to help your career."

Melissa interrupted. "I won't accept this! This is—"

Jess slammed her fist on the table. "No! Shut the fuck up! Let me continue, bitch." She cleared her throat. "Finally, I'm sure you tried to hook up with Brendon, but you didn't succeed because he can't fuck women. You bitch—you knew he couldn't fuck women, so why the hell did you set me up with him? You sold me someone damaged and broken, who just wants a good charade of a marriage so he can keep his secret life. I bet he even confided in you, you manipulative cunt. You aren't just a disgraceful friend, you're a disgraceful human being. Brendon, if you were on in this, then you're the scum of the Earth, too. If not, then I wish you well in life."

Melissa was breathing hard. Jack was smiling, and Brendon didn't disagree.

"Pack your shit and leave!" Jess yelled. "*Now! Both of you,*" she screamed, and they were all startled. "Pack and leave before I throw your asses on the road. You have ten minutes."

Melissa looked at Jack. "Are you going to let her do this?"

"Yup," Jack said. "She said it all loud and clear. Go on now."

Melissa stood up, and Jess added, "by the way, Jack is breaking up with you. If you ever contact him, I'll snap your fucking neck." She hugged him, and they moved sluggishly to the couch where he gave her a smooch. "And he is an amazing lover," Jess added. "I've never had an orgasm like that with anyone."

Jack leaned closer, keeping his arm around her. "We haven't slept together yet."

"I know." Jess replied, "Isn't that even better? Anyway, once they leave, we're taking these clothes off. No, we'll rip them off." She kissed him. "They have five minutes, I'm counting, then we're going to get physical."

Once Melissa and Brendon left, Jess and Jack went at it like animals. They fucked everywhere. They were like a couple on their honeymoon.

Usually, I removed the chatter from the video files I saved in the final edits folder, but I wanted to keep the evolution of this relationship. Seeing a territorial female defend herself this way and claim the male was phenomenal. It wasn't a typical thing that happened in nature, but I believed that there were species or tribes with females who were this strong.

I wanted to find my perfect companion: strong like Jess, beautiful like Sylvie, and hungry like Laurie. A partner having all those qualities would undoubtedly believe I was an apex warrior, and she would support me in spreading my message.

I took out my tablet and wrote a chapter about my ideal partner, her role and her strength, and when done, I went back to the outline and added:

Manifesto outline:

The alpha female: pure, hungry and dedicated to the apex warrior.

RAIN

Chatting with Xeris_Light2323 had opened my eyes. I created a morning ritual for myself. I breathed and repeated that I should take what was mine like a true apex warrior, an evolved hunter. Fear had no place in my heart. I would move through this world leaving a legacy behind me. My children would roam this place, and if they captured or killed me, I would have my alpha female carry on my message. I would leave her with fridges of stored sperm. The children would be as plentiful as rain.

Melanie used drugs more regularly, and she was knocked out most of the time. In the early morning, I left to pick Sylvie up from school—yes, pick her up and not drop her off. That day we planned to have penetrative intercourse for the first time. The other night she had gotten too horny. She wanted to do it right away. Those were the moments when she wasn't afraid she would hurt. She always worried that losing her virginity would show in some way.

I decided to go to one apartment. I chose the apartment where the two couples had just stayed. When Sylvie got in the car, she was all giddy and hyper. She was so excited. She wore makeup, and I got mad at her and told her to clean it off. Stupid. I didn't know why she would put any powder or cream on that beautiful face. She told me she had removed all the hair, and I was happy about that.

The first time wasn't so good—she moaned in pain—but the following two times were fantastic. She asked me why I saved the condoms, and I made up a story about the proper disposal of plastic and biologic waste, but I couldn't wait to tell her the truth about using the semen.

We watched TV, made food and chatted. I brushed her hair, and I got sad we had not met sooner. She was one of a kind, and I knew then she was the one for me, but she had to choose in what way.

"Are you sure you want to be with me long-term?" I asked. "What if you decide you want someone else, or you don't agree with me?"

"I don't know," she said. "I feel sure right now. I want you and only you. Like, I know my friends say you really don't love the first person you're in a relationship with, but this doesn't have to be the rule."

"Okay," I said. "I promise to love you as much as I can. See, we have here a good apartment, so when you move out, we'll spend some time in motels and hotels and eventually settle down here. We can have our own get together with friends. I don't know. Maybe..."

"Maybe what?" she said. "Don't be an ass. Maybe what?"

"No, I have to do this the right way."

"Come on. You know me. You can tell me anything."

"Okay. Give me a minute." I went to the bedroom and got a small box from a drawer. "Be gentle, babe." I leaned over and kissed her forehead, and she grabbed me and kissed me. A few more seconds and we'd be fucking again, but this wasn't the time.

"Stop. Wait. This is important."

"Okay," she said.

"I know we've only been together for a month, but we won't have this chance again because today marked the first time we did it. I was like ninety-nine percent sure, and now I'm one thousand percent sure." I went down on one knee. "Sylvie, will you marry me? Wait, don't answer. I have loved you since I first saw you, but over time you've stolen a piece of my heart. I can't imagine a day without you. When I'm away for an hour, I miss you, and I think about you every second."

"Oh, my god! I'm too young! I don't know what to say. Yes, I guess. Sorry—a definite yes, but not now." She took the ring and cried out of joy, and I couldn't be prouder. She was my example for the world that you can love and you can commit, and you can find happiness at any age. "The ring's a little too big," she said.

I took the ring back, and she made a sad face. "You've made me the happiest man alive. I know the ring's a bit too big because I bought it for the future. The law won't allow us to get married right now, but I couldn't have lived with myself if I didn't propose to you today." I hugged her. We had sex again, and then again.

In the afternoon, I wanted to go home and check the status of everything. The following morning I had a session with Dr-Anna45, and afterward, I had to go by Laurie's place. I wanted to stay here and sleep next to Sylvie, but unfortunately not possible. My heart ached.

On the way to the car, she was walking funny and kept adjusting her pants every few steps. I told her to stop because it looked suspicious, and she said she was in pain. I asked her to endure it. She was afraid her mom could tell she just had sex, and I told her to deny it. She asked what to do if Melanie forced her to show her vagina. I told her, if it came down to that, to tell Melanie that she'd met a boy from another school and slept with him.

Luckily, Melanie was hammered, as usual. She lay in bed like a dead body, her breathing shallow and infrequent. An effect of the drugs, I guessed. I thought to myself that I would kill her if she died before I could put my plan into effect. *Silly, right?* I stood over the bed, looking at her with disgust. I said to her that I should strangle her, take the life out of her worthless body. She couldn't hear me.

I went down to sit with Sylvie.

"I want to fuck you in my bed," she said. "That way I can lie in your smell all night."

"Ahh. You bitch, in your clean bed," I said, and we laughed. I told her I had to go now, but I'd be back by midnight, and I'd wake her up in her bed. All she had to do is rest until I came back in a few hours. I clarified I couldn't stay over, and if I did, it wouldn't be next to her. She said she preferred I didn't stay over in that case.

I went home, to my basement where I focused the most. I thought about what Xeris_Light2323 had said, "Let them prove themselves to you." The *lala* effect with Sylvie would fade soon enough, so I had to move on with my plan, and she'd have to prove herself. Otherwise, she'd have to make way for someone else to take her place.

Xeris_Light2323 had thought my sperm donation plan was devious and smart, but he said I could do things better if I had some help. He told me that the sperm donation would result in few children because of the demand and rate of selection, whereas every dedicated woman could bear ten or more children for a man like me. I agreed.

He said I wasn't truly dedicated to my mission, so I stopped doing things that weren't helping make my vision come true. No more flashing, much less unnecessary stalking, no more sniffing women on the metro, no more groping in clubs... meaningless. I aimed to pass my genes and have as many children as possible, one day the warriors might again roam the Earth in numbers.

I planned to find women compatible with biological builds and drive, like Laurie, who were suitable for giving me children. To do this, I planned to expand my custodian business and start working for another landlord like Mrs. Sharbadian. The total apartments I looked after became eight. Other handymen had a full complex to look after, but I didn't do it for the money.

And I made a plan to find a suitable alpha female. I smiled when I imagined us planning hunts together. For this, I remained a volunteer in the support group for families of drug addicts, looking for women like Melanie to get to their daughters. Over time, I wrote criteria with which to filter the women I met according to their social background, family, friends, etc.

My manifesto was in its final stages, and I needed soldiers to protect me and help me spread the message. As Xeris_Light2323 had said, "You'll find your people hanging out in the same places where you hang out." Except that he was wrong, because warriors like me underwent chemical castration, were in prison, or attending sexual offender programs. Luckily, the state made it easy for me to find them. I accessed the public sex offender database and selected the strongest and most vicious among them. Soon I would contact my soldiers, my brothers, and we would recruit others.

I only needed one more thing now: to take a life. Something I hadn't tasted yet. When I did, I might undergo another transformation and reach my ultimate potential.

I took out my tablet and entered two new topics:

- The secret plan to protect the old marriage
- Uniting the brothers / soldiers

I drove back to Melanie's place and went upstairs. She was still knocked out. I went into Sylvie's room and snuck into the bed next to her. I was glad I hadn't woken her up while coming in because I was hard and wanted to wake her up just before I put it in. The way I imagined it, but as I slid down her panties, she woke up. "Baby. Thanks for coming back," she said.

We heard footsteps. Shit, Melanie was awake! I quickly hid under the bed. She opened the door and asked if everything was all right. She'd thought she heard something. Sylvie acted sleepy as if she'd just woken up. My heart didn't beat, I didn't feel fear. *I became fearless.*

She left, and we heard a rustling in her bathroom. We knew she was taking another shot. We waited for fifteen minutes. Great memories.

I made sure Mel was asleep. Sylvie and I made love, but we kept it quiet. Not that Melanie would hear a thing, but just because it was more fun this way.

"When do you think you want a baby? Like if we wanted to start a family. How many kids do you want?" I whispered to her.

"Two children, a boy, and a girl. I don't know, maybe in ten years—no, wait, fifteen years. I want to work a bit, maybe learn Spanish, and then okay."

"What if I wanted kids earlier than that?" I whispered.

"How much earlier?" she asked.

"Next year. We'll wait 'til after you move out. Afterward, we can do it."

"Nooo." She giggled. "That's too early."

"Listen, we agreed that you'd be home schooled, so we won't get caught. Getting pregnant early is better than working or going to college. You don't lose all that time." I winked.

"Why do you want children so soon? I thought we wanted to have great times together," she said.

"Yeah. I'm just making conversation. I don't know why I want children. I just feel I want everything from you, to do everything with you. A big wedding, too. We'll plan it for a few days after your eighteenth birthday." I kissed her. "See what the stupid laws do to love? How many couples break up before they can get married because they're young? And how cruel society is to blame them. You see how your friends are afraid to say the word love. They all say 'I like him' and 'I'm into her.' What a shame."

"I never thought about it like that," Sylvie said, "But it's true."

"I guess it's all a scam. When people only lived to be forty, everything was right. You know, like two or three hundred years ago, our relationship was natural and normal. Now the religious groups and the government don't want people to marry early when they live to be eighty or older because then divorce rates will be much higher." I secretly wished I could show her the truth I knew.

"Wow," she said. "You really know so much."

"This is science, babe. I'll show you what the true philosophers have written on the secret Internet. It's called the dark web, and many smart people hide there because the government can't get them."

"I've heard of it, but I thought it was about guns and drugs. Later you'll show me, not tomorrow. You didn't tell me, how many kids do you want?"

"Fifteen or twenty," I said, waited for a few seconds for her reaction.

Fuck, I scared her.

"I'm joking," I said, "but I'd like a big family, like five or six children." It wasn't easy for anyone to accept those numbers. There were so many people on the Earth, many were worthless, but society and law-makers prohibited us from cleaning the world of the worthless. Back in the day, we could remove the weak.

She laughed. "You're so funny, Sam."

"Okay. I have a tough one for you. I'll explain it more tomorrow, but now for fun only. Okay?" I said.

"Okay. Shoot." She licked my ear. I was so proud of her. We'd already done it five times today, and she was still trying to get more. Such a special young one.

"Stop. Tomorrow we'll do as much as you want. So here's the thing. Would you accept sharing me with other women?" I asked.

"Hell, no. You're mine. Mine mine mine mine mine. Muahahahaha!"

"No seriously. I'm not saying I want to cheat on you, and I promise you I don't need to because you're the most amazing thing that's ever happened to me. I mean, if there was a major reason like a zombie attack and all the men who fought were dead, no one would be left to be with the women. Or, no, I have a better one. What if a virus wiped out all the men, and only *I* survived? Would you share me?"

"Then I'm obliged to, to save humanity. Why do you say these things? You're making me sad. I'm starting to think you want someone else."

"Don't be naïve. I'm only thinking out loud with you for a reason. Just a fantasy. Later, I'll explain to you about the genetic profiling that will begin soon. Don't be down, babe. These are pearls of wisdom you won't find in books."

I bid her farewell and left the place. How disappointing, a real letdown. I'd thought she might be more open.

HEALED

I woke up and saw my new screens for the first time, I smiled. When I sat in my chair, I had two on each side for a total of six. The responsibility of looking after this many apartments required a new set of equipment.

I'd also bought a racing seat with a steering wheel as if I were a hardcore gamer. I was so excited how the upcoming days would unfold, but at the same time, I longed for the day when someone worthy would join me in the basement.

I checked the screens. No one was awake except the couple in the new building under my responsibility—apartment 1215. The woman thought she had outsmarted me. She'd told me she was a single parent, and the father of her daughter had custody, so I let her rent the apartment at the rate of a single person. That same evening she had her boyfriend move in, bringing over his own lamp and his bags.

I'd run out of patience with them. They must leave. They didn't work; all they did was smoke dope, invite friends over to play cards and video games, they didn't even fuck a lot. Probably once every two days. I had to rewind a lot to find their glorious three minutes of action. I would take pleasure in driving them out of the place.

That day, I planned to chat with Dr-Anna45. She remained my last source of anger and frustration. If I could kill her, that would be the best thing. I'd be hitting two birds with one stone, getting both revenge and the only taste I hadn't experienced yet.

A message came in.

Dr-Anna45: "Hi, Kevin. How are you? I'm looking forward to our discussion today. How've you been?" A smiling face.

Dr-Anna45: "How was your week? Anything major take place?"

"Hi. I'm good. Great. I've never made it this long, and I want this time to last."

Fuck you. I want to break your fucking bones. I wish I had never even contacted you.

"Tell me about you. How are things with you?"

Dr-Anna45: "I'm okay. I guess I could be better, but I've realized we must accept the things we can't change. So, what happened this week? How are your girlfriend and work friends?"

"Work is fine. My boss wanted me to take on more responsibilities, so she expanded my area of coverage. I recommended we tighten security a bit, so we installed a few cameras at the entrance and whatnot..."

Dr-Anna45: "That's huge! Go on, please."

"GF is great." I typed something about her wonderful daughter, but I erased what I wrote. No need to flare her. I just wanted her to get stuck in the honey like a hopeless bug.

"Truthfully, she's wonderful, but god bless her soul, she still gets depressed. I suspected that she was using drugs again because she vomited and sweat a lot, but it turned out to have been a stomach bug." I hit Enter.

"I asked myself if I would stick around if she used again, and I realized that, yes I would. I must live a life where I can help others and think about their needs. I used to think life is either kill or be killed, but now I consider us more of a group. We should be there for each other."

Dr-Anna45: "Wow. I'm proud of you. You're a hero. Well done!" A big heart.

I continued. "I'm truly grateful to you. I was pessimistic when we started. I didn't think anyone could accept me. I was afraid to share, but once I did, you helped me learn new things. I'm healed."

Shit. A bit over the top. Healed is a big word.

Dr-Anna45: "My pleasure to help. How long has it been now?"

I knew it, I blew it. I hoped she didn't think I faked it.

"It's been 44 days. Today's the 45th." Fingers crossed emoji. "Listen. I said healed, but I know this is only wishful thinking. You know what they say: *You are what you believe you want to be.* I'm actually still in a lot of pain, but now I understand how to control it. You showed me I have a choice." I hit Enter.

"I don't want to hurt anyone. I don't want anyone to go through what I've gone through."

Dr-Anna45: "Have you needed any pornography during this period?"

"Yes, but not the illegal type. I found some with women who looked young and are legal, but without hair."

"And I'm active with my girlfriend. I always know how to get her in the mood."

She typed for a long time. I got worried.

Dr-Anna45: "What if she didn't want it? What do you do if she isn't in the mood?"

Well, she typed a lot for such a short sentence which meant that she thought well about it. *Okay, fuck you again.* She was talking about good old rape.

"Then I respect her wishes. I've never done anything against anyone's will, and I never will. Can I ask you something?"

Dr-Anna45: "Shoot. You're free."

"When a man or a woman does something to another person against their will, does the person they're doing it to really not enjoy? I thought there was some pleasure even if they didn't want the sex."

Dr-Anna45: "Seriously? Noooo. They don't find any pleasure in it. Not at all." Angry face.

Oh goodness, how emotional.

Dr-Anna45: "Sex is an expression of love or attraction, or at least fun. When you are forced, against your will, you feel afraid, sad, and violated. I can guarantee you, there is no pleasure at all." Angry face.

"Don't be angry with me. I'm still learning. Consider it an academic talk."

I swore, I never imagined I could hate anyone as much as I hated her.

"So they don't come at all?"

Dr-Anna45: "NO." Angry face.

"I just ran a quick search. Apparently, they can. I can send you an article about orgasms during rape. The victims themselves confirmed."

Dr-Anna45: "Let's agree it's forbidden, illegal, and we don't do it, and then postpone this topic for another time. Now I want to ask you about your childhood." Hands together in gratitude.

Condescending bitch.

"Sure. I just wanted to make a point about the strength of biology, but we can talk about whatever you want. I owe you a lot, and I trust you with my life. Ask me what you want. I also decided to come forward, but with you, after we meet. So, I'll answer you, and then you tell me about the guy you loved. Deal?"

Dr-Anna45: "Deal. When you were a child, did you have an accident, for example, on a bicycle, and hit your head?

Were you beaten as a child? Did anyone hit you on the head?

"Why are you asking?"

Two minutes earlier, I had thought I couldn't possibly get any angrier, but I could. She was talented at infuriating me.

Dr-Anna45: "I'll tell you once you tell me. It explains a lot by the way, and I'll throw in a story."

Dr-Anna45: "My story about the guy I loved and how I lost him."

"Not enough for the truth—the full truth from my childhood."

Dr-Anna45: "Then what would be enough? I think I know what will be."

"Hehe. Yes. Coffee. In a public place where you'll feel safe, although there's no reason you shouldn't. If you want, we can visit jail and rent one of the cubicles where family members visit inmates with the glass between them."

Dr-Anna45: "You crack me up. Indeed." Laughing face with tears.

"So it's a deal?"

Dr-Anna45: "Yes."

"Okay. Here it goes. When I was about six or seven years old, I used to peek in on my parents while they were having sex. Sometimes they thought I was asleep, but I wasn't. I used to squint and look. A curtain separated the bedrooms, and sometimes they left it open." I hit enter.

"My mom was away for work, she flew a lot from one city to another. He used to invite his friends over, and he liked this young one. Lucky to be their only child, I used to get a lot of attention from them and their guests, and a lot of candy." I hit Enter.

"I used to see him sleep with this other woman. When he'd finish, he'd tell me I had to be a man and keep his secrets, men stood by each other, and that when I was old enough, I'd understand. I didn't understand what cheating meant. Anyway, I didn't say a word."

Dr-Anna45: "Okay. Go on."

"Then mom would return, and they'd have a fight. I remember very well. The screaming, the crying, the flying plates; the memory now annoys me a lot. I used to sob and try to get between them because my mom used to be violent with him. The neighbors called the police on them one time, but they did nothing because she had hit him." I sent.

"Then, to get revenge, she started going out with one of his friends. They used to come home as well, and as with just curtains as room separators, I could see them."

Dr-Anna45: "Thanks for sharing. It's an important part of your history, so it'll be important for your therapy. When did they hit you?"

I hated when she was right. *The beating, where to start.* Her talk about history and therapy was very patronizing, as if she perceived every part of me.

"Wait, I'm getting there. So, the first couple of times they didn't see me. Then the guy saw me. I forget his name, something like Germaine. Let's call him that. He waited 'til my mom got into the shower, and he called for me, saying he knew I wasn't asleep. So I went over to him. I remember so vividly. He was smoking something nasty-smelling. He told me that if I said a word, he'd cut my throat in my sleep." I hit Enter.

"He pulled me closer, grabbing my short hair with his strong fingers. I could smell the alcohol on his breath. He ordered me to say, 'I understand, sir.' I didn't. So he hit me with his knuckles on the head, not a full punch but still very painful. Once, twice, ten times. 'Say it, you stubborn motherfucker!' I wouldn't. I cried of pain, and I felt like choking because I didn't want to say it." I hit Enter.

"I tried running. He held onto me. He pinched me in my butt and back, and he no longer asked me to say anything. He only threatened and hit. This became a habit, every time he came over, I'd get a beating. I'd shiver with fear while they were sleeping together, and when she moaned harder or he grunted louder, I knew they were about to finish, and I'd get my beating."

Dr-Anna45: "Oh, god. I'm so sorry about that. How do you feel about this memory?"

"I don't feel anything, honestly. It's something that happened, and I don't need to feel anything about it. The funny thing is that I didn't remember this until a few years back. I went throughout high school not remembering it."

Dr-Anna45: "You don't feel sad or angry, or have any feelings of guilt?"

"No. It used to anger me. But after growing up with that, I decided not to feel anything about it."

Dr-Anna45: "When did you remember everything?"

"I don't recall specifically. A few years back."

Dr-Anna45: "What happened? Is there more?"

"So then, I started growing white hairs among the black ones. Not very many, but they were enough. I wet the bed, but not too often. My mom wanted to take me to a doctor, but my dad said he could fix it. He told her that some manly activities like hunting would be enough.

"He took me on a hunting trip. When we got there, he drank a few beers, and after that, he insisted I tell him what frightened me. I made the biggest mistake and told him everything, and he lost it. He hit me, he bit me, he went batshit crazy all over me in the forest.

"We took the car and drove to the nearest phone to call her. She answered, and he told her he would kill her. He shouted, and he hit me on the head, back, legs, pretty much everywhere, much worse than Germaine had."

Dr-Anna45: Face with eyes opened. "Police?"

"By the time we got home, she'd fled the place. For two years he stayed mad at me. He hit me every now and then, especially and aggressively when he got drunk. He told me I had no honor because I didn't know how to protect my women. He called me a weakling. I skipped school for two weeks after the incident, because of the bruising. No police."

Dr-Anna45: "Then?"

"He died. May his fucking soul turn in its grave for eternity. My mom returned. She was so sweet. She asked for my forgiveness. A lot."

Dr-Anna45: "Where is she now?"

"Upstairs."

Dr-Anna45: "You live with your mom?"

"Hahaha. No. She died. Heaven." Cloud picture.

Dr-Anna45: "I'll be brief because I've got to leave. I used to love someone a lot, an artist. I left my husband for him. Our one-year anniversary was coming up, and he had one of his not-so-good moments, so I prescribed him something. Not supposed to, but I did anyway, I tried to help him. I loved him so much and couldn't see him suffer. He took half the bottle and died." Crying face.

Dr-Anna45: "I don't know whether or not he committed suicide. I think he did take his own life, but I hate that people think so as well. I lost my license... I hope this is enough. No, you won't find the story on the Internet, they sealed all the records."

Dr-Anna45: "I was lost. I did drugs..."

"I'm so sorry for your loss. You poor thing."

Dr-Anna45: "It's okay. Life is hard. Then I met someone, and although we both had problems, we were a good fit, despite the odds, but then I went back to my husband."

Dr-Anna45: "I have to go now. Let's talk next week, and we'll meet for coffee like I promised you."

"No. You didn't tell me about the hitting, and why you asked about it. You promised." I swore if she left without telling me, I would cut her into a thousand pieces when I caught her.

"Is the beating and my childhood the reason I like young girls young women?"

Dr-Anna45: "Oh, okay, quickly then. No, not that. It essentially relates to your emotions. You don't feel many emotions, and you don't identify with other people's emotions. Like if someone is sad, you know, you just don't care, and this is the main trait that sociopaths and psychopaths share. This emotional void is filled with intense desires."

Dr-Anna45: "Gtg bye. The term and definition don't matter. What matters is that it's a fact, and we need to deal with it."

She logged off.

The news shocked me. She called me a sociopath, a psychopath. *Me?? How dare she?* I boiled with rage. I trashed the whole place; two screens and the racing seat didn't survive the attack. *What did she mean I don't feel many emotions? That I don't feel for other people?*

FOCUS

The days passed quickly, and I enjoyed every moment. Work was becoming more rewarding, and my mental clarity was unimaginable at this stage.

Dr-Anna45 gave me the address at which to meet her, and it was only a three-and-a-half-hour drive from my place. I told Sylvie I was going on a business trip, a conference related to telecommunications and new management systems. During my absence, she was supposed to draft the letter to her mom, and once I was back, we would put our plan into action. The letter would tell Mel not to look for her and not to take drastic measures.

I packed my clothes and tools. I was ready to know who this Anna was. We agreed to meet in a café at 11 a.m. I was there at 9, looking at the landscape and studying the traffic. It wasn't a busy shop. It stood among a few stores and a supermarket with a generous parking space.

I parked in the sweetest spot after rounding the place a few times. From where I was, I could see the entrance to the café and still have a view of the parking lot. I assumed Anna would arrive half an hour before the appointment and then sit in a different place than we had agreed upon to give herself the chance to leave if she sensed something wrong with my appearance.

I'd had to control my temper during our last discussion. She had explained to me about emotions and how I lacked the ability to empathize with others. I told her to share a photo of herself so I could recognize her, but she didn't want to, and I told her I didn't want to share my phone number.

"What if we could not find each other?" I asked.

She agreed we need some sort of identification cues, we thought together about solutions, and finally, we decided to wear something yellow.

Time slowed down. I was focused, in hunter mode. Everything moved in slow motion. I felt like a jaguar. I took out my binoculars and relaxed back in the car seat. I recorded in my tablet the plate number, model, and color of each car parked in the lot. I was worried that she would stay in the car, just as I had.

A Mercedes sedan pulled into the parking lot. A woman in a yellow shirt with a jacket climbed out and then took a hat out of her bag. She was very good-looking, of eastern

Asian origin. What I found weird was that her hair was both blonde and black at the same time. *Crazy people. That's her!*

She went into the cafe wearing a hat and holding a book. *Stubborn.* She chose the corner booth and stayed in it. I could see well with the binoculars. I wished the cafe was ones of those places where they wrote your name on your cup, but it wasn't. As far as I was concerned, her name was Anna, even though it was definitely a fake name.

I walked unnoticed to her car and placed a magnetic GPS tracker on the bottom. I decided to send her a message that I couldn't make it. If she had the website's app on her phone then good, and if not, I assumed she would wait half an hour and leave.

I wrote: "Hi. The policed stopped me. They said my car was stolen about six months ago, and I told them I bought it about ten months ago. They're checking the ownership papers, they took me into the station."

"The station is about twenty minutes from the café, but I don't want to keep you. We'll try again soon. Kisses." I sent it.

I also sent her my picture wearing a yellow shirt, up to the neck, and a crying face. I wrote, "Sorry" under it. I saw her reach for her phone. Now I knew it was her. I was relieved. She took her coffee and book off the table and left.

Three days, and I was lurking around her place. I had switched the plates from the dark sedan I rented, and I intentionally covered the whole car with mud, so the color was unidentifiable. The neighborhood didn't have cameras.

Anna lived in a regular suburban house, like mine but fancier. She lived with a man and a small girl, probably her family.

I waited until both of them had gone out with the child and then broke into the place. They didn't have a security system, but the house was made of brick with heavy doors, not the usual cheap sliding. I picked the lock without leaving a trace and then went through my usual routine, I took a used pair of panties and set up the camera.

I placed a couple of bugs around the bedroom and a small camera on top of the closet. I wanted to know Anna and her husband's sexual routine and how they did it. I also needed to practice his voice. It was crucial for my plan—I wanted her to enjoy it.

Our next session was coming up in two days. I wanted to be back in my basement for it, so I was hoping I'd have the chance to act before the session. Ideally, her husband would be out of town, but in case that wasn't possible, I needed to know his schedule exactly. I'd followed him to work. He had a lame nine-to-five job. On one occasion, Anna met him for lunch. They sent the girl to preschool for a few hours during the day.

I decided my time inside the house should not be more than one hour, two hours maximum. I would make it look like a robbery, for the cops. My heart raced at the idea. I closed my eyes, turned on. I jerked off, cleaned up after myself and left for the motel, but before I left, I placed a magnetic camera on one of the garbage cans so I could keep an eye on them tonight.

I needed two hours of sleep and a shower. I wanted to be clean for my doctor. Sylvie was nagging me to return, and she told me that Melanie wasn't doing well. I was scared the bitch would die before I got back, and then Sylvie would end up with social services.

The next morning at 7 a.m., I was doing my usual surveillance. The husband left, and a half hour later, Anna dropped the girl off at preschool. I went into the house and waited for her. I closed a few of the shades upstairs and bagged jewelry and cash. I put on a generous amount of her husband's cologne. There were a few ways this could go down, and I was prepared for all of them.

I wore my ski mask, the one that had a small sheath over the eyes, black surgical gloves, and shoes with disposable blue covers. These covers made it hard to detect the shoe markings at crime scenes, and they silenced the noise while walking. I placed my bag under the bed.

I took my time looking at her stuff, her clothes and what she had. I took many photos and a short video of the house layout and the lovely family.

Let's see if you still feel jolly when I'm done with you.

The car pulled into the driveway. A few seconds and she would be inside. I wondered what she would do today: aerobics and a shower, or make breakfast, or just watch TV. I waited upstairs. I was glad the stairs didn't make noise in case I needed to go down.

Breakfast it was. I hid under the bed. I regretted not having a camera downstairs. The time didn't pass quite as quickly as I desired. She finished and came upstairs, but I was reluctant to make my move. I was right, she took off her clothes and put an exercise outfit on. She was a bit too thin under the clothes. Her spine and ribs were visible. She went back downstairs.

She finished in half an hour and came back up. She stood in front of the mirrored closet and looked at her body. She tucked her stomach in, she stood on her toes, maybe to check her ass. I didn't want her to take a shower and come back out in a towel—I wanted to rip the clothes off her body. I got out from under the bed slowly and stood up without a sound.

"Oi." I had been practicing an Irish accent, and as a robber my voice was deep. She saw me for a second in the mirror before I grabbed her around the waist from behind and used my leg to trip her. I didn't let her fall down; instead, we stumbled on the bed where she landed face down. She shouted, "Stop!" I placed my hand over her mouth.

"It's been some time since I did something saucy for you," I said.

"Henry, is that you? Oh my god. I'm scared, baby," she said.

"Enjoy it, babe. Of course it's me. Who else would it be? Don't ya know my smell?" I relaxed my grip on her. "Do you want me to stop? Play along, you'll enjoy it. You always tell me you want me to do something spontaneous. Dangerous."

She was reluctant. I sighed in disappointment and said something without the accent but a bit high pitched. I hoped that flew over her head. "Maaan, I took off for this roleplay." I relaxed my grip more and waited for a second.

"Sorry," she said.

Yes. Touchdown. Perfection.

"Don't say a ward," I told her. "I was nicking this place as a fierce fella, then you fine thing came along. I couldn't feck off. I want you too badly, I have to be a bad boyo."

"You scared the shit out of me," she said. "What are you wearing?"

"Shh. I said no wards."

I wanted to kiss her neck, but I thought about the DNA trace. I started groping her ass, I had heard her asking him to do that during one of their steamy nights.

I ripped off her blouse, her sports bra, and then her tight yoga pants. I ripped off a piece of the pants and gagged her with it.

"You'll get de time o' yoohr life," I said.

I already had a condom on under my clothes. I unzipped, keeping my pants on. I waited for her to come, and then I got very rough. I hit her to injure her, and she moaned. As I was coming, I pulled her hair, and she started crying.

I pulled her two hands behind her back and pressed on them with my knees, then I choked her until she passed out. I had planned for five minutes to clear the place, during which I removed the bugs and the camera. I left no trace left behind. That should be about the time when she'd wake up.

I waited for her to come around. As she was waking up, she turned, and I jumped on her. I tied her up, face down. She tried but couldn't scream because of the gag.

I leaned close to her ear, and I whispered to her, "Kelly, Dr. Anna. Fuck your will. I hope you liked it as much as I did."

I trashed the bedroom and the living room, taking valuables. Before I left, I went up and hit her back more than fifty times with a belt.

Payback bitch, for every time you made me angry.

I drove back home, and along the way, I threw her belongings in several different dumpsters far from her house. Maybe the jewelry would show up in different pawn shops in a week's time, throwing the cops off.

I wondered whether she knew it was me or not. *Surely, she knew.* I wondered if I should go back soon and kill her. Maybe. If she annoyed me again.

DREAMS DO COME TRUE

Sweet revenge relaxed me, made me a different person. I took what I wanted, and nothing could stop me. The major news coverage of the attack came a week afterward, they said a woman had been attacked, the mother of a four-year-old, but they didn't release her name. The police had nothing, and they wouldn't find anything. I thought to myself the attack wasn't a Ted Bundy move— this was me making a point, showing her what was right. As expected, she missed our next session, and honestly, it didn't bother me. I just wanted to speak to her one more time to tell her, "Fuck you."

I made a few visits to Laurie's, but I spent most of my time with Sylvie. She had written the letter to her mom explaining she would leave home, she couldn't tolerate living with her anymore, and that she'd bought bus tickets to move away. She asked Melanie not to look for her because she'd end up in a foster home, which none of them wanted. She also told her mother she loved her, but that this was for the best for both of them.

I didn't go to Melanie's place again. I wanted to be away when it all blew up, as if we had broken up. Sylvie often came to the apartment, we made love, and we agreed she would give her the letter the following morning.

I gave her the bus tickets and money, and she argued that she didn't really need to take the bus. I told her that if the police looked for her, they would see her on the security footage from the various stations. She argued more about the motel but came around eventually. I told her I'd pick her up between two to four days from then, depending on the police. She easily agreed to leave her phone, and I gave her a burner replacement promising her a smartphone soon.

She left the letter in the morning and went on her route. She texted me once she was settled, but said she was afraid to be alone. I expected a call from Melanie, she had no one, but she didn't call.

That evening, I went to Melanie's. She was wasted and hadn't eaten in a few days. She was in a confused state—she didn't make sense. I had expected a totally different reaction from her. I'd thought she would sob and shout, then call the police, but she did nothing, and I thought she would O.D. within a year or less. The enemy of the addict was money. Having the resources for drugs brought the demise of such people. *Worthless shit.*

I didn't know what to do. I would certainly tell Sylvie that her mother hadn't shed a tear over her, might make her feel better about leaving.

I decided to call the police myself, and after being transferred and waiting for half an hour, I got to someone. I asked about the wait, and they replied this wasn't an emergency, but anyway I explained everything.

"How old is the girl?"

"I guess sixteen or seventeen. Something like that. I'm not sure, honestly." She would turn fourteen in a few months.

The lady on the phone transferred me to another department, and I asked about the waiting time and received the same response. I'd thought the fuss would be more prominent like you see in movies about missing people. The guy who answered explained to me the difference between runaway cases and missing people cases. He said about a million runaway cases are filed a year, and the actual number of runaways crossed three million.

"We can't track down every rebellious teenager, or everyone who fails a class and decides they can make it on their own. Most of them return home on their own, and sometimes, it's better for them to leave."

I became ecstatic about this revelation, a significant break for me, the loophole I needed, they don't look for runaways, as in murder - no body and no crime! This was the path to finding my Alpha in case Sylvie wasn't the one. I texted Sylvie and told her I could pick her up tomorrow morning, and the news made her happy. I didn't tell her the details of my phone call, better to let her think the police were searching for her so she'd stay inside, which she needed to do for the plan to work.

A week passed, and then another, and Melanie kept sinking deeper. I felt so happy living with Sylvie, and she was so much fun to be around. Spending this much time together made me realize that she was great and everything, she would help me transform, but sadly she wasn't my Alpha. She was stubborn about sharing me, so how could I ever hope to take her hunting with me, let alone help me spread my message.

I had to keep searching for my Alpha.

I asked her to pack an essentials bag and to get ready for a special night out. We would sleep in a motel then take a hike through the woods together the next morning before dawn.

That day, I visited the place alone, a perfect location with no cameras, and I could park within meters of the room. I rented three rooms for three days, and we would stay in the one in the middle. That way, we heard no one, and no one heard us.

We came back together that evening, around eight. We had dinner. We joked and laughed. She said, "Why are you looking at me like that?" I answered because she was so special. I'd never imagined that someone would love me like this, so much that they would leave their home for me. We were on the run together, a dream come true.

We made love, we drank juice, we watched a movie. She was sitting next to me on the bed in her undies and a bra.

I told her to put her clothes on, "Why? Are we going somewhere?" she asked. I told her no, but I wanted to have sex with her, and I wanted every detail to be perfect.

"But you have to be patient," I said. "We'll do something rough, okay?"

She nodded and said, "Ooh la la! Teach me what you want, Sam. Everything."

I didn't do anything differently, but I took my time. I enjoyed the salty sweat on her body. When I was inside her, I put my hands around her throat and squeezed. She couldn't take a breath. I released, and she felt the pleasure. She came a second, then a third time. I hadn't yet.

We rested a bit then started again.

"I want you to come again," I said to her and she nodded." I pressed harder on her throat, but this time, I didn't release, and I had the best orgasm of my life.

She gasped for breath. I leaned forward and told her I loved her so much. She scratched me with her nails, tried to pull my hands off, punched me. I leaned back, and said, "I swear to you I'll never love anyone like I love you. You're part of something huge. In a way, you made me what I am." Her arms fell down gradually, and I kept on pressing until she had no pulse.

She lay there, and I stood over her body for an hour. I slept next to her, only for one hour. I didn't need more; elite warriors didn't need more. When I woke up, her body was cold and stiff. I kissed her on her forehead. I brought a suitcase from the trunk of the car and crammed her into it, cracking her bones in the process. I cleaned the whole room with bleach spray, put the suitcase in the trunk, and drove home.

I had redecorated my basement for her arrival. She was a special guest, my eternal companion. I painted the walls yellow with stripes of red, but not too thick. On one side behind the screens, I made them vertical, and one the other two the stripes were horizontal. Nothing could be done about the stairs, but come to think of it, I thought I should dismantle the stairs and create a different entry point.

I'd dug the hole a few days before so it would be ready when we arrived. I placed her in, mixed the new cement, and filled the hole.

I thought a lot about Xeris_Light2323. I wanted to reach out, but he or she never stayed in one place for too long.

I typed a new message and sent it out on a few platforms.

Thank you. Now I have seen it all, and I have done it all. We should work together. Reach out. Let's find the people who belong together...

A day later, the response came. Let's do it. We need to discuss this. I'll send you the details for a secure place.

PART

5

JASON

BREEZE

Life had gotten better, and so had I. I didn't drink as much as I'd used to, and Cynthia kept tabs on me. I jogged with my dog, buddy, in the neighborhood, and I gradually gained some weight. I startled myself when I looked in the mirror: I'd grown a beard and sometimes forgot to trim it.

I couldn't have said that life was a breeze, though. Not a day passed when I didn't think about my family every few minutes. The great times were when I forgot.

I felt terrible for Mathew. He wasn't discussed on national TV or social media as a missing boy, and he wasn't on the back of milk cartons. Luke and Danny Miller explained that the circumstances of the kidnapping defined how much the public engaged with the children. Evidently, our circumstances weren't good.

I knew deep down, but I'd never wanted to consider the possibility that he might have been taken by a criminal ring that trafficked children to abuse them. I had heard something about such a ring having a website with thousands of children for customers to choose from. Customers would take a flight to the ring's place, somewhere, and do what they wanted. How shameful. What a tragedy.

Alternatively, black market organ sellers could have kidnapped him, but I wondered who would find a match in my son. Unless the criminals tried to enrich the bank of donors, also possible. However, these motives didn't fit with the nature of the crime committed against us.

I tried calling up the police. "This is Jason Stankovic. I want to follow up on my son's case. He's missing."

The detective responded that old leads went cold, and nothing new had come in. He said, "Have you considered hypnosis, to help you remember... what you did."

I was furious and didn't hold back on him, but he hung up on me. They didn't work cold cases, and that was final.

Someone else on the force told me that of the thousands of missing children cases, they prioritized the most recent ones in which the children still had a chance of being alive. *Yup, alive*. Without any emotional consideration, they'd tell a father there was a 99% his child was dead without imagining the toll it took on him. I was beyond sad, not depressed, crushed. My chest was so tight and painful; I thought I was having a heart attack.

I checked online for informative sources about child abduction. Although a big range of probability, a tab on one website named "know by days since day zero" scared me, and showed ridiculously small numbers for after 2 years of disappearance. I decided it meant nothing, I chose to believe Mathew was still alive and we would be reunited. I read pages written by other parents. They all talked about how the doubt, the *not knowing*, is the toughest part. I didn't agree. I feared someone abused Mathew and killed him, *this* was the worst.

Cynthia was my backbone during this period. I joked and told her she could do the thinking on my behalf, and I would do whatever she planned for me. This covered eating, dressing, and exercising. I much preferred her place, both the view and the neighborhood, but because of Buddy, I stayed at my house, and she slept over most nights. I hadn't asked her to move in yet, but I would soon.

Danny Miller did her job well enough—as instructed and nothing more, I wished she would go the extra mile, but that never happened. She shortlisted six guys in the end, a garbage man among them, but Danny didn't even want to hear my suggested theory. She said, "You're the boss, no need to explain. I only get you what you need. Whether or not it makes sense, I don't care." I never tried to include her in my thinking again, but she was reliable and trustworthy.

She confronted half these men with photos and recorded their facial expressions when they first saw the pictures of Lea and Lisa, and according to the experts who analyzed the reactions, none of them had ever seen my girls before. She also confirmed they don't keep crime memorabilia or a trophy in their houses. When I asked her how she knew about what they stored in their homes, and whether she broke in, she answered she had ways of knowing what is inside without breaking in. She said, "My men can be your everyday plumber, city inspectors for gas leaks and what not. We didn't break any laws, they showed us around their place."

The other three were an enigma. Two of them were believed to have left the country, and Danny said that was normal—even kidnappers went on vacation or fled the country. I thought to myself that an abuser who wanted to kidnap a child might find it more successful outside the country, in places with less security.

Danny argued that offenders could have traveled to wherever they wanted and rented sexual services. "They can even buy children in some places. You don't know what a crazy jungle it is beyond the borders. If purchasing didn't work, then they would abduct children in countries where the average number of children per household was huge."

The only elusive suspect was the garbage man who had used a fake name that wasn't listed in any criminal databases. His colleagues' memories of him were fading, they recall he made unusual advances to a woman at work, and afterward, he disappeared. He vanished as if he no longer existed. I asked Danny to spare no effort in figuring out who this man was.

She agreed to send agents to track down the two people who had left the country. She had some recognized achievements as a PI, and she always used the practical approach of both a field agent and a consultant. I had faith in her work. The bills tripled; we had agents in multiple countries now, including the people following up on leads about Mathew. I was sure Luke saw the statements, but he didn't discourage me, he knew I had to do everything I possibly could.

Time passed by, we had no success abroad, and Danny kept searching for the garbage man. I promised not to obsess over any leads, but this one got to me.

I went to the bloody group meetings for sex addicts and offenders, and it seemed okay, none of the attendees seemed creepy. This was a new part of my life. After a few meetings, I realized that someone had done me a favor by placing me in a good group, predominated by sex addicts rather than offenders. The people in the group were regular struggling artists or businessmen describing how they'd fallen into pornography addiction, or this is what I assumed. They could have been offenders, but during the meeting, they would only highlight their addiction.

"Hello. My name is Jay." I sighed. "I'm an addict." It never got any easier to say that, even though it is easier than saying I was an offender. I thought someone would call me out for being something else, for not being an addict, but no one did. I spoke about the overwhelming options on the pornographic sites, how I had to see it all, and how my addiction had started. Others described how they'd developed rituals: they'd cook dinner and masturbate before and after, hide in a bathroom stall at work...

I kept my head low, listened, and avoided participation. I enjoyed listening to the stories, and the determination of some people to get laid surprised me. It was better than reality TV. I was disgusted by one person who used his sex addiction to justify his cheating, but nobody else seemed to be annoyed. The group even gasped when he said that he hadn't known he was an addict. I didn't buy it because he displayed no signs of shame or remorse.

The dullest part, which didn't come until near the end of meetings, annoyed me the most. When people shared why they thought they had become sex addicts and how controlling their addictions had helped them reach their potential, like a before-and-after weight loss commercial. I imagined myself speaking: *Before becoming an addict; I had a family. After becoming an addict, I lost my family. They committed me. Did I mention the accusation of sleeping with my daughter?*

We met three times a week, and I couldn't help feeling the meetings were a waste of time. I simply wasn't a sex addict, in fact, I was below-average when it came to sexual drive.

It was my turn to clean up the meeting room before the next one started. It took two minutes to arrange the chairs and remove the SAA sign, but I had to wait for the next group.

I imagined meeting someone from work. In the beginning, I'd thought they might be here for something as bad as I was, but then I thought they might be coming for a regular group, like bridge or bingo. I always worried about someone in the following meeting recognizing me, although I'd forgotten which group came in next.

"Hi," a man behind me said. My heart pumped an extra beat, but I stayed calm.

"Hello," I stood up.

"Oh, sorry," He jolted a bit. I hadn't stood up quickly, so he shouldn't have been startled, this kept me wondering about his reaction. I hoped he didn't recognize me from somewhere.

He shook his head, then said, "Do I know you from somewhere?" He gave a fake laugh. He kept smiling, also fake, tiny wrinkles appeared at the corners of his eyes—a clear sign of a labored smile.

"I'm about to leave. Am I supposed to give the key to you?" I asked. His face was familiar, but I didn't recall him from work or Lisa's office. He actually looked like me when I was healthy, not mind-blowingly similar as though a doppelganger but same built, features, and hairline.

"Yeah, sure." I handed him the key. "I want to ask you something, and I'm sorry if I'm being a pain, but you're in the SAA group, right?"

I nodded.

"So, about the group here. How big is it? And is it totally private? Like, do people mess up and leak something out?"

"It's cool," I told him. "Privacy is very important. People leave their phones outside, and people can use fake names. There are eleven of us in the group. I recommended it if you're searching." I was so eager to leave before others started coming.

"Yeah, I'm thinking of joining. Do you think it works? You know, in controlling it?"

For the first time, I looked into his eyes, and they were still as if they were lifeless or empty.

"I don't know, works very well for me," I replied. "You can drop your contact details in the box, and they will contact you." I hoped that would end the conversation.

"Yeah. I might." He turned and walked a couple steps. "One more question. Last one—I promise. Do they take severe cases? Are there any severe cases that can't be controlled? In your group, specifically."

"I am not sure, some must be severe. This is a support group, doesn't matter how severe, and I don't think they turn anyone down." I said, and he nodded. His disappointment surprised me, maybe he didn't want to label himself as a severe case.

I added, "Listen. I don't know for sure, but I think most of the people in the group didn't have severe addictions. Each one has their own story, and they use the group for their benefit as it suits them. Probably one or two who had severe addictions and got better along the way. For god's sake, one guy is a cheater and by no means an addict, and he still finds the help *he* needs."

He hissed and shook his head in disagreement. "Worthless shit." He sharply pronounced the S.

I frowned at him.

"Not you." He laughed, also fake. "I mean the cheater."

I smiled back out of courtesy, although I didn't find it funny. We walked to the door.

"I gotta go. What group are you in? The one coming next?"

"Alcoholics. AA," he said, and I left.

He'd lied. The next meeting was NA. I'd just seen one of the group's leaflets: Tuesdays at 9 p.m. Perhaps he wanted to hide which substances he abused, addiction is a private matter.

The encounter with the stranger unsettled me for no apparent reason. I had a few drinks, and smoked a lot; I enjoyed the fact that Cynthia wasn't coming over that night, felt like a cheat night.

I was dozing off, on the couch watching comedy reruns, and the guy's dead eyes flashed in my mind. I drifted off but didn't fall asleep, in between sleep and wakefulness, I suddenly remembered where I'd encountered the stranger before. The guy who had attacked me in my home said, and in the motel, he'd pronounced the same sharp S when saying worthless shit!

It is him!

Who the fuck is this guy?

I jumped to my feet and grabbed the whiteboard from the other room. I erased the upper part and wrote a few words:

Worthless shit — assailant = Garbage man?

SERENDIPITY

I stayed up all night replaying what happened after the SAA meeting, during the attacks and planning my next move. I tried to see the situation through impartial eyes, I wanted to know whether I was making sense or not. I didn't have anyone else in my surroundings to help me check, no friends, and heartless family. I thought only of Kelly so I called her, but her number had been disconnected, I decided to try again later.

I erased what was written on the whiteboard. Cynthia would be coming over for lunch soon. I decided to stake out the anonymous meetings for the next two days and at least try to take a photo of the guy on my phone. Worst case scenario, I'd volunteer to clean up and hand the keys over at the end of my session, and I would wait for him to come like last time.

The stakeout was a failure, totally different groups were there. I had to wait for the following day. That night, I confided in Cynthia, and asked her about the possibility this was the same man. She said the probability was low, and being a control freak, she asked me a hundred questions.

In my session the following day, I wasn't listening and got called out as if it mattered. The group that would come after us took all my concentration. Volunteering to handover the key made another member happy, so at least the plan resulted in something good.

The thirty minutes seemed like a day. I gave the key to someone, not my guy, and waited for all the members of the group to join. Five minutes, then ten minutes, and almost everyone had arrived except him. I waited a bit longer outside the room, then decided to leave. The place didn't have a CCTV I could look at, and they didn't keep a log sheet or anything of that kind, besides he wouldn't write down his real name.

I walked to the car, uncertain about what to do next. I noticed that all the cars in the lot were clean, or at least not very dirty, except for a sedan with dark windows. Dirt covered it completely. I thought to myself that when left for such a long time, dirt might damage the paint. Then I looked at it again, and I thought I saw a man with binoculars inside. Once I sat in the passenger's seat, he disappeared, either he ducked down, or I'd imagined I saw him.

I turned on the car, adjusted the way I parked for a better view of the building, and then turned it off. I looked closely, but there wasn't anything visible inside the car. I could have imagined it. I hadn't slept more than an hour, and I was on edge.

I don't know. I couldn't be certain.

I lit a cigarette and rolled down the window. I didn't know what I waited for. I thought that maybe there was another entrance to the building, and I'd better go back in and check again whether or not he had come.

I could just walk up to the fucking car, he couldn't attack me here. I encouraged myself - assuming I hadn't imagined all of this, and assuming someone hid in the car.

I had covered half the distance to the sedan when I saw its lights come on, and then I heard the car's engine start. He peeled out of the parking lot in a reckless manner, but I recorded his plate number.

I didn't need more evidence to know something was wrong, other people needed more evidence, but not me. Many times, intuition proved accurate about such things. I circled around the block, got a coffee to go, and returned to the parking lot. Unfortunately, the car hadn't returned. I drove around for an hour, but kept returning to the parking lot, without any sighting.

I called Danny to request that she find a sketch artist who could see me within the hour. I admired that she had the professionalism not to ask me why or what for. The artist came to my place, and we worked on the sketch together. After he finished, he said, "Sir, I have to warn you before others do that there is a resemblance between you and the sketch."

I told him I agreed and smiled.

I called Danny again, and she agreed to put surveillance people on a large radius around where anonymous groups assembled, without limiting the search to the NA. I also asked her if she could run a check on the plate numbers through one of her old friends.

I knew he would disappear. As the week passed, I went to three meetings, and he was nowhere to be seen. Danny reported that the license plate had been stolen. It couldn't get any fishier than this.

I decided to tell Luke and Cynthia everything. I prepared my whiteboard, hiding the written information with sticky white cardboard. The order in which I planned to deliver the information was the attack, the SAA weird guy questions, the sketch, and the encounter at the parking lot.

Before I started, I decided to put emphasis on the phrase the man had used, "worthless shit," because of how peculiar it was. If they were receptive, I'd test the possibility whether this mysterious man AKA garbage man was the criminal who infiltrated our lives, possibly through befriending Lea.

Once Cynthia and Luke were seated, I poured them each a glass of wine. I didn't pour one for myself.

"I beg you to keep an open mind. This is a casual discussion, and there's no need for anyone to get worked up," I said.

They agreed.

"And please do not interrupt me. I'm only going to talk for five minutes, and then we can discuss." As a joke, I added, "And the event will be followed by dinner."

As I went through the presentation, I noticed them giving each other ambiguous looks, and I knew they didn't buy the story.

"Honey, I'm so proud of you for doing this," Cynthia said afterward. "It's been a long time since we've seen this kind of energy. You're a natural leader and a persuasive presenter."

I didn't like her comment, which was patronizing and condescending. I felt like a sick person who had received praise. *There are no losers, we're all winners. Here's a trophy for your effort.*

She could have at least acknowledged that I had tried telling her about it all a few days earlier. She thought of her image in every situation, pragmatic to an annoying extent, I never thought of her as a genuine person.

Luke stood up and said, "I'll play the devil's advocate, so bear with me. So, you're saying that a guy who attended NA is no longer going to meetings. That is not big news. Also, someone who might be getting a blowjob in the parking lot fled the scene when you approached the car. And..."

"What do you mean? Are we going to blame it all on my imagination? Huh?" I tried to be as calm as possible,

"No. not at all," he said. "I mean the devil's advocate would look at these events as separate ones and not connected. However, the fact that your attacker and the man at the meeting used the same phrase, with the same intonation, is a strong point in your favor."

A brief win! I knew it would work. I enjoyed it, but it faded away quickly.

"It's a common phrase, but when you consider the unusual pronunciation, then it seems more likely that the two men are the same person."

"But," he continued, "we can estimate that 5% of the population uses this phrase. Do you agree?" I nodded. "Combined with the sharp S, that number drops by a quarter or a half. So, we're speaking about a small percentage, but numerically a very large number of people, even if we just count the people living in this city. Right?"

"Yes, agreed, but not every one of this population attacked me and claimed to be an CCB agent, wired my place, and then tried to look me in the eye again. In fact, thinking about it now, the incident in the meeting might be part of the stalking. Perhaps he wasn't even part of the meeting after mine—he said alcoholics and not narcotics." I pointed to the chart. "That's not a coincidence. That's targeting."

"I agree," Cynthia jumped in.

"That is good," Luke added, "but not good enough. This could just be a sick person who's interested in your life or wanted a story, or maybe just a nosy person. Even if we assume there's a connection, that it's the same person, that doesn't mean he is the killer of Lisa and Lea, does it?"

We fell silent for a while. They drank, and I topped them up. I brought myself a glass from the kitchen, and I heard them whispering, but I couldn't make it out.

"Jason," Luke sighed, "I love hanging out with you. You're a brilliant person."

Uh oh.

"But bro, what you presented today won't make sense outside this room. Yet. I don't know, later on it might yield something. Although for now, it's only speculation."

He looked at Cynthia as if asking her to jump in, but she didn't, I thought she would leave all the dirty work to him.

He continued. "Our focus right now is to getting you in better health, and searching for Mathew outside the country, and of course inside as well. Keep doing what you're doing for your recovery, and pass your orders to Danny. She can take care of it all."

Cynthia was nodding more quickly now.

"Let's make a plan," she said.

"Okay," Luke said. "First, Danny will continue working on what you asked her for, and we'll add to that a couple of people who can surveil the meetings and centers. Second, let's get you some security, someone who can look out for you, at least from a distance."

When I sat, Cynthia hugged me under the arm, and she put all her weight on me. She whispered that she was sorry, and I knew she was sorry for discouraging Luke from being enthusiastic about my theory. She asked me to cheer up, and she said she'd make it up to me. I was pissed because I didn't have a next step. I had focused so much on the storytelling that I'd forgotten the planning part. At least I could look forward to her I'm-sorry sex, she probably had something astonishing in mind.

It still surprised me how my days had changed from before my family died to now. Previously, I'd had two operating moods: a busy one with an ultra-productive schedule that started with the morning news, followed by breathing, stretching, and sometimes yoga. Then, to the gym or a heavy cardio sessions, followed by more breathing sessions and meditations. Then, either work or leisure, and whichever of those I chose was well-planned and executed to perfection. I'd thought this regimen brought out the best in me.

The second mode had gone into operation when the discipline, the busy mode, broke down on its own, without a warning or a signal. Amid a yoga session or while finishing breakfast, I would get the idea to not go to work. *Today I'll retreat to my cave where I think*, but there wasn't much thinking going on. It was mostly sitting, not feeling interested in anything. Anhedonia, they called it, lack of excitability... nothing could move me.

Now, I lived in a totally different mode. I didn't care much about what was going on unless it involved finding Mathew. I couldn't accept that he was gone. I had accepted most of what had happened, but I couldn't live with myself knowing that there had been a time when I didn't remember him or couldn't acknowledge his presence. Correction: his disappearance.

I choked on the thought that he wasn't with me. Every few minutes a tide of sadness overwhelmed me. I missed him a lot, and I was helpless. *It's all my fault.*

I remembered his tiny hands. I used to put them in my mouth and say "I can eat you up!" He'd be frightened for a second and then laugh so hard... I would steal his nose, and he would say, "It's ooookaaaaaayyyyyy. You need it because your nose is..." He would giggle.

"It's what? Confess," I would say.

"It's... It's ugly!" He would break into laughter, and I would tickle him, and he'd laugh harder. That laugh was the purest and most fascinating sound in life.

A week went by, and there was no sign of our person of interest.

I asked Danny to place ten additional people on all meetings, venues, and centers, and they were given the locations of the centers and copies of the sketch we'd made. We also agreed to make a special schedule for each team member so that they would visit the same center a few times a week and hang around during peak times.

She asked how long this would go on, and I said one month. The decision was arbitrary, I could decide as I went along. I asked her not to tell Luke, and she said she wouldn't inform him, but he'd know from the billing statements. I agreed to pay for the additional force with cash. Luke would see the withdrawal but wouldn't know for what it was used.

I didn't have a rationale for our plan, just a hunch. Despite what I'd said to Luke and Cynthia, I didn't think the guy came to the meeting venue to see me. It was probably a coincidence—I could tell from his reaction when he recognized me. He had another motive for being there, and I wanted to mess it up. Basically, that was the plan.

It didn't take long. A few days after the men were deployed, someone knocked on my door. I woke up and waited; the knocking persisted, so I went down and opened the door. It was a courier, the kind you paid to deliver things by hand.

I received a yellow folder, the type you put a few papers inside. I thought, *What a cliché. Why not text me?* I opened the folder and saw a small paragraph typed on printer paper.

I didn't hurt your family, and I don't know where your boy is. I told you this before.

Leave me alone before I hurt you. I'm a private person who doesn't want anyone interfering in their life.

We have no business together. Pull the men off my trail before someone gets hurt.

Note: You're very trusting of the people around you. I wouldn't be.

LAUGH

The following afternoon, I went to a nearby hardware store and printed on a small metallic plate: *I'll find you, I promise*. I hung it on the front door. Luke and Cynthia thought I was referring to Mathew. But I was communicating with the person who sent the folder, who for me had become the number one suspect. My theory was that if I could provoke him enough, if I could get him to attack me, this time I would subdue him. I was sure he'd seen me hanging it; he had tabs on me at all times. I also suspected that he'd bugged my place, and that was why he had sent the letter.

I gathered the only people in my life in one room: Danny, Cynthia, and Luke. I showed them the folder and read the letter to them. I didn't suspect any of them would have cheated me or stabbed me in the back. We had been through thick and thin, but there was no harm in seeing their reactions. Gladly, nothing stood out. I briefed Danny not to mention anything about our deployment of a total of fifteen men roaming the city. It seemed aimless, but I was following my hunch.

I planned to call him names in front of the group and suggest the potential motives of such a person. If he fit the profile, and if he was listening, then surely, he would act.

"I know what kind of person this is. This is a monster, some coward who works in the shadows, someone who leeches on the weak, on children."

They looked at each other. I spoke loudly and paced the room as if I were Sherlock Holmes, I wanted to make sure he could hear me wherever the bug was placed. "I'm not saying he's the one who killed my family, but I'm declaring to you, and the world, that this guy is a pedophile who might have taken my boy. I have this intense feeling that Mathew is being held captive by this sick person. For me, it's intense, for you it's not, but we can agree that even if there's a slim chance, we have to do what we can with full force."

Cynthia and Luke looked down at the floor. They weren't entertained. They probably thought this exaggerated confidence was the first sign of a breakdown. I saw a sincere worry in their faces. However, Danny listened intently. She was remarkable—you could ask her for flying unicorns, and she would take you seriously with no judgment.

"This letter was written by someone very weak. Potentially a psychopath. Someone who lacks empathy, who doesn't feel the pain and sadness of others. Look how he accused you of being unfaithful. I bet you this is someone who suffered in their childhood, abused, or maybe was locked up like an animal."

There was some back and forth within the group, but I achieved the intended objective. We agreed to continue with the plan, but to be vigilant.

I asked them if I should call the police and tell them about what was going on. They looked at each other in dismay, and we ended up deciding against it. After they left, I asked Danny about it, and she said the police would say I fabricated the letter for attention or blame it on my other personality, which from their point of view was a reasonable possibility. I hated the fact that this motherfucker got to listen to this part.

"We don't need them. We can have our own law enforcement, or even better," I said and winked at her, "buy your people that new equipment from your special ex-Army contacts, you know, the stuff that lets them listen through walls."

She seemed to understand that I thought someone might be listening. "Also, hire a few strongmen and make sure they always patrol in a pair. If they spot him, I want them to follow him to his house and capture him."

I took out a new phone and texted her: "The house is probably bugged."

She said, "Understood, sir. We'll have fifty men working the streets, and we'll pay them upfront for a few month?"

"Yes. Can I recommend a reward of $250,000 for the person or persons who capture this man? Alive."

She said such bounty hunting would not be possible.

I texted Cynthia to say that I needed a couple of days to myself. I also told her that she meant a great deal to me, and I couldn't have improved without her.

I wrote: "We should move in together. I'll ask you properly when we meet. Kisses."

A final text to her.

I was excited. This could lead me to Mathew. It truly could.

I downed a whiskey, and I dozed off for an hour afterward. The doorbell rang. I didn't want to get up, but I did, waiting at the top of the stairs. It rang again.

I went down, and it was the same courier. I was still sluggish but focused enough.

"Hey, this one came in urgently for you." I signed for it and he left.

Same yellow envelope. I opened the folder and took out the letter:

You didn't listen. Now you'll pay. You disrespectful worthless shit.

I smiled as I read it, now was the time for my next move.

I took Buddy out for a walk. I bought a new burner and pretended to make a long call on it. Once back in the house, I called Danny, certain that the stranger would be listening to our conversation.

"Listen, Danny, another letter came and I got a bit scared, so I called the police and they told me to relocate somewhere safe. They're going to stake out the house and apprehend him when he comes in. ... Yeah, here in the neighborhood. I know someone who rents furnished apartments with no questions asked. ... No, this is a done deal, don't send anyone, the police have got it. This guy is so stupid that I'm sure they'll get him. Listen, they told me to stay off the phone because this place is bugged."

I was sure he laughed, thinking he was smart.

I packed a bag. I would feel bad if he hurt Buddy, but then I told myself that he wouldn't come here. He would follow me.

I left the house and walked causally down the street, crossed at the right place, paid the man, and took the keys to the apartment. Once inside, it occurred to me he might have placed a GPS tracker in my bag or shoes, so I cut through my bag's zipper lining, and I found the device. Afterward, I cut open the heels of my shoes and found another tracker. Then removed all my clothes and put on a cotton shirt and a pair of shorts. I smiled.

I've got you, motherfucker.

I called George, my all-in-one man from the pub. I got worried that he might have left the job and I hadn't known the pub news in some time, but when he picked up I was happy. I asked him to come to the building, but to approach from the back. I grabbed a few hundred dollars and went down the fire escape.

As instructed, George brought me sunglasses, a baseball cap, and size eleven running shoes. We went around to the front side of the building, and I climbed in the car and asked him to go around back on foot and stake out the fire escape.

We waited for an hour, burner phones in our hands, getting excited every time someone went up the stairs. Another hour passed and a courier went up the front stairs, that meant another folder.

Why isn't he attacking? I suddenly got anxious. I hadn't planned for this. If he didn't come, what would I do next? I had already provoked a dangerous person.

"Another letter. Maybe he knows I left the apartment and wants me to go up and get it," I said to George.

The man exited building and went around the block. I thought of asking George to go up and get the letter.

"Jason. The courier guy, was he wearing an orange tucked-in t-shirt and an orange cap?" George asked.

"Yes."

"Well, he came from around the block and now he's climbing the fire escape. Is this our guy? Do you want me to stop him?" he asked.

Shit, this was going down. "No. I mean, yes, he could be our guy, but leave him alone. Wait until he gets higher on the stairs, and threaten to call the police, but keep your distance."

"Okay."

Sneaky. So, he was dressed like a courier.

A minute later I heard George, "Hey, dude! Hey! What are you doing up there? Thief! One two three four. Hey, people on the fourth floor, someone is breaking into your apartment! I'm calling the police." He paused, then said to me over the phone, "It worked. He's coming down." He was panting.

"That was very good. Well done. Well done."

"He's down. Going your way, running now. I'll circle around the building."

"Okay," I said. "I see him now. He's no longer running. He's getting into a car."

"What do we do?" George was still panting. He reached to the car and got into the driver's seat. "Let's follow him."

"Are you sure you're okay with this?" I said to him and he nodded.

The guy drove a small French car, the kind that were half the size of a regular car. It probably ran on electricity. We followed him for fifteen minutes, during which he drove to a ten-story parking garage where he exchanged cars.

If I were ever in doubt, at that moment I became certain that this person was a criminal of high caliber. No one has the time or energy for switching cars unless they were playing for very high stakes. A burglar who wanted to steal your Blu-Ray player wasn't going to worry about switching cars.

I insisted that I continue alone from that point on. George protested, but I couldn't let him risk this kind of danger, he yielded saying he would grab a taxi.

I kept my distance while following my target, and recorded the plate numbers of both cars. I didn't see his face, so I couldn't match it with the person whom I had met after the SAA meeting.

It wasn't a long drive, but the last twenty minutes exhausted me. Now that I was alone, I panicked. If he was a psychopath, then he was also a paranoid person who would check his mirrors every few seconds. I kept asking myself if he had spotted me, but I couldn't be certain. We reached a calm neighborhood that had low-rise buildings on one side and small suburban houses on the other. The birds were chirping, and a few children played on the sidewalk. Many people would say they'd like to live here. It looked like one of the nicer neighborhoods.

He pulled into one of the houses on the street. I slowed down a little, then continued past without looking at him or the house. I looked closely at the next few houses, memorizing the house numbers.

What should I do?

I called George. "Hi. Thanks a lot, buddy. I owe you. I need your help to get this done."

"Sure", he said.

"Pass by a sporting goods store and buy me a taser. Not a regular one, a long-range one."

"Are you sure of this?"

"Yes, just get the taser, meet you at the pub," I said. "One more thing: Get me a crowbar."

I went to the pub and George came. I asked him to go to the apartment where we met to get the shoes and go my house, and then to call me when he is inside. I told him what to say exactly during the call, and I promised to send my location after I break in, but he was only allowed to send it to the cops if I didn't check in with him every hour. He asked me why I wasn't taking a gun instead of the taser, and I told him I only needed to attack from a range and I might kill the guy with the bullets.

My plan was to get the guy out of his house for a while and then break in to see what he was hiding inside, careless of the ramifications of this illegal act.

I drove back to the neighborhood. It felt odd to be there after the sun had set. The street was much quieter, and no birds singing and no children playing.

A few minutes later, George called, and I hoped he remembered to put me on speaker.

"We got him on the security camera at the apartment entrance," George said. "The hidden one."

"We got the bastard." I said. "That's great. Meet me at Danny's office. She has a friend in the police department who can run the video through facial recognition software."

"Give me forty-five minutes and I'll be there," he said. "I need to get something first."

We hung up.

A few minutes later, I saw my person of interest leaving in his car, and I walked toward the house. I told myself I hadn't thought this through, what if there was another person in the house? I could be shot on the spot.

I looked for cameras. I suspected this guy was the type who had a security system installed. Surprisingly, there was no installed security on the outside of the house or the windows, either.

Well, fuck me. A crazy and meticulous murderer would have kept his place like a fort. What if he wasn't the guy?

Only one way to find out.

I decided to climb up the drain to the balcony and start with the bedrooms.

NEVER SAY NEVER

I got the crowbar from the car, went around to the back of the house and climbed up the drain and jumped onto the balcony of the second floor. I planned to break the door down if it didn't open. I had the taser in my pocket.

What was I looking for? I knew I wanted to find something incriminating, but I didn't know what. A gun? A body? A hostage?

I had moved on him very quickly, I should have waited and planned it properly, or even better, come with backup.

If this was the guy who had attacked my family, then I had to get my revenge. If not, then I would accept my punishment, and this would mean prison time. Only if I were caught.

Standing on the balcony, so dark no one recognized me, I felt the cool breeze and drew in a deep breath. Phone on vibrate, I texted George: "Is he still there?"

Immediately, he replied. "Yes. Waiting in his car. He punched the steering wheel a few times."

I replied: "Text me if he moves."

I got scared, and my hands were shaking a bit. After a few tries, I wedged the crowbar in and the door cracked open; you could hear the air hiss. I slid the door open and gladly no alarms went off.

I searched the room quickly—under the bed, the closets, the bathroom... I acted like a madman grasping for air. I paused and decided to follow a method for covering all areas, thorough in each part and avoid coming back to searched areas, then to think of uncovering hidden places. I checked my phone's clock to keep tabs on the time. Ten minutes passed and I finished searching the upper floor, nothing in either of the two bedrooms.

Disappointment filled me. So far, the guy was not a killer.

I carefully went down the stairs, a few made a creaking sound, but I couldn't do anything about that. I watched for cameras, the small ones that might be used to spy on nannies. The house was ordinary, very much like any place in the area, neat and well-kept. I walked slowly into the kitchen, bathroom, and then the living room.

Nothing! No guns, no memorabilia, no hostages.

What the fuck am I looking for? Take a moment to think. Cover every room. Where is the laundry room, where is the garage?

While moving into the kitchen, I saw two locks on the basement door, and one lock was hooked with a small chain. This was it. *Jackpot.* Why put two locks on the door unless he was hiding something major downstairs? I lost interest in what else might be on this floor and focused on getting into the basement.

Mathew could have been down there, cold sweat formed on my forehead. His... his body could be down there. Another innocent child could be down... *Focus.*

The door didn't budge despite my forceful kicks. It was made of solid wood, and when I knocked on it, I knew it was reinforced. "Anyone inside? Hello? Can you hear me?" I put my ear very close for few seconds, but I heard nothing.

I kicked again, and again, until my leg hurt. The locks would not break like this, I need a tool or something to break them.

I searched below the sink and found a small hammer, went back to the basement door, and knocked the locks off, one after the other. The door still didn't open. There was still a deadbolt lock. I jimmied the door with the crowbar, and it unlocked. I took a deep breath.

I opened the door gradually and took one step inside. I saw a camera on the low ceiling and a motion detector on the floor—it was too late to avoid them. The camera was only few inches away from my face. I raised my hand and flipped it the middle finger. I was sure that he had gotten a notification and would soon come back home. I just hoped that he'd missed the notification.

I was scared. This guy wasn't normal. He really could be a psychopath, a killer. I went down the stairs. I took my phone out and sent George the location. He replied that the guy hadn't moved.

The basement was lit by a dim light, and I didn't find a switch with which to turn on anything else. There were two large desks with six large computer screens and two computers. There were only a couple of chairs, and in the corner lay a trashed gamer seat, like the ones used in arcades for racing games.

I took photos of the setup, and then noticed another camera in the corner. I went back to the desk and got a piece of paper from the drawer, in which there were more than eight phones. I wrote on it: *u sick bastard. I got u mother fucker.* I went to the camera and flashed the paper, flipping him the finger again.

There was nothing else in that room. The yellow walls with red stripes were ugly and looked like clumsy work. I didn't think there would be a passage from the basement to anywhere else, but I had to check. Looking closely at the paint, I saw what looked like closet doors. This could be the passage. I wondered if someone was inside, Mathew might be inside.

I couldn't help but imagine that I would rescue him, and we would flee this place together.

I sprung the doors open. There was something electronic inside on one side, a plastic box topped with a few bottles sitting upside down on their caps. On the other side, there was a fridge. I opened it before thinking. Afterward, I thought it could have been a trap. There were hundreds of small urine-collection cups, wrapped in pieces of cloth. I opened one of them and smelled it.

Fuck. Yugh, semen.

My phone vibrated. I took it out and my heart raced. George was panting again.

"Where have you been?" George demanded. "I called you. You scared the shit out of me. He moved a couple of minutes ago, and he wasn't happy."

"Okay, how long ago?" I asked, holding the phone between my ear and shoulder.

"Only a few minutes. Sorry, I lost him, he moved with his lights off, and I couldn't find him."

"It's okay. I don't want you to follow him. I want to capture him. I sent you the location. Don't come, and don't call the cops. Wait for me to check in after twenty minutes. No, make it thirty minutes." I hung up.

I panicked a bit. Semen, hundreds of cups of semen. *Shit, the cameras.*

I moved a chair under the camera, waived the crowbar at it, and then pointed at the fridge and electronic container. I mumbled, "I'll fuck that up." I thought maybe there was no sound and he couldn't hear, so I ran to the closet and started hurling the cups on the floor. I tried to topple the fridge, but it didn't work, so I left the door open.

I went back to the camera and knocked it down, raced up the stairs, and knocked down the camera there. I was relieved that he had no eyes on me now. I hid down behind the stairs, and waited. I thought I breathed heavily. I tried to calm myself down.

I looked at the phone clock, and tried to calm down. I had the taser in one hand and the crowbar in the other. The firing distance was fifteen feet. I thought I could hide in the corner and wait for him to come down, but the room was between thirty and thirty-five feet across from one corner to another; if I shot at him from too far away, I could miss my chance. I only had one cartridge with me; the other was in the car.

I could throw the crowbar to create a diversion and then shoot him. The five minutes passed. I could hide in the house, and once he went down the stairs, I could jump him. *Why jump him? Shoot him!* I stood to go up, but then I thought he could have parked down the street and come by foot, and I wouldn't have heard the car. He could be hiding upstairs and waiting to attack me.

I crouched in the corner and waited. I heard footsteps upstairs. I was right—he'd parked down the street so the car's engine wouldn't announce his arrival. I opened the phone and sent all the photos to George. I typed: "He is here. Wait for me to check in twenty minutes from now."

Suddenly the lights, which were already dim, died. I guessed he was on the top of the stairs. My heart beating strongly, I breathed through my nose. The lightbulb in the fridge was the only one lit in the room. It shed a cone of yellow light across the floor. I couldn't move from the corner without stepping into it and being exposed. I didn't hear him come down, but he might have.

I rested on my knees, the taser pointing forward.

"Come out, you worthless shit. I'll kill you."

His voice was deep; he reminded me of Batman or Bane, I couldn't be sure. The voice came from the stairs.

"You'll pay," he said. The voice was now in the room.

There was a scratching noise on the floor. He could be holding a bat. What if he had a gun? He would kill me.

"Where is my son, you motherfucker?" I said, regretting it immediately. "I called the cops. I sent them what you have in the closet before I smashed it."

I heard sudden footsteps racing toward me, but I couldn't see. I fired the taser. *So much for planning.*

I hit him in the head, he jolted and hit the floor. I was so relieved, but had to kick him few times on the head to knock him out, he was capable of overturning the situation once he had the slightest chance. Once he was out, I took the phone out and texted George that all had gone well, and he should call me every thirty minutes for updates.

He was very heavy, muscular. I didn't have anything to tie him up with. I'd expected things to go otherwise, to find evidence of his murders and then call the cops. I should have planned better.

I removed the laces of my shoes and tied his hands, but it felt like that wasn't enough, so I took his shoelaces and tied his calves to the chair where I seated him.

DEBT

I lit a cigarette. They were wrinkled, and a few were broken in the pack. Still, it was a moment of triumph. I wanted to enjoy it as much as I could before he woke up. He wouldn't be out for longer than five minutes, and I'd spent some time tying him up—not that securely, come to think of it.

He woke up, and I made a point not to say anything to see what is the first thing that he would say.

"It is not me," he said. "You have the wrong guy. I'm a gamer, man. Come on. Cut me loose and leave. I won't bother you anymore."

I exhaled and smoke filled the room, I sat in the second chair and rested. What he just said made me more inclined to believe he was the one.

"I'm telling you, I didn't hurt your family. I don't know anything about you," he said in a soft voice. I didn't reply, this wasn't the real him. I knew there was a dark man underneath this polite exterior, so I decided to wait.

Not one minute later, he shouted, "I said cut me loose or I will fucking kill you! You motherfucker! You're a worthless shit!" He was spitting and trying to maneuver out of the chair.

That didn't take much time, I thought. He's already lost it.

I waived the crowbar as a threatening message, and he settled down. I was sure he could get out of the laces if left alone, but he wouldn't try while I was there with a weapon. I could break his arms and stop any attempts to escape before they even started.

"Where's my son?" I said. "Think well before you answer. I won't leave an unbroken bone in your body. Where is Mathew?"

"I told you, man. I am a gamer, I don't know anything about him. I didn't hurt your family. I swear," he said, looking fragile and weak. I knew that this was also an act.

"What is that in the fridge?" I said.

"Nothing. I don't know," he said, shrugging his shoulders.

I stood up and hit him on the shoulder with the crowbar, and he grunted. "No lying," I said and sat back down. "What is in the cups in the fridge?"

"I'm a gamer. Some days are good and some are bad. I store my sperm and sell it to sperm banks for money." He paused. "Some people need it, you know. They can't make their own, or it isn't good."

I didn't reply.

"Remember when I saw you in the meeting?" he asked. "I was going to check out SAA. I started masturbating so I could donate, but then I got hooked. I was checking if SAA would work for me."

"Really," I said. "I thought you were a CCB agent. What about the Be Your Best Motel?"

He was taken by surprise for a second.

"What motel?" he said.

I hit him on the shoulder, thigh, and both knees. He grunted.

"Listen. I won't get tired. I'll keep hitting you."

"Okay, I'll tell you everything. I knew your daughter, but I had nothing to do with her or your wife's death. I loved Lea."

The next blow was to his head. Blood started trickling down his face. He didn't scream—maybe he was stunned that I had it in me. I was surprised, too. A raging anger filled me when he uttered her name.

I switched on the computer. It was password-protected. I asked him for the password, and he gave me one. A screen notification popped up: the password was incorrect. I assumed the computer would allow only three wrong entries and then lock, but it could also have been set to lock after just two wrong entries.

I hit him with all my power, focusing on his shoulders and avoiding making any new cuts. I sat down and he gave me another password and I entered it, but before hitting Enter, I glanced at him sideways. He was looking at the closet, as if he expected something to happen there.

I didn't press Enter, instead, I walked to the closet. I asked him about the plastic container, and he said it held a server. I asked him about the bottles, and he said they held coolant, but when I looked closely, I saw that the bottles had fuses attached to their caps.

I removed the bottles carefully thinking to myself they might be bombs. Each bottle had a seal on its opening, like a thin film. These were weird bottles, metal, with nothing written on them. I asked him what was in them, and he insisted it was coolant.

I knew he was lying, the coolant had to circulate to do its work. I put the bottles on the table and erased the password he had given me, and he suddenly charged at me from the chair, but I knocked him down and gave him a load of punches. I hit him until he passed out.

I ran upstairs, hoping to find some rope and I saw a laptop bag lying on the kitchen table. I went into the living room and found that he had a back pack containing a ski mask and zip ties. *Bingo.*

Cautiously, I went down downstairs with the computer bag and the zip ties, and he was still lying on his side, still tied to the chair. I placed as many zip ties on him as possible. I opened the bag, and inside were a laptop and an electronic notepad, exactly like the one Dr. Thompson had given me when I was in the facility.

I sat back down in front of the screens and wished I had something to torture him with, some way to get him to give me the password. So far, all I knew was that he was a man who stored his semen in his basement, and he owned a ski mask and zip ties. I could call the police, and they would do a better job of investigating, maybe search for evidence and DNA; however, I would be arrested along the way and I would face severe consequences. The police wouldn't question him about Mathew the way I wanted them to, my son was out there and I must find him.

I searched online for torture methods, all of them required supplies, and few were truly cruel. I went upstairs and searched for something to use, but all I could find was lemon and salt. *Squirt it into his eye.*

I waited patiently, but along the way I panicked about not finding anything and assaulting the man in his house. After some discussion, I told him I would not leave unless I see what is on the computer, otherwise I would stay here. At that stage, he offered up the password without me even asking for it. I entered the password on the desktop keyboard and threatened him that if it didn't work, I would break all ten fingers and all ten toes.

It logged in, the desktop was empty except for one folder, I double-clicked it and it was empty on the inside. I try the changing the hidden feature, but nothing appeared to be hidden. This was the moment I realized the defeat, I panicked to the thought of police and facing Cynthia and Luke. If only I preserved the good thing I had with Cynthia.

The man started babbling, but I could not focus on what he said, I was sure he mentioned untying him and leaving. I reached for the electronic notepad and powered it on and entered the password used for the folders, it worked but prompted a fingerprint validation from the garbage man. Once in, I saw he had many text files saved in a folder labeled, "Manifesto: Rise of the Elite."

What a sick motherfucker.

I threw down the notepad and opened the laptop, and suddenly one of the screens turned on by itself. The other three screens followed. What I saw was horrific: he was filming people, in their homes, and it was live. Each screen was split into eight smaller ones.

"Wait. It's not what you think, this is paid service, these people willingly accept to be recorded. You have to know that."

Yeah right, as if I believe you.

His shirt was now bloody from the cut on his forehead, and his eyes had started swelling.

I checked the desktop of the laptop, and there was a folder I clicked on and it had several folders inside, named by year. I opened the 2016 folder and scrolled down. I saw her name in caps: LEA. I double-clicked.

"What you see doesn't mean I hurt her or her mom. Man, I told you, I loved Lea."

There were fifty-two items in that folder, and all of them were videos of them having sex in the studio. I was so sad, I cried. It was horrible to see. "You fucking sick bastard!"

I returned to the 2016 folder and started opening other folders within it. They all contained footage of him having sex with women, or videos that looked like they had been made by secretly filming women in their homes. I spent an hour looking through them, and George called three times to check in. There was nothing else, but surely this would be enough to get him investigated for what happened to my family and convicted for whatever other shit he had done.

"Listen, man," he said. "No one got hurt. All of this is just for me. I don't sell it, and no one sees it except me. I told you, I didn't hurt your family. I was angry at you because I thought *you* hurt Lea, that's it. I really loved her."

"Shut the fuck up!" I yelled.

"Let me go, and I won't press charges," he said. "I told you, I did nothing. I didn't do anything to them."

I jumped out of my seat, cut off part of his shirt, and stuffed it in his mouth. It wasn't the best gag, but it worked. He was still loud, but no longer comprehensible.

I didn't know what to do next. I was curious to know what was in the bottles. I removed the film on one bottle and held it close to my nose. It smelled like vomit, I poured a few drops on the desk, and they made a hole and released an awful smell. It was probably acid, certainly something corrosive.

I lit a cigarette and thought. I right-clicked inside the folder, and changed the option to "Show all files." More folders appeared, with names like "on the road" and "my special one" and "experiment." My heart gave an extra beat,

Mathew. What do I want now, to see him or to know he didn't hurt him?

I opened "on the road," and it had many folders inside it, all filled with videos of pranking old people, hitting women, and video footage taken on buses and subways.

I found folders with people's names. I looked through very quickly—I wanted to see if there was anything on Lisa, Lea, or Mathew. I found one called Kelly, and my heart skipped a beat. *My Kelly? Definitely not her.*

Seeing what he had done to her, I punched him few times and kicked him on the floor until he started spitting blood. All I was thinking was, *don't kill him, Jason. Don't kill him. Don't kick the head.*

I still needed him to tell me where Mathew was.

I opened "the special one" and saw him choking an underage girl while having sex with her. The "experiment" was him with a boy, and I was glad it wasn't Mathew, but I was so sad to see that happen to someone. How damaging and how unfair to commit such an act on a defenseless and vulnerable soul.

I wanted to kill him, he deserved it, and I would probably be excused, but I knew from his demeanor that he was hiding more. "Where is Mathew?" I asked him more than fifty times and he insisted he knew nothing about him, and he never took him away. He even mentioned that he has no motive now to hide anything else, especially that I have seen everything on his laptop.

I looked at the laptop, not knowing what else to do, how to squeeze the truth out of him. There were a few icons on its desktop, one was titled, "the elite paradise." I double clicked, and it opened another video feed.

There were three women in what at first appeared to be a jungle with many trees and a small stream of water, but it looked like the jungle was in a cement warehouse or a deserted building. The three women had chains around their necks, and one of them was pregnant, they looked weak and lethargic. One of them was watching TV.

"Jesus Christ," I said.

The three women were startled, and the one watching the TV shut it off rapidly. The three of them quickly sat on chairs and straightened their backs.

"Shit. You sick motherfucker," I said.

They looked at each other as if they heard me.

"Can you hear me? Where are you?" I asked. There was no way they could hear me. What kind of twisted simulation was this?

They stood up suddenly. "Please let us out!" "Please!" "Please!" One started crying. The pregnant one fell to her knees begging. She had a very big bulge, she was probably in her seventh or eighth month. "Let us out before he comes back!"

"Wait a minute." I called the police and gave them the address. I said I had a man tied up in his basement, and I could see three women held in captivity via video feed on his laptop. They said they were coming.

"What are your names? And do you know your location?" I said to the women.

I texted George: "The police are on their way. Call Luke. Tell him to come here. Tell him I got the motherfucker."

"Melanie Salva," said a very thin woman who didn't look at all well. She was swaying from side to side. "We don't know where we are."

"Laurie Makenzie," the pregnant woman yelled.

"Christelle Sherlie." Her voice told me she was young.

"The asshole impregnated me! He's the guy who looks after my apartments. Tell them his name: Andy Manger. Andy Magner!"

"Don't worry," I said. "You're going to be saved. The police are on their way."

I had a few minutes before they would arrive, I begged him to tell me where Mathew is - was. I thought this was his only leverage at this point, and he'd probably try to use it to get a deal.

I wondered where he was keeping Mathew. Was there another live feed for Mathew, like with the women? If the guy went to jail, who would feed Mathew?

I took a few pictures for leverage, but while taking them, I asked myself about the purpose of what I was doing in the moment. Almost two years had passed, and no progress had been made. I'd had to take care of finding this creep on my own. How could I trust the police now?

I sat on the floor and rested my back on the wall and thought of one thing only, they are GONE. This monster took my family. I lost them all, including Mathew.

END NOTE

END NOTE

Protect your children and promote the protection of all children. Predators are smart and manipulative, they feed and act on people's trust.

The vast majority of abusers are within the close circle of the family. Be vigilant. Never break your rules even if you trust whoever, never let your guard down.

I am sorry if some parts of the novel made you angry. I also felt bad about thinking like this for a brief time.

AUTHOR'S NOTE
Thanks again for reading the book, appreciating your time.

If you enjoyed it, I would be immensely grateful if you could rate it and post a short review.

My email is Authorjaykerk@gmail.com, drop me a message if you want.